The Shah of Texas:
~~A Historical~~
~~An Historical~~
~~An Novel~~
A Novel

Charlie Green

Illustrations by John Green

ISBN 978-1-7377808-8-5

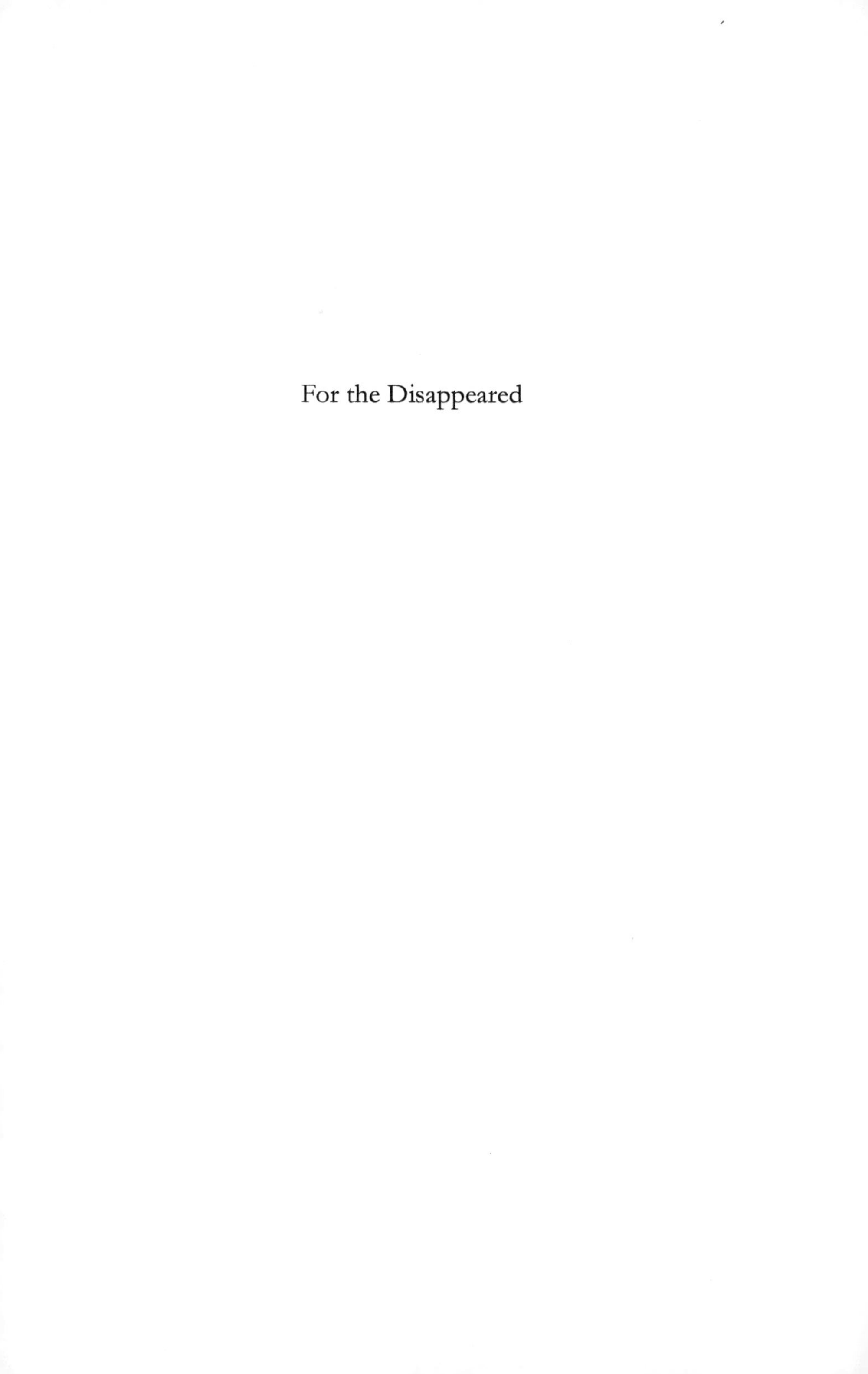
For the Disappeared

"I'm guided by the beauty of our weapons."
— **Leonard Cohen**, "First We Take Manhattan"

"I am tempted to quote the great Leonard Cohen: 'I'm guided by the beauty of our weapons.' And they are beautiful pictures of fearsome armaments making what is, for them, a brief flight over this airfield. What did they hit?"
— MSNBC news anchor **Brian Williams**

"Everybody says sex is obscene. The only true obscenity is war."
— **Henry Miller**, *Tropic of Cancer*

"News is a rough first-draft of history."
— Attributed to **Philip Graham**, publisher and eventual co-owner of *The Washington Post*

"The first draft of anything is shit."
— **Ernest Hemingway**

"Shit runs downhill."
— **Origin Unknown**, or your alcoholic uncle, or your mother speaking of your uncle, alcoholic or otherwise

"As a dog returns to its vomit, so a fool repeats his foolishness."
— **Proverbs 26:11**

"The fool doth think he is wise, but the wise man knows himself to be a fool."
— Touchstone, **William Shakespeare**, *As You Like It*, Act V, Scene I

"'By art is created that great Leviathan, called a Commonwealth or State—(in Latin, Civitas) which is but an artificial man.' —Opening sentence of Hobbes's Leviathan."
— **Herman Melville**, "Extracts," *Moby-Dick: or The Whale*

Promised Landings

Promised Landings

Today was a day, Adiel S. Thomas told herself, that would live in infamy. She almost went to get the morning paper before peeing, but first she'd have to find change, and the nearest newspaper box was a block away, and there was always the danger of running into either Otis or Cody, one of her chatty next door neighbors, whose chattiness always squeezed her bladder. So she peed, knowing Otis could hear through the wall if he was in his bathroom. Such was life in her one-bedroom in the Promised Landings Apartments.

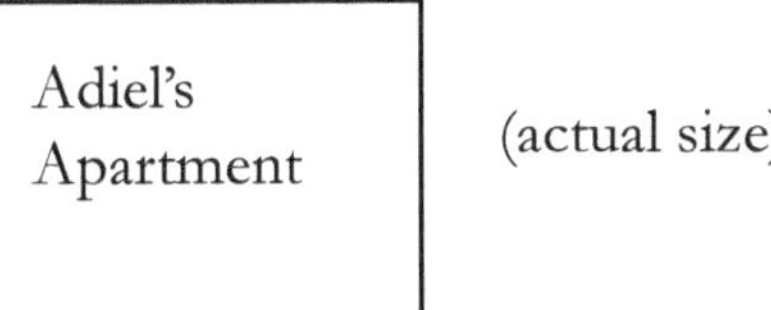

(actual size)

Adiel didn't want to be giddy—after all, the infamy would be the revelations and photographs of torture by military members of the Great Independent Nation of Texas at the Garza West facility in Beeville. The Shah of Texas would be exposed, the unnecessary violence of the war would be exposed. But she had the co-byline with Cy Jost. Cy had done the bulk of reporting before having a massive stroke and passing away two weeks prior, but she'd worked with him, her first real story, and finished it off. Sure, he'd gotten the photos, he'd had all the contact with the source—she didn't even know who it was. But her name would be attached, she'd discovered the identity of one of the soldiers in the photos, and Margot Nought, the Executing Editrix of the *Texas Morning Sun,* had already told Adiel she'd have to defend the piece on TV. TV!

But once she grabbed some small, sticky coins and clopped out in her flip-flops and got the paper, she discovered the headlines weren't what she'd expected. One about successful simultaneous air strikes against American military bases outside Baton Rouge and Wichita, another about the psychological toll on Texan soldiers of facing the ongoing barbarism of America, yet another about the growing powerhouse that was the Texan oil industry. Adiel flipped through, shedding newsprint on the sidewalk and drought-yellowed grass. Nothing in the A section, where it would have been; she flipped the Sports section into the steel trash can (Adiel didn't care about scores or standings in the TBA and TBD leagues*). With the A section, Style section, and Classifieds under her arm, she flop-jogged back to her building. The plastic slaps echoed off the buildings.

Margot Nought had told Adiel the telephone extension to her office, a little badge of importance. Still, after dialing the newspaper's 800 number, that meant pressing buttons on her phone: 8# for editorial, 4# for executing editorial, then Margot's, the Executing Editrix: 1, #, *. Margot was number one. The number was a closely guarded secret among the *Morning Sun* staff.

"Margot Nought," she answered, "To what do I owe the pleasure?" She said all this with the casual professionalism of a band performing its hit song with dry pride for the thousandth time.

"Where's my story?" Adiel felt sweat in her armpits. The receiver was hot already against her ear.

"I'm afraid you'll have to be more specific."

"'Atrocities at Garza West'?"

"Ah, Adiel. It's you. Good morning."

"Where's the story?"

"I said, 'Good morning.'"

Adiel flumped on her couch, the cushion that had more stuffing. "Good morning, ma'am."

"Thank you. The niceties matter."

Adiel wanted to believe they did, but that was a challenge this morning. "Yes, ma'am. So what happened to the story?"

"Bob Toose called late last night," Margot said. Bob Toose was the Shah's Secretary of Conflagrational Elucidations. "The Shah will be making a major announcement today regarding the war at his ranch."

"Bob Toose knew about the story?"

"That's not clear. But he wanted to let me know personally about the announcement so we can have a reporter in the front row."

---

*Texas Baseball Association and the Texas Basketball Division, repectively.

"You want me to cover it?" Adiel threaded a loose brown string of the armrest under her thumbnail.

"No. But I decided to push back the story. How long depends on today's announcement."

Adiel slumped, then lay back and pressed a throw pillow on her face. Through the pillow, she said, "I couldn't sleep last night. Why didn't you call me to let me know you were pushing it back?"

"Adiel," Margot said in her tone of parental finality. "The news is not about us."

Adiel completed the call with niceties and walked the phone receiver back over to its cradle. "Fuck!"

On the other side of the bedroom wall of her apartment, her neighbor Otis yelled, "You okay?"

On the other sides of the kitchenwall, her neighbor Cody yelled, "What did Otis say?"

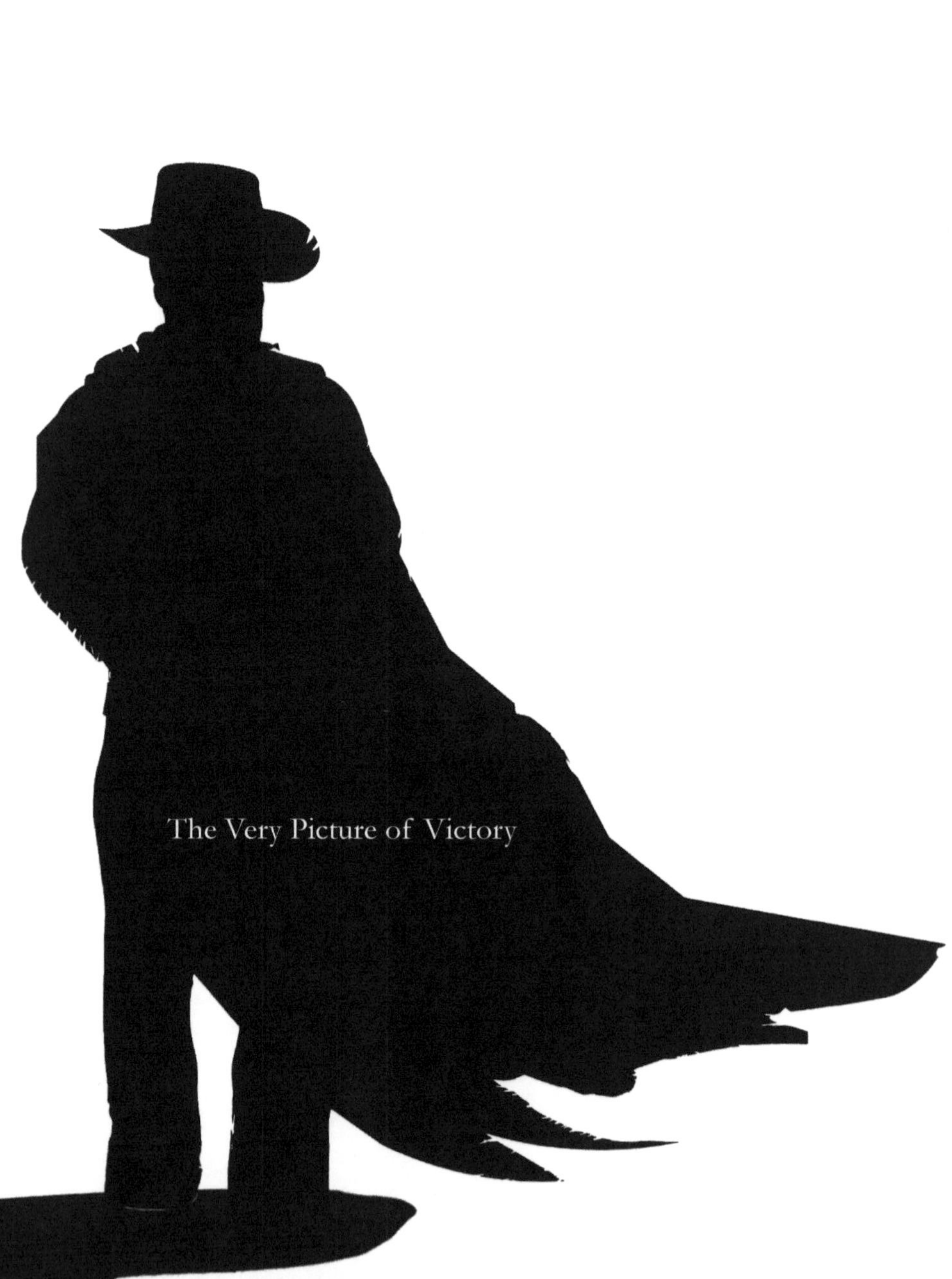
The Very Picture of Victory

The Very Picture of Victory

The Shah clipped on the belt buckle, which was modest but had a glint. "These jeans have been dirt-rolled?"

The guard nodded. "Of course."

The haberdasher carried in the platter of hats.

"Atom smasher!" the Shah yelled.

"Haberdasher, sir."

The Shah grinned. "You know I know that."

"Yes, sir," the haberdasher said. "Very funny."

Bob Toose was sitting on one of the two sofas that faced each other, re-re-re-re-reading the Shah's speech, pen in hand. "Sir, this is a very important speech. It's important to be serious."

"Bob, I know that. I went over the speech last night. I went over it again this morning. I'll be great."

"Sir, you've said that before."

"Question. Is it pronounced 'air-uh' or 'ear-uh'?"

Bob narrowed his already narrow eyes. "Either one is right, but for this, I think 'ear-uh' is best."

"That's what I thought."

They were in the Grand Office of the Shah at the Great Ranch of the Shah. This Grand Office replicated the Grand Office of the Shah in the Freedome in Houston. Over the mantle in the Grand Office in Houston hung a reproduction of a painting of the First Shah, the father of the current Shah. (The original hung in the current Shah's home.) It depicted the first Shah, in eighteenth-century battle regalia, sitting atop a white horse, a saber glinting across his thigh, pointing in the air as he led the Texan soldiers that he had freed from the hell of American prisons. (The first Shah had not seen battle, nor had he been involved in the military strategies. As the Texan history textbooks with reproductions on their covers point out, the portrait manages to be heroic and realistic all at once. In the original version, the first Shah looked too much like the Statue of Liberty, and they ordered the new painting because, as he said, "I'm not womanly.") In the Grand Office at the ranch hung a reproduction of the reproduction:

The haberdasher placed a caramel-colored felt hat on the Shah's head. The color matched the Shah's pre-scuffed leather boots. "The very picture of victory," the haberdasher said.

The Shah ran his pinched fingers around the brim. "Nah, the felt's too uppity."

"You are the Shah, sir," Bob Toose said.

"Let's try the straw," the Shah said and bent his head forward.

The haberdasher crowned the Shah with a straw hat. "This, sir, is the Diamond Jim."

"Breathtaking," Bob Toose said.

The Shah shook his head. "It's poking my scalp. It'll distract me. What about that one? What's it made of?"

"That's fur felt, sir. The Desert Condor."

The Shah bowed his head forward; the haberdasher placed the hat. "Oh yeah," the Shah said. "That's the juice." He turned to Bob Toose. "You think Dick will like it?" He was speaking of the demi-Shah, Dick Dick Dick Dick Dick. (He came from a long line of Dicks.)

"In matters of the hat, Dick Dick Dick Dick Dick defers to you."

"I'm the Shah, right?" He serioused his face. "'My fellow Texans, my fellow God-fearers, my fellow lovers of liberty and justice and peace, I come before you today a humbled man. We've been at war a long time, longer than anybody wanted, with America, and today I come before you to say that war is over. And Texas has emerged victorious.'" He chuckled. "Told you I practiced."

Bob Toose closed the binder. "All right, then. You're sure you're okay with the horse?"

The Shah smiled. "I'll be fine. I've rode a lot of carousels."

The white horse could not be startled. His trainers had given him the ultimate calm: he'd learned to tolerate whistles, gun shots, uncommonly loud laughter, the screams of women and cowardly men. The Shah felt at ease with the animal, one hand on the saddle's soft horn, the other hand tipping the brim of his Desert Condor to the media arranged at the gate of the ranch. When the horse came to a rest beside the stage, two ranch hands approached and helped the Shah dismount. He removed his hat and swatted it against his thigh, releasing a cirrus of dirt from his jeans. All in the wrist. They said he was stupid, but if he was so stupid, why was he the Shah?

The speech was on the teleprompters, but the Shah spoke largely from memory.

"My fellow Texans, my fellow God-fearers, my fellow lovers of liberty and justice and peace, I come before you today a humbled man. We've been at war with America a long time, longer than anybody wanted, and today I come before you to say that the War of Texan Independence from the Surly Grip of America is truly over. And Texas has emerged victorious.

"Hostilities have ended.

"Bombs have stopped falling.

"Soldiers have ceased firing weapons.

"Western values have won again. The Ear-uh of Texceptional-ism continues in stronger strength than it ever has.

"And those of us who had no control over the war, who had to watch it unfold before our eyes, who watched in horror as innocent Texans died at the hands of American evildoers, we are so thankful that we've been able to show them who's boss. We did it. We won!" He raised his hat in the air. The gathered crowd, a mix of media and invited guests, cheered. A guard at the side of the stage pulled out a lasso and swung it around in the air.

Once the cheers settled, the Shah resumed. "We are empow-ered to move forward in peace, engladdened by this victory over our enemies, the dreadful Americans, who would stop at nothing to see the destruction of our way of life. But our way of life won. We won. We thought to be aggressive—B. E. Aggressive, as our soldiers said each morning and each time they went forward into battle, and like we Texans said in our hearts and prayers each and every morning. We defeated our enemies, who now have to pick up what remains of their losses and try to move on the right way, the Texan way, even though they're Americans. We want them to adopt our way of life, the right way to live, as it will. If you were. You see, Americans don't know what their military does. They just lap up what the government tells them. Not like Texans, who love the military for good reason. We're truly free, and y'all support the war because y'all know it's right." The Shah had to glance back to the teleprompter. Though the sun was just past its noon height in the sky, the Shah said, "Good night, and God Bless Texas."

Despite Their Savagery

Despite Their Savagery

Maude Lynne, syndicated opinion columnist for the *Houston Times,* couldn't believe the speech. The Shah had ridden in on a white horse as a soldier pulled the reins, both the Shah and the soldier dressed all in denim, except for the Shah's hat—a lovely number that signaled his role as leader. The first Shah had been so regal and majestic, but his son, the current Shah, had an authenticity that rose every time he buffed his hat against his thigh and released dirt from the downhome ranch work he did. Even as the Shah, he was down to earth.

She could nearly smell his musk from her divan, even over her own perfume, Eau D'Or: the Goldwater. She'd never seen a speech like this. It would go down, she knew, among the cavalcade of the world's great orations, watched and re-watched by generations, studied across the world. Among the parade of the world's great orations. No, among the pageant of the world's great orations. Well, parade or pageant, *tktk,* she thought. Once she set herself to writing, her prose would celebrate and ride in the wake of this great moment.

Someday, even the Americans would appreciate his speech, despite their savagery. Ah, yes: there was a line for her column.

Maude Lynne had been a speechwriter for the first Shah. Before Texas declared its independence, she had been a fierce believer in the centuries-old American experiment; after independence, she became just as fierce a believer in the Era[*] of Texceptionalism. Greatness mattered, and if one had to serve as handmaiden to the englorification of human greatness, one would.

Her telephone rang. In the age of push-buttons, she kept a rotary telephone. If only she could freeze the world in a time of perfection and forestall unnecessary change.

She sat in her chair for telephonic discourse and crossed her legs at the ankles. On the other end of the telephone was Bob Toose.

"Miss Maude Lynne?"

---

[*]In her head, *air-uh.*

"Mr. Robert Toose. To what do I owe this pleasure?" *

"Unfortunately," he said, "despite the Shah's wonderful announcement, no pleasure, and I have only a moment. Sometime soon, the *Texas Morning Sun* will run what they claim is an exposé on the practices of a teeny minority of our soldiers against the inhuman cockroaches of the American military."

"Those dastards!" she said.

A pause. "The soldiers?" he asked.

"The *Texas Morning Sun!*"

"Yes, it's dastardly."

"Were they going to run this story to spoil the spoils of our victory?"

"Yes. Yes. They were going to run it to ruin our victory."

"Whatever can I do?"

"We will need the power of your pen," he said. "The enemies of the Shah will try to marshal the grotesque; we will need you to marshal patriotism."

Maude Lynne sat a little straighter. "Anything for the Shah. Anything for Texas."

In a quiet voice, he said, "Good girl."

"One would like to see you soon," she replied, her voice downshifting again into arousal.

"One will," he said. "One will."

Maude Lynne reset the receiver in the cradle. She went directly to her chest of drawers, spritzed the air before her with Goldwater to glide through, and went to her writing desk. She took a deep inhalation of Eau D'Or. Anything for the Shah. Anything for Texas.

---

*If there were world enough and time, we would linger over how the practiced elegance of Maude Lynne's "hello" downshifted into arousal in "pleasure." Sadly, there is world enough, but no time.

The Engorged Eagle Skies

The Engorged Eagle Skies

Adiel couldn't believe the speech. Utterly empty stagecraft. The white horse, the Shah and his guard in denim, the dust that came off his jeans. She could almost smell the bullshit through the television—she'd say that when she talked with her newspaper colleagues about the speech, the ones who could be trusted for their cynicism. Maybe even Texans could see through it. Couldn't they?

The Shah's people had timed it down to the break: after the speech, as he rode off into the distance, the screen faded to black and stayed that way a moment. Adiel saw her reflection.

READER: As happens in novels, I must provide a description of Adiel S. Thomas, as she is the protagonist of this history. However, yr. hmbl. srvnt. is male and aware enough of the faults of male writers in describing female characters, so I would like to offer you options. After all, once a novel leaves a writer and goes into the reader's hands, it is truly yours. So, first: the blank page. Allow your ample imagination to create any necessary physical form of Adiel S. Thomas:

Or, should you mistrust your imagination and prefer that the writer craft detail that directs the reader, use the following, borrowed from the hallowed canon of our greatest literatures:

> She is awfully pneumatic, like meat. For my own amusement sometimes I like to think of her part by part. . . . One breast is smaller than the other, like junior and senior; her pelvic bones are not well covered, she is a little gaunt there. But her body looks gentle and pretty. Her breasts are as firm as ever, they haven't changed since she was seventeen. Her arse is amazingly round too, without a trace of fat; unquestionably she has a beautiful body. When she is angry, her breasts pulse with resentment. Thankfully, her breasts always enter rooms before the rest of her and establish her mood and psychology. They are poignant; they stand out straight and true. She is a little squirrel that loves to fuck.[*]

Ahem. Now then. Allow us to carry on.

---

[*] Or, in lingua franzen of our day: Tiddies and furgina, am I right boys?

From the black screen arose an inset image that then filled the screen: Neil O'Chisholm, the jowly-but-not-too-much-so anchor of W-ANK, Texas flag pin affixed as ever to his lapel. "Well," he said, "there you have it. An indubitable image right there, the Shah giving the speech of his life, riding off gain-victoriously."

The sound from Adiel's throat can barely be translated into English (her only language) and looks like this: ерунда [transliteration: yerunda].

"You just kind of get a feeling in your spine," Neil O'Chisholm said, "when the Shah gives a speech like that, when the Shah's marching band plays 'Ah, the Shah,' and he rides in on that white horse, and in that hat—it must be his working hat—you just get a thrill up your legs and through your fingers. Such a simple man, with simple values. You can almost smell the heroism."

"You've got to be fucking kidding me," Adiel shouted.

Otis, on the other side of the bedroom wall: "What's up?"

Cody, on the other side of the kitchen wall: "You okay?"

"I'm fine, y'all," she said and turned off the television.

She got dressed and ready to head into the office. She would plead with Margot to publish the Garza West article and photos—it was as important now as it had been before the announcement, if not moreso—then probably be demoted to the Metro Houston beat or, worse, to obits. After all, the news wasn't about her.

As she gathered her purse to leave, her telephone rang. After her "hello," a voice said in a bad, inconsistent Mexican-Spanish-vaguely-Latino accent, "I see you. Don't leave yet."

Adiel looked around her apartment for anything resembling a camera, but there was none. Her blinds were only split an inch down the center.

"You won't find it," the voice said, "but because of Garza West, you're being watched all the time. You're being listened to right now."

Adiel's arms trembled; her stomach carbonated with anxious nausea. "Who is this?"

"Thees," the voice said, its fake accent exaggerated even more, "eez El Poya Grrrrande."

"Oh, God," she said. "You're the source."

"Yes," he said, his voice returning to the mild fake accent.

She had never met Cy Jost's source and didn't know his name, but he had told her the details: the bad accent that got worse when he announced himself, the sombrero he wore when they met, presumably to make the source incognito but having, in fact, the opposite effect. Cy had even told Adiel the code for meeting places on the off-chance the source contacted her or, God forbid, anything happen to Cy. But God had not forbade, and here she was on the phone with the source.

"What do you want?" she asked.

"Where is my story?" Menace laced his voice.

Adiel sat on the floor, back against the door of her apartment. "My editor pushed it back. Because of today's speech."

"Relax," he said. "We will make it appear soon. And I have more to give you. The engorged eagle skies. It nests mainly in the cedar. Do you understand?"

Adiel took a breath. *The engorged eagle skies. It nests mainly in the cedar.* "Main and Cedar? In the parking deck?"

"*Dios milo,*" he said. "Okay, just this one time, but do better next time. Tomorrow at sundown, the parking deck at Main and Cedar. Level 10."

"Okay."

"Don't write it down. Just remember it."

She hugged her purse to her chest and raised her knees. "Main and Cedar. Level 10. Sundown."

"*Jesu Crisco,*" he said. "I told you you're being watched and listened to. And it's pointless to hug your purse. It won't protect you."

Adiel scuttled behind the sofa, the cord dragging the phone off the kitchen counter with a plastic clang and an echoey ding.

Otis: "You okay?"

Cody: "What was that?"

"I'm fine," she yelled. "Just a little clumsy." Quietly, into the phone, she said, "You're El Polla Grande?"

"I am indeed."

"The large chicken?"

"Almost," he said. "Almost."

The Champagne Room

The Champagne Room

In the Grand Office of the Shah's Great Ranch of the Shah, clear tarpaulins had been draped over the couches and carpet. The Shah, Bob Toose, and Holly Unlikely, the Secretary of Conflagrational Interventions, sprayed each other with champagne from bottles and from hoses that pulled out from the wall. The people were begoggled, yet a cork had hit the Shah's cheekbone, leaving a small bruise. He didn't care. They were champions! Champaign-ions!

The Shah pointed the foamy mouth of a champagne bottle at the reproduction of the reproduction of the portrait of his father. "I finished it for you, Poppy." He doused the reproduction as if his father were in the room celebrating.[*]

Out in the hallway, spurs jangled and shined. (The spurs had been chosen for their jangling and shining.) Earpieces crackled. The Guardians of the Shah, all down the hallways of the Palace, stood up straighter. Word had arrived: Dick Dick Dick Dick Dick was coming.

Dick Dick Dick Dick Dick rarely appeared at the Palace, tending to communicate instead via messages typed by his long-time assistant, Scheissetete[†]. When Dick Dick Dick Dick Dick came, something was wrong.

Down the hall strode Dick Dick Dick Dick Dick's personal Guardians, all in denim suits, black shirts and ties, and black-framed sunglasses, even their earpieces black. Their footsteps were crisp on the gold-trimmed red carpet, their steps making choral *hishes*. As they passed, the building's custodians silenced their vacuums, the typists poised their fingers above their keyboards, the document shredders pulled back the flaccid papers. Among the Guardians, at the center of the formation, walked Dick Dick Dick Dick Dick, stately, plump, buck, a mulligan, snarling, and hunched. Just behind him followed a thin man in a black suit, white shirt, and narrow black tie, his short white hair in crisp formation: This was Scheissetete.

---

[*] For those worried about the finish of the painting, should anything happen to any of the reproductions, there were more reproductions lying in wait, soldiers in the Great Army of Government Art ready to take the place of any that were lost.

[†] Scheissetete rhymes with "nice jet," as in "Scheissetete's nice jet flies wet."

The celebrants didn't hear the convoy, so they were mid-splash when there entered the tip of Dick Dick Dick Dick Dick's formidable phalanx. Dick Dick Dick Dick Dick's Guardians took a bit of bubbly on their lapels. When the Shah, Bob Toose, and Holly Unlikely saw Dick Dick Dick Dick Dick's protection, they formalized their celebration, standing up straight and pouring champagne into the as-yet unused flutes. Bob Toose offered a glass to Dick Dick Dick Dick Dick.

"Leave us alone," Dick Dick Dick Dick Dick said. The Guardians went into the hall and shut the door. He refused the champagne. He nodded, and they all sat on the tarped sofas and took off their goggles. The polyethylene crackled beneath them. The Shah felt his jeans wet, then start to soak from bubbly.

"We have a problem," Dick Dick Dick Dick Dick said.

"But we won," the Shah said. "I went out and told them, we won."

"I think he means another problem," Bob Toose said. "Some bad news." His tie was now a headband around a bust of the first Shah; his dress shirt was unbuttoned to the rising convex of his abdomen[*].

Dick Dick Dick Dick Dick told of the article that would appear, any day now, complete with photographs of torture at Garza West. "I don't know when," he said, "but the *Texas Morning Sun* is running it soon. My sources tell me they were going to run it today, but your coincidentally timed victory speech bumped it."

Holly Unlikely wiped the inside of her goggles.

"Who reads the *Morning Sun*?" said the Shah. "I don't read that."

Thus began an explanatory back and forth:

Bob Toose: "Well, many people do, apparently. Largest paper in the nation."

The Shah: "But I don't read it."

Dick Dick Dick Dick Dick: "But the people who read it are going to read this story."

The Shah: "Is it long?"

Dick Dick Dick Dick Dick: "Long and detailed."

---

[*]His gut was awfully pneumatic; it was a little pug that loved to fuck.

The Shah: "No one will read it."

Dick Dick Dick Dick Dick: "It's got pictures."

The Shah and Bob Toose: "Shit."

The photos were graphic, Dick Dick Dick Dick Dick explained. Holly Unlikely nodded. Dick Dick Dick Dick Dick rose, tarpaulins crinkling, and gazed at the portrait of the first Shah, to whom he had been an early advisor. In the extant (and textbook-ready) photographs from the first year of the first Shah's reign, Dick Dick Dick Dick Dick stands as part of the flank to the Shah's right, a half-head shorter than everyone else, in large, square glasses. He was, then, the Private Secretary of the ███, the Domestic and Foreign and, in case of need, Interstellar Surveillance Agency of the Great Independent Nation. But he hoped to be named the first demi-Shah of Texas. When the Shah named another advisor his demi-Shah instead, Dick Dick Dick Dick Dick took a backseat in the administration and focused on his pet project, the Blueprint Underscoring Liberty, Laissez-faire economics, State's rights, Historicalism In Texas. But the current Shah had always liked Dick Dick Dick Dick Dick. During the first Shah's administration, he told the now-Shah little side jokes before and after meetings, which the current Shah didn't quite get but understood would be quite funny if he did. Also, the man snarled at the Shah's father when necessary—so when the first Shah died and the son rose to become the second Shah of Texas, he tapped Dick Dick Dick Dick Dick to be his own demi-Shah, erecting Dick Dick Dick Dick Dick to power. Sadly, not once in their regnum had Dick Dick Dick Dick Dick told a joke. At least, he hadn't told one the Shah understood to be a joke.

Dick Dick Dick Dick Dick said of the photos that were to be published, "Your father would have understood that we did what we had to do."

"It was a war, right?" the Shah said. "I mean, what did we do?"

Bob Toose raised a finger. "Plausible deniability! Don't say anything, Dick. What the Shah don't know can't hurt him."

Holly Unlikely said, "It's going to be in the public domain. Everyone will know, including him. Copies have been leaked to the networks."

"Right, but if he knows about it before the news comes out,

then we don't have plausible deniability."

"But if he doesn't know about it before the news comes out," Holly Unlikely said, "then the government looks incompetent."

Dick Dick Dick Dick Dick said, "And we can be incompetent, if we have to, but we can't look incompetent."

The Shah interjected. "So what don't I know?"

"A lot," Dick Dick Dick Dick Dick said. He took a deep breath that rattled in his chest. "Allegedly, Texan soldiers tortured prisoners at the Garza West Unit in Beeville. Allegedly, Texan soldiers whipped and beat American prisoners. Allegedly, soldiers smeared American prisoners in feces and even forced the prisoners to eat it. Allegedly, the soldiers had stripped and beaten and cut the prisoners and generally defecated on their human rights. Allegedly, all kinds of things. And, allegedly, there are photos."

Scheissetete grinned.

"Are the photos alleged or real?" the Shah asked.

"The photos are real, but it's alleged they're of Texas soldiers doing these things to American prisoners."

"Ah," said Bob Toose, "real but alleged. That helps."

"I don't understand," the Shah said. "How can photographs be real but alleged? They're real or not real, right?"

"Well," Bob Toose said, "the photos are real—they're undoctored, right?"

"Right," Dick Dick Dick Dick Dick said. "So far as anyone knows."

Holly Unlikely said, "But who can even tell these days? I once saw a delightful photograph of a bear firing a shotgun at a man. It turns out it was forged."

"So they're of a thing that exists. But they're only allegedly of what they say they're of."

"Well," said Dick Dick Dick Dick Dick, "that's where we have a pretty big problem. Allegedly, the *Texas Morning Sun* also has some memos that allegedly have some pretty high up signatures on them."

The Shah leaned forward. The tarp made a noise; his nethers were cold and wet from champagne. He spoke with veuve. "Whose signatures?"

Dick Dick Dick Dick Dick and Holly Unlikely glanced at each other. Bob Toose seemed to understand.

The Shah stood, his jeans adhering to his legs. "Whose signatures?"

Holly Unlikely said, "Do you remember when I advised you that we didn't have to follow the Geneva Conventions because we were a new country and hadn't signed them yet?"

The Shah pursed his lips. "Vaguely. Yes."

"And you made the determination that I was right?"

The Shah's eyebrows scrunched near each other like boys who want to appear tough but don't actually want to fight. "Was this one of the times when you said let's do this, and I said okay?"

"Yes," Bob Toose said. "You made the legal determination."

"No. She said this is a good idea, and I said okay."

Dick Dick Dick Dick Dick: "But you signed the document that said Holly advised you, and you made the determination. And you saw my signature, and Bob's, and you decided it must be okay."

"This was the paper with all the positives and negatives, the neverthelesses and all that?"

"One of them, yes," Bob Toose said. "The one that said we didn't have to follow the Geneva Conventions, but of course we would, unless we needed not to."

"I'm confused," the Shah said.

"That's the point," Holly Unlikely said. "It says we don't have to follow the rules, but we will, unless we have to break them."

The Shah flumped back down on the damp tarp. "Well, did we tell them to do the stuff they did in the photos?"

Scheissetete grinned at the mention of the photos.

"See," Holly Unlikely said, "that's where we have an out. We didn't specifically say they could or couldn't do all that stuff."

"So what do we do?" Bob Toose said.

"I feel like I'm going to throw up," the Shah said.

Dick Dick Dick Dick Dick crossed his arms. "I say we bomb the offices of the *Morning Sun.*"

"We can't do that," the Shah said. "It's the *Sun!* You can't bomb the *Sun!*"

"He's right," Bob Toose said. "What about the networks?"

"We could bomb them, too."

"I feel sick."

"We can't just bomb the media," Holly Unlikely said. We have to infiltrate them instead."

"What do you propose?" Dick Dick Dick Dick Dick asked.

"Some of them we don't have to worry about," Bob Toose said. "They're on our side. We just have to get them to say the right things." And Bob Toose had power over the power of the pen.

"It must not appear that you're trying to affect the network's news content," Dick Dick Dick Dick Dick said. "That's what you must do, but you must not appear to be doing that. That would be stupid[*]. "

"Oh, good," the Shah said. "I'm not going to have to be sick at all."

---

[*] This is a work of fiction. "Quotations, names, characters, businesses, places, events, locales, and incidents are either the products of the author's imagination or used in a fictitious manner." Any resemblance to actual Nixons, living or dead, or actual events is purely coincidental.

Grande

Grande

Adiel S. Thomas hadn't wanted to be a journalist. Since the age of eight, she'd read newspapers and magazines daily, but grudgingly. Every morning of her life, her silent father read the newspaper, front page to comics to classifieds. After her mother died, Adiel read it with him, just to be in the same room and in the hope he'd be a little less silent. While he solved the Jumble, she shook her head at the op-eds that he had already shaken his head at.

One morning, when she was ten, just before Texas declared itself independent: "Did you read Maude Lynne's column?" she asked, wanting to savage Maude Lynne's scroll of cliché.

He nodded. "Same old, same old."

"At her wedding, I bet she had something old, something used, something trite, and something bruised."

He grunt-laughed. She'd extracted that much from him; a victory. Ever after, when she asked if he'd read Maude Lynne, he said, "Something old, something used, something trite, something bruised." Routine was their intimacy.

In college, she majored in history, vaguely hoping to go to law school. She liked reading! She liked arguing! Until, in her junior year, she met a group of law-school students at a party (two dudes and one woman, the two dudes eying every female body, Adiel's included[*]).

"Yeah," they all said (not in unison, but at various times), "if you like reading and arguing, law school is not for you." The only pleasure in law was sadistic. So she ordered another shot and went home with the handsomish one of the two dudes because he muted his earnestness with jokes, then made out with him for a while and ignored his calls thereafter. In the messages he left on her machine for a week, his earnestness became unmuted.

To her friends, she sometimes described things in the form of a newspaper article—"It was revealed this week that Adiel S. Thomas has listened to the messages of an unnamed law student but refused to return his calls. Two anonymous sources have cited his emotional tur-

---

[*] Please refer to pages 22-23.

moil and referred to Ms. Thomas' 'cold-heartedness.'"

After her graduation, the *Texas Morning Sun* hired her as a copy editor. Heavy turnover and her tenacity about detail moved her up to the Metro desk. Margot Nought confided to Adiel that she was concerned about Cy Jost (but did not confide what about him concerned her) and moved Adiel to the desk catty-corner from his to assist with the Garza West story.

Thankfully for our narrative, Adiel had time to recall the above summary narrative of her life in relatively linear terms; given the power of omniscience, I've cut out the irrelevancies and shifted some things around. She had this time to recall as she waited in the parking deck at Main and Cedar for El Polla Grande, looking out on the Houston skyline. Buildings, cranes, 1970s American cars and a few recent imports from Japan, a Mercedes or two. Texas had one working automotive plant, and it had produced cars for General Motors before the war. The Texas government had sold the building to a group of oilmen, who had renamed it General Sam Houston Motors but hadn't yet gotten around to producing cars.

Twin domes drew the eye: the Astrodome, and the new seat of power in the country, the Freedome.

When Adiel squinted, she could see elevators going down in the skeletons of future buildings, hard-hatted men leaning against the walls. What did they talk about? Did they even talk? What would they say when they saw the photos from Garza West? Adiel felt at times she couldn't imagine the lives of certain people—the enormously wealthy and powerful, but also those who lived out in the sticks, those who worked in physical labor. Every time she thought she knew what they were like, they surprised her simply by thinking and saying a thing she wouldn't have expected. She remembered something Cy Jost said: Most of life is a failure of the imagination.

"Meese Thomas?"

Adiel startled and turned. In the shadow cast by the parking structure, between a dusty blue Chevette and a boxy Datsun, stood the sombreroed man who must be El Polla Grande. A la Hal Holbrook in *All the President's Men,* which was banned from screening in Texas, he wore a trenchcoat and smoked something lit orange at the end. But a cigar, not a cigarette. A really fat cigar. The enormous sombrero was threaded in the full range of Roy G. Biv.

Adiel said, "You can drop the accent, whoever you are."

"Nonsense. It helps keep my secret."[*]

Adiel stepped closer to him, but he held up his hand. "I must remain secret," he said. "Mr. Jost understood that. It is for both of our safeties."

"He told me he knew your identity."

"Rats," El Polla Grande said. "And now he is deceaséd."[†]

"Fair enough. What do you have for me?"

"I have good news and new news. First, your story will come out tomorrow."

Adiel felt her smile erupt. "Fantastic! How do you know that?"

"I am the source," he said, "and I have my sources. I am grande." He spread his arms wide, knocking the sombrero from his head. "No!" he yelled, bending down to hide. "I have defenestrated my somberero!" When he stood back up, it was again on his head, tilted further forward to shield his face.

"Don't worry," Adiel said. "I didn't see your face. You're still anonymous."

"Of course I am," he said. "I know what I'm doing. I am El Polla Grande. The new news: I will have another scoop for you soon. Troubles abound. They say the war is over, but it is not over. They declared victory to delay your story."

A whining tire announced itself coming from the deck above. Both Adiel and El Polla Grande squatted behind cars to hide. When the car rolled past, Adiel saw an exhausted businessman rubbing his eye with the heel of his hand. Once his car disappeared, they both stood again.

---

[*]From here on out, except for occasional moments, imagine his accent at whatever degree you'd like. I hate writing it out, and phonetic spelling in novels always grates, as if there is some standard pronunciation undiluted by region other than the bland television-Midwestern accent. For example, Maude Lynne speaks in the regionless but presumably Northeastern cadence of William F. Buckley; Adiel speaks in a practiced non-accent that veers to Texan when she is excited.

[†]The occasional linguistic variance is essential, I hope.

"We must be careful," El Polla Grande said.

"They can't just lie about the war being over," Adiel said. "That's criminal!"

"Yes," he said, "they can do it, and it is criminal. All you can do is try to stop it."

"How?"

"I will be coming to you with more pictures. They will do war, and war will make damage. I have my sources. Pictures will show the brutality. I will remain anonymous, but you, Adiel S. Thomas, you will make yourself a name. It will not be as wonderful as the name I have made for myself, but it will be a name."

Adiel's shock at the news set itself aside for pride. "Wow."

"Congratulations."

She shook her head, felt herself doing so showily. "No. I mean, wow. I can't believe the war isn't over."

Adiel couldn't see his face from the lips up, but from the way his chin moved, she knew he was grinning. "Most journalists," El Polla Grande said, "are better liars. You should practice."

WOR

Reader, you may be wondering: how did Texas and America come to be at war in the War of Texan Independence from the Surly Grip of America? (Or, as Americans called it, the War Against the States.) It's a common question, one Texans could ask every day; up to and through the events of this novel, the nation had always been bombing, always aiding bombers, always trooping, always aiding troops, always running covert ops. Texas became an inveterate covert opper, a/k/a copper, policing the world.

For the sake of clarity, here's the basic narrative students learn in Texan schools: for decades, Texas wanted to establish its national independence from the United States, and the leadership of the first Shah finally allowed Texas to tear itself from the clutches of the evil America.[*] The Shah, humble as always, did not want to become the Shah, but led by the needs and desires of God, Freedom, and Texas, said in that order, he did his duty.

It is probably most useful to start with a poster inside the front cover of every Texan high-school history textbook[*]:

---

[*]Style note: After Texan Independence, all Texan officials were instructed to refer to the United States of America only as America, in order to linguistically undermine said Uniting of said States. Texan media followed suit.

In terms of fairness, one usually would include an example from history textbooks in American classrooms, but they haven't been updated since 1972[*]. The real history is more complicated, as histories are once in a blue moon, and the causal connections less obvious. Here are some important notes:

1979: The not-yet and future Shah the First works in business, where he exerts considerable financial power but less of the political power he had in various and sundry government roles, im- and ex-plic-it. A run for the American presidency seems possible but exhausting and hopeless. And after the Vietnam War, the American government seems exhausted and hapless [†]. Still, he wanted his apotheosis—he attended the finest schools and wore the finest suits; he knew the word apotheosis and he wanted his. Fortunately for him, Fate interceded on his behalf.

So how did he become Shah? There are two explanations: an irreducibly complex confluence of events, or the single cause, aka the Franz Ferdinand.

The irreducible complexity: Texans never saw themselves as Americans but as Texans, and a string of American failures created the animus and animosity to make that happen:

• the Shah of Iran had to flee his country, and the Ayatollah Khomeini took power;

• Adolph Dubs, the American Ambassador to Afghanistan, was kidnapped and killed, and many felt the American response lacked a certain fortitude, testicular and blastacular;

• as the Texan not-yet Shah the First and his supporters knew, the CIA began providing weapons and funds to Mujahideen fighters in Afghanistan under Operation Cyclone;

• in April, the Red River Valley tornado killed dozens, including 42 in Wichita Falls, leading many Texans to doubt the power of the Great American Weather Machine and leading Texans in the

---

[†]Several states bordering Texas also used the Texan history textbook.

[*]According to these textbooks, the United States continues to win the Vietnam War.

[*]According to the news, the Vietnam War was a tie, meaning the United States won, because the tie goes to the runner.

know to see more than coincidence in Operation Cyclone and the Red River Valley tornado;

• the Salvadoran Civil War began, and instead of nuking El Salvador, the United States began funding the Salvadoran government, inefficiently favoring slow terror over fast terror;

• the Nicaraguan National Guard killed ABC journalist Bill Stewart;

• on July 15, President Jimmy Carter gave his famous "malaise" speech, in which he did not use the word "malaise," and which briefly raised his approval ratings;

• the following day, Saddam Hussein replaced the President of Iraq after being the de facto leader for years, and quickly began a purge of the Ba'ath party;

• on November 4, Iran took American hostages;

• finally, the final straw of finality: on November 12, Jimmy Carter announced a halt to U.S. oil imports from Iran while Houston's oil boom boom-boomed, and he ordered that Texas oil companies would provide America's oil under market price.

The poor, put-upon leaders of oil companies complained that Jimmy Carter wanted to take Texan oil for peanuts. They meant it metaphorically, but Texans took it very literally, believing that Carter wanted to enrich himself by trading his peanuts for oil. Texans rebelled by buying all the peanuts from grocery stores and stomping on them in the streets.[*]

Polls overwhelmingly supported Texan independence. Governor Boon E. Hoolihan claimed to support independence but refused to act on it. Publicly and privately, he counseled moderation. So, privately, on November 13, police directly overseen by Dick Dick Dick Dick Dick quietly and loudly assassinated the Governor. Quietly in that the public never knew; loudly in that people several offices down the hall heard the Governor's screaming and desk-kicking, and even further down people heard the single gunshot. They knew it was an assassination because it wasn't a bevy, a gaggle, an assembly, a party, a cluster, a murder of gunshots.

------

[*]Peanut futures rose.

After news of the Governor's death (publicly reported as a heart attack), the not-yet Shah the First gave a powerful public speech that local stations reported widely and praisingly: America had become a parasite grown to the size of a host, bleeding every man, woman, child, and nation it could. Such bleeding had made Texas anemic when, if Texas was a country, it would immediately become the most powerful in the world. And you know what? As of now, Texas was an independent nation, and he'd be honored and humbled to lead it. And in honor of the great Shah who had been deposed by the terrible Ayatollah, he declared himself the Shah of Texas. Thus the not-yet Shah the First became the Shah.

The Franz Ferdinand cause for historians: More simply, more to the point, and less reported and understood than all the above causes: The single, impossible origin of Texan Nationhood arose on January 26—*The Dukes of Hazzard* débuted on CBS. The sight of the General Lee rekindled that deepest of desires: Texan Independence. As the show became a hit, all the Bo and Luke Dukes of Texas yearned for (usually metaphorical) automotive flight away from the evil clutches of the buffoonish Boss Hogg, imagined broadly as Jimmy Carter or, alternatively, America, because America wasn't what she used to be. The Duke boys did what they wanted; they did what was fun and right. The spirit flew and grew. By November, the image of waiting in lines for gas grounded their imaginative and literal vehicles, and when the now-Shah announced their freedom and his now-Shahhood, they rejoiced in their freedom. He became the patriarch, their Uncle Jesse.

Had *The Dukes of Hazzard* never aired, Texas never would have declared its independence.

Maybe the Shah should have publicized the assassination of the Governor instead of intoning sadly that the Governor had died of a massive stroke. Said Governor could have been immortalized as a neo-Franz Ferdinand. Instead, the United States government was puzzled. The Shah was ready for. . .

WOR!*

Instead, the Shah received from the American government what many now understand most immediately as:

$$\bar{\ }\backslash\_(ツ)\_/\bar{\ }$$

There were diplomatic disputes, and fights among families that were Texan by origin but American by address, and vice versa (could one be both American/Wyomingian† and Texan at the same time?), but these didn't rise to the new Shah's hopes. Freedom only mattered if the free could fight or pretend they had fought for those freedoms. War *must* be fought. Freedom should not be gained with ease or, worst, a mocking shrug, especially for Texans long hungry for true freedom, and especially if they noticed no differences in their relative freedom.

So the Texas National Guard—a National Guard now in the sense that Texas was a nation—lined up at interstates and started shooting any American who drove in. They let cars with Texas plates cruise on by because they were good, God-fearing, honest-to-God Texans: the license plates said so.

America now took seriously the secession of Texas from the States and the cessation of Texas as a state. Texas insisted that America sign with it a Desistance of Hostilities. Grudgingly, and under the impression that Texas was, in fact, not leaving the Union, America signed, condemning America and Texas to war because one must sign a peace treaty before war breaks out and for no other reason. And as there was now a peace when there had been no war, America sent its troops to the border; one cannot stop a war without troops. The soldiers were, legally, men and women; in the American press, they were boys and girls. But if one country mans their border in response to the first country manning their border, the first country has a right to retaliate. Those are the rules of war, as set down in *Robert's Rules of Border.*

---

*An overworked telegrammer, excited by the prospect of war, made a small typo in the message to President Carter. Whomst among us hans't?

†Wyominger? Wyoman? Wingman? Why me? If only one could contact the residents of Wyoming to know.

Between the Texas National Guard, sundry Texan police, and American troops who went AWOL so they could become Texan troops, Texas had a good-sized army with small arms, like a formation of Tyrannosauruses Rexes. Thus the Shah agreed with his War Secretary (a position appointed before there was a War to Secret) to send a battalion into Louisiana. The incursion went badly, but the Shah's experience in gov't allowed him to turn the situation into a PR win for Texas. Their men and women murdered our girls and boys, and child-acide must always be punished. Texans now had Texan news stations that told very different stories. Out went the Brinkleys and Chancellors, the Jenningses and Walterses; rather, in came Neil O'Chisholm, Hugh Succop, their hairstyles and voices speaking calm and terror into Texan lives, depending on need.

When America threatened Texas with a real war, the Shah knew they were outgunned. They could never be outhearted, but America had weaponry, if not the spine, to empty every heart in the heart of Texas. And when Ronald Reagan took office with his Vice President Alexander Haig (campaign slogan for the pair: "WE ARE IN CONTROL HERE"), the threat of actual war became actual.

The Shah was savvy enough to let Dick Dick Dick Dick Dick handle some of the financial details. America needed oil; Texas needed weapons. So even though they skirmished, they traded. Meanwhile, Iraq and Iran began their eight-year war. America sold weapons to Iran to fund Contras in Nicaragua; Texas sold their own newly acquired weapons to Iraq in exchange for weaponry, then exchanged Iraqi weapons with the U.S. for more American weaponry so America could examine Iraqi arms.

If you find the exchanges described above confusing to follow, a visual guide follows:

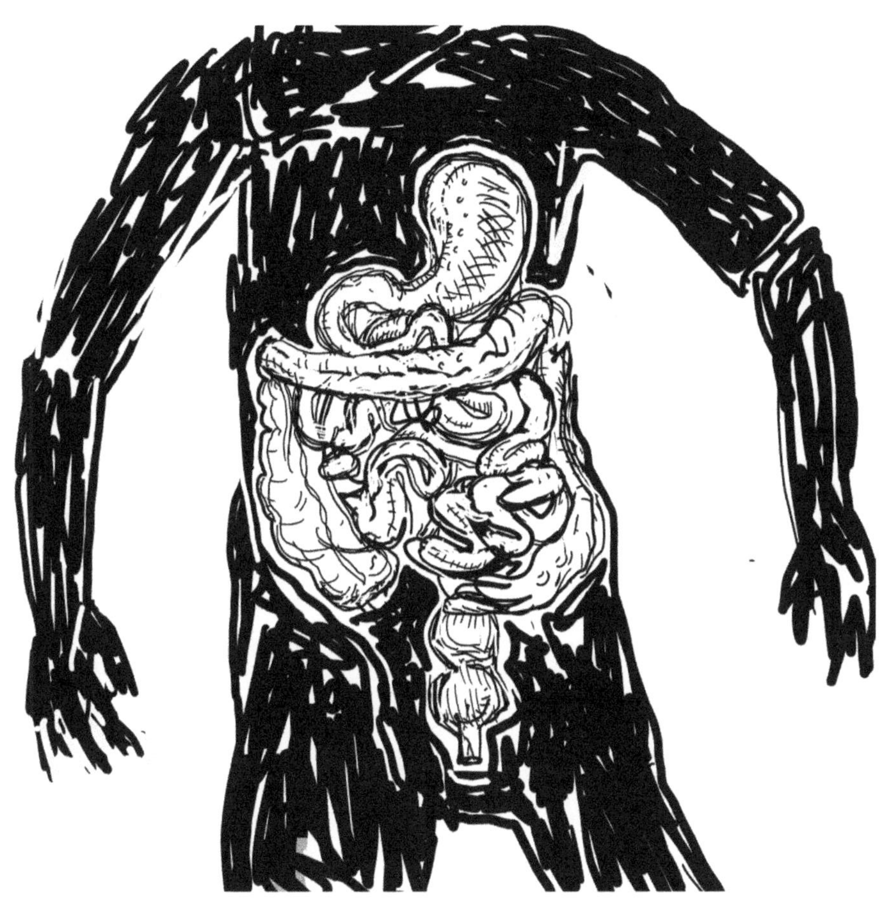

Both Texas and America needed to project strength, for strength is not an abstraction but a projectile. So their war consisted of soldiers firing rubber bullets at each other and planes bombing empty buildings. Both governments could say: "Look what we did to them"/"Look what they did to us!"/"We have spread our freedom to them!"/"We will rebuild!" Both countries saw the benefit of loss and economic redevelopment. Of course, war being what it is, and competence being scant, soldiers died and were maimed, civilians died and were maimed, buildings that were both physical and symbolic were made only symbolic. War continued this way, with little particular movement on either side, until 1984, when America allowed Texas its independence so they could defeat them on the truest field of conflict: the 1984 Olympic Games in Los Angeles.

Almost all Texan athletes were already contracted to compete for America, leaving Texas with an Olympic team of cast-offs and benchwarmers. Until, that is, they discovered a pocket of ethnic communities between Amarillo and Lubbock, where the athletes had prominent Eastern European accents and spoke little English. American news outlets began calling the newly independent country "Soviet Texas," which led to the state's current slogan: "So Be It: Texas." Nearly all of the Texan athletes were disqualified because they tested positive for steroids and brisket[*]. Texas won the war; America won the Olympics.

For three years, hostilities simmered. Americans called Texas toast "fat toast." Texans called American cheese "freedom cheese." But there was no violence of note[†].

On October 19, 1987, Black Monday, stock markets around the world crashed. The first Shah remained heavily invested in the Dow Jones and Texas' new stock exchange, the Bull Market. Looking at his investments and doing the math, he misplaced a decimal and tried to commit suicide by leaping off the back of a sofa. He sprained his wrist. Luckily for his death drive, he proceeded to have a massive stroke. Usually, someone else would be in the Grand Office of the Shah. However, he was alone. Everyone else was elsewhere on hold, waiting to talk with their brokers. He was discovered by his secretary at 11:00 a.m.; she had gone into his office to give him his post-coffee peppermint and tickle.

Grief struck the Freedome. Within the hour, Dick Dick Dick Dick Dick made the public announcement of the Shah's death, interrupting the popular Texas soap opera *Specific Hospital*. He also intended to declare—to no one else's prior knowledge—that he was taking the

---

[*]Music connoisseurs may think here of the "lost" Tom Waits bootleg album *Cigarettes and Brisket,* a 3 a.m. recording of Waits trying to order off menu at an International House of Pancakes.

[†]Meaning, of course, that there was violence, but not *war* violence.

place of the new Shah, but as soon as he began speaking, he realized he couldn't be the public face the first Shah had been. Dick Dick Dick Dick Dick hated people, both individually and as a whole, and he could not fake it. But with the stock ticker spelling out S.O.S. in Morse code, the country needed stability, so he announced that, following the draft Constitution of the Great Nation of Texas, a draft that existed un-written with various laws in the minds of various lawmakers, the Shah would be replaced by his son. So the Shah replaced the Shah.

The new Shah hadn't been raised to be Shah. He hadn't been raised to be anything in particular and was the commissioner of both the TBA and TBD sports leagues.

America wanted to take advantage. Americans were excited for the oncoming fall of Texas, because the Shah's son, the new Shah, was a dimwit. And not their kind of dimwit, either. A real Texan. Texans worried for the same reasons, but they trusted that, in spite of his dim-wittedness, he would surround himself with brightwitted people, as dimwits are wont to do.[*] With the stock market tanking, they needed a pretext for war. Months later, a suitable pretext arose. On July 2, 1988, Texans were enjoying their usual day-to-day lives; the top two movies in Texas were *The Karate Child* and *The Muppets Take Manhattan*[†]. Then, on July 3, 1988, an American surface-to-air missile shot down Iran Air Flight 655, killing the 290 souls on board.[¥] In retaliation and fairness, a Texan surface-to-air missile shot down Iraqi Airways Flight 187, killing the 273 souls on board.[§]

---

[*]Citation needed.

[†]Texas had not built its own Hollywood, so, for a fee, they purchased the rights to air American films, usually with alternate titles such as *The Karate Child. The Muppets Take Manhattan* had been rebranded as a war film, with the Muppets taking Manhattan on behalf of the Texas National Guard. The overdub of the new script was poor; Texans loved it.

[¥]After a long struggle, we decided on the phrase "souls on board" here, as pilots and air-traffic controllers have long referred to "souls on board" to refer to the number of persons on a flight. In flight, we are souls.

[§]If one sings "Souls on Board" to the tune of Duran Duran's "Girls on Film," one uncovers a jaunty note in death.

Tensions spiked* between America and Texas, leading to actual attacks on actual military bases. Given the proximity of military bases to sub-urban and ish-urban areas, civilian lives and populated structures took much greater violence, motivating both pro- and anti- war sentiment in both nations. As a joke, recorded and later broadcast, Ronald Reagan said before a speech, "We begin bombing in five minutes." In response, the Shah recorded and released his response, scripted by Dick Dick Dick Dick Dick: "We began bombing five minutes ago." For Texan media, Reagan's joke was incitement, the Shah's joke an example of his superior strength and sense of humor.

After a week, tensions unspiked a bit, until Iran fired two rockets at an American ship in the Persian Gulf. The rockets turned out to be duds; they damaged the hull of the ship but injured no one, save for a sailor who was shaving at the time. (His stiff upper lip went home wrapped in an American flag.) In clearing the rockets, sailors discovered two things: a) the rockets were American, a common discovery in these times, and b) said American rockets had been sold to Texas and, evidently, then sold to Iran. American forces were outraged to learn that Texas had turned powerful American rockets into flaccid duds, for America only made weapons of the greatest strength and efficiency.**

Internally—both in his private offices and in his body—the Shah was angry about the error. Then the real, real war between Texas and America began.

Under the banner of free speech and a free press, criticisms of the Shah and his government arose, some legitimatish, some non-legitimate. The Shah, in the shadow of his father, was flailing. It became clear that the Shah needed a domestic victory. And beneath that lay the schools were terrible and in dire need of reform. Texans did not want to make the ever-so-common mistake of paying teachers exorbitant salaries with summers off; instead, schools would discover the destinies of their students earlier in those students' lives and categorize them sooner. No more wasting money on waste. School would prepare them better and more aptly for the work of their lives. Students who

---

*Cf. thousands of newpaper and magazine headlines.
**Citation needed.

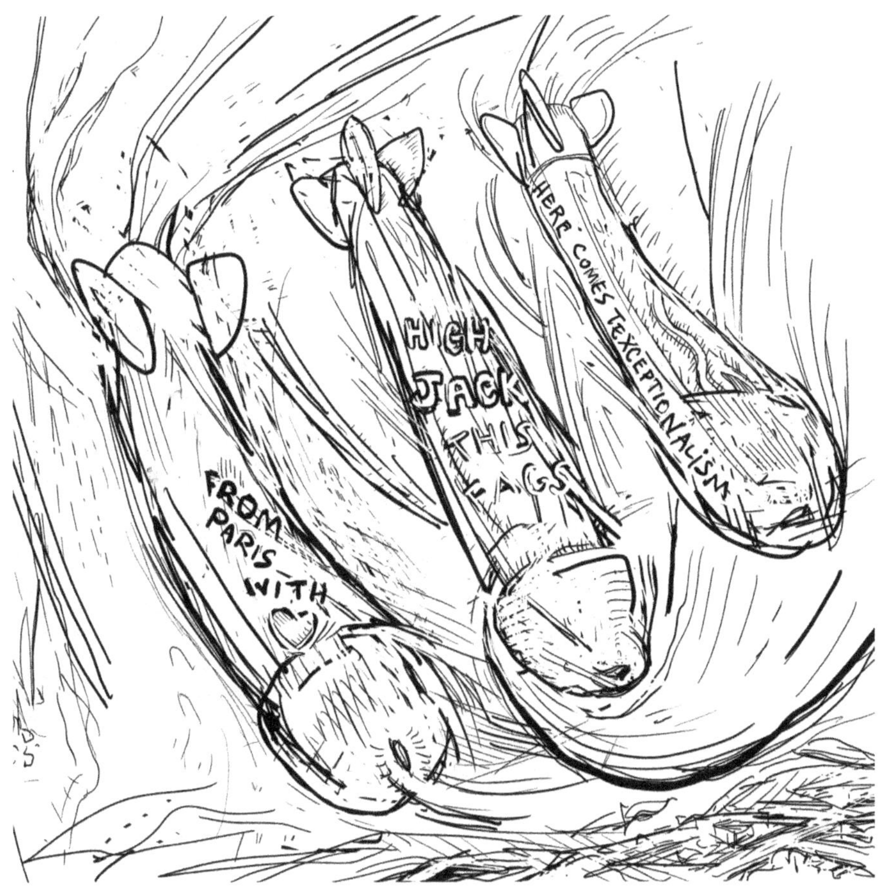

deserved options would be given options. Unlike the failed American experiment of opportunity, Texas would be the merrytocracy it had always been.

Of course, Texas had seen school reforms before, long before the first and second Shahs, long before Independence. But the second Shah, guided by the twin wisdoms of Bob Toose and Dick Dick Dick Dick Dick, made two savvy decisions: first, students had to pass a test to enter the next grade, but no student would ever repeat a grade.[*] Second, the natural link between education and the military would be

---

[*] A teacher had once threatened to make the Shah repeat a grade, and only his father's intervention in getting the teacher fired led to the Shah moving into the next grade as he should.

more formal: students who did not pass the test but could not repeat a grade would move into their work-study in the military under a new program, Superior Texans Undergoing National Guard Training.

Elder Texans loved it, and the Shah loved Texans loving it. The military refilled with soldiers, and the Texas National Guard achieved greater success in the war with America. That war is the one that, in this narrative, our Shah has just announced has ended.

As of the present time of this novel, the two warring teams are in the midst of a long, ongoing draw.[*]

---

[*] Some readers, when they start a chapter, flip forward to see how many pages there are left in the chapter. Other readers flip ahead to the end of the book, then read the whole thing.

The Ballad of Bob and Maude

The Ballad of Bob and Maude

Bob Toose fingered the doorbell. As he pressed, its light went dark; it lit again when he let go. He was a master of the communicatory arts, well above his fellow man, but he did appreciate how the little things made him giddy. He wanted to use the just-really-stellar knocker—dark wood, gothic design with bulging eyes, large as his hand—but it intimidated him. Plus, he didn't want this visit to begin with an ominous knock. Given the news from Dick Dick Dick Dick Dick, he wanted to be as omininity-free as possible. He did, though, trace it with the finger that had fingered the doorbell.

The door, a thick, pocked oak, swung open. Maude Lynne smiled at Bob Toose and put her free hand to her pearls. She had a hairstyle that would have been appropriate and tasteful across several decades: never in style, never out of style. An enduring status quo.

"Mr. Robert Toose," she said. "What a darling surprise."

"Ms. Maude Lynne," he said. "My pleasure as always."

She invited him in, offered coffee and tea. He declined—his visit was business, not pleasure. Above the fireplace in her sitting room was an oil painting of the first Shah, standing at a quarter-turn, right hand Napoleonic inside his suit jacket.[*]

Maude Lynne led Bob Toose to one divan and sat on the facing divan. "I see you've brought your briefcase. This must be serious business."

"I'm afraid it is. Did you watch the news?"

Maude Lynne raised her chin as if she were setting it on an invisible windowsill. "I rarely watch the evening news. Why bring such a dreary end to such a lovely day? The Shah's speech needs no gilding."

"Unfortunately, some are going to try to tarnish his speech." He pulled from his briefcase an envelope with the calligraphic words "Classified and Confidentialized" on its front.

Maude Lynne's eyebrows betrayed a joie de vivre that contained nearly too much joie and vivre to be proper. "Oh, Robert, you flatter and tease me."

---

[*]For art buffers: The style would be best described as paleo-classical.

"Oh, how I wish," he said, unsheathing a stack of 8x10 photographs from the envelope. "A certain media outlet will publish these."

The image on top depicted a laughing Texan soldier pouring what appeared to be old porridge into the mouth of a prone American prisoner.

"Oh my!" she said and put both her hands to her pearls.

"Sorry," said Bob Toose. "That wasn't supposed to be the first one. Some of the photos inside are worse. Do you want to see them?"

"Dare I? Do I need to?"

"I think it's important that we know what we're dealing with."

As he showed her the photos, she kept her fingers at her pearls, teasing them in her fingertips. "Oh heavens," she repeated. "Oh my." Once he had shown the entire set, returning to the first image, she asked, "Who would do such a thing?"

"Allegedly, Texan soldiers."

"No, no. I mean, who at the *Texas Morning Sun* would force these into our eyes?"

Bob Toose shook his head. "Head byline is Cy Jost."

"Cy Jost? Didn't he die?"

"He did, and obviously none too soon."

"How dreadful, Robert! The gall, to speak from beyond the grave."

Bob nodded. "He had some help. The other name on the byline is Adiel S. Thomas." He said this as if Maude Lynne might know who Adiel S. Thomas was, but she shook her head. "She's young," he added.

"Oh!" Maude said. "How I hate the young!"

"Me, too. But we were all young once."

Maude rolled her eyes. "I was never young."

Bob re-sealed the envelope and returned it to his briefcase. "And now we have to get out in front of this—this story. The Shah needs your help."

"Anything for the Shah. Anything for Texas."

Bob Toose reached out and held her hand.

"Oh Robert, I want you. Here and now."

"In your sitting room?"

"Heavens no," she said. "Not on the divans, you silly man. Let us repair to the boudoir."

Getting Down to Brass Tacks

Getting Down to Brass Tacks

Dear Reader,

There are, of course, many terms for intercourse, categorized below by varieties of experience:

The sex act: intercourse, sex, fucking, making love, coitus;

Construction: nailing, screwing, caulking, wetwalling the drywall, polishing the marble, laying, laying the pipe, fitting the fixtures, wetwork, re-tiling the sink, flogging one's box, servicing, making a service call;

Sporting and gaming: balling, screwballing, touching home plate, the grand slam, the grand salami, playing hide the salami, the naked bootleg, high sticking, crowding the box, personal foul—giving the business, banging down low, rolling snake eyes, running the two-minute drill;

Education: knowing, matriculating, loading up on debt, cramming, fluffing to reach the minimum word count;

Finance: making a deposit, doing the deed, doing one's taxes, auditing, notarizing, adding up credits and debits, grossing and netting and grossing again;

Home décor and cleanliness: mopping, swiffering, laying down a rug, adding a rinse cycle, burying the wick, dipping one's wick, putting junk in the crawl space, furbishing, refurbishing (for use by especially energetic young men with quick recovery times), arranging the furniture, lacquering;

The filmography of Harrison Ford: raiding the lost ark, the last crusade, bullwhipping the Nazis, going to light speed, blowing up the Death Star, patriot games, clear and present danger, regarding horny, getting frantic, graffiti-ing, using the force, getting inside the Tauntaun to stay warm (and I thought they smelled bad on the outside!), hiding among the bearded Amish as in the Oscar-winning 1985 film *Wetness;*

Miscellaneous: buggering, rogering, bumping uglies, making a baby, making feet for children's shoes, making the beast with two backs, shagging, boinking, shaboinking, deliberating, flabbergasting, getting laid, getting lucky, getting short or long shrift, getting some stank for the hang down, the horizontal bop, having a go, dicking, lay-

ing, boning, burying the bone, romancing the bone, crawling, cream-
ing, winding back the clock, diddling.

(Nota bene: the list is not exhaustive, though compiling it was.)

You may, at your leisure, choose the term you deem appropriate for the act in which Bob Toose and Maude Lynne were about to
engage. We find the sex act so deeply personal that we prefer to leave
most of the next two pages to your discretion. Imagine away, as you
wish. We would be remiss, of course, if we failed to provide any linguistic guidance, and so, below, we have offered just a redacted touch.

Kiss

                                               nipple

                iceberg

slinky

     crack

                                  trickle-down

abrogate

                  deregulate

                              milk pearl

                three-hole punch

                              portastrophallic

rind

armoire

titular

coil

stifle

muff

the disappeared

If necessary, reader, take a moment for yourself before we move forward.

Outlaw in a Polo, Etc.

Outlaw in a Polo: Brief Interviews with Serious Men (and One Woman)

It is not within the characterological elucidations of this history to include the lives of those uninvolved with the machinations herein. That said, some may wonder about the views of Everyday Texans™. With that in mind, below are quotes from a few E.T.'s™.

Question: How do you feel about Independence?

Autry Barrow, owner and proprieter, Barrow's Wheels, a chain of car dealerships: I feel great about it. Inspired, even. After all, we Texans are fiercely independent, so it's only natural that we'd finally realize our ultimate fate: Nationhood.

Buddy Hogan, oilman: Why, it's our right! No man is an island, but every man is his own nation, endowed by God. By God, it's only right. After all, we Texans are fiercely independent.

Babe Didrikson Perot, wife: Why, I'm delighted! Finally our boys and girls can pray to their God and pledge allegiance to their true country! It's a historical first! I'm just so honored to be part of such a fiercely independent nation.

Question: How do you feel about the war?

Barrow, owner and proprietor: I feel great about it. Inspired, even. After all, the greatest thing any one of us can do is serve our country and, if necessary, sacrifice ourselves for it. Sacrifice is holy. Now, I'm too old to serve for Texas, and I didn't serve for America because I was Texan, first and foremost. So I have to live every day with regret that I cannot do the greatest thing any one of us can do. Instead,

I pledge to do every day what I must, the second greatest thing any one of us can do: support our boys and girls in uniform.

Hogan, oilman: Why, we all know that war is hell, a scourge of man. But it's a scourge that is our right, endowed by God. And if we must go to war, I will support the scourge until the end, because it's only right.

Perot, wife: Long live Texas!

Question: Are there any dissenters?

Unnamed interlocutor: I'm sorry, we're out of time for questions.

After Publication

After Publication

Margot Nought, Executing Editrix, held her chin and narrowed her eyes. Adiel still awaited Margot's editorial judgments with the same internal squirm. At least she had learned, chided by Margot many times, to stop flicking her fingertips while she waited for Margot's decision.

Margot nodded. "You're going to have to clip that. Veronica?"

The intern nodded. She pulled a binder clip from the bowl.

"No, honey," Margot said. "One of the big ones."

Adiel yawned—not tired, but nervous, needing oxygen. She heard the clinks in the ceramic bowl behind her as Veronica pulled out a larger binder clip.

"Adiel," Margot said. "Shoulders back."

Adiel put her shoulders back, as instructed, and felt Veronica pulling on the back of the blazer Adiel wore. Then Veronica clipped it.

"There," Margot said. "Now it fits."

Adiel had last worn a blazer, stiff with shoulder pads, for job interviews. She had donned one for her interview with the *Morning Sun*, and here she was, prepping for her first TV appearances as a reporter. They had set up in Margot Nought's office, in her appearance nook: sitting in front of the bookcase, the depth of field set so a bored viewer could read the book titles. (Margot Nought's history of the war, *For Country, God, and Country*, was displayed with the cover facing out, her serious face gazing out very seriously.) Adiel would be doing a series of remotes. Most of the stations were based in Houston, within walking distance, but it was simpler to sit in Margot's office for all of them than to meander around the city, sweating on each walk and freezing in each studio.

"Remember," Margot said. "There's a brief delay. Don't react. Keep your face flat. Don't do that little smirk you do."

"What little smirk?"

"That one. Doesn't she do it, Veronica?"

From behind Adiel, Veronica pulled Adiel's hair behind her ears. "Yes, ma'am."

During the interviews, Adiel's nerves faded. The anchors asked the same questions: why this story now, wasn't this anti-Texan, who were her sources, had everything been confirmed. And Adiel gave the same answers, shaped by Margot as they had been. This story now because she wanted Texas to be the most Texceptional it could be; it wasn't anti-Texan but out of patriotism for this great nation and our greatest soldiers, and to honor her late, great colleague Cy Jost; she couldn't reveal her sources, and everything was multiply-sourced. Between the interviews, though, she felt like a boxer: Margot her corner man with nerve-inducing instructions ("what did I say about that smirk?"), Veronica re-gracing Adiel's hair and blotting her face.

Once Adiel was done, she took off Margot's blazer and handed it to her. While it was in Margot's hands, Veronica unclipped the back. At her desk, Adiel was met by one of the secretaries, an older woman whose skin, thinned hair, and voice were all yellowed by years of smoking. Adiel should have known the woman's name but didn't. Hers was among a dozen names Adiel was told her first day, forgot, and never asked about again for fear of looking like an idiot and insulting these nameless people. The woman handed Adiel a stack of papers torn from a message pad. "Congrats, dear" the woman said in a flat, mentholated voice. "Your first death threats."

"Not my first, but my first set, I guess."

"Come work the phones with us for an hour," said nameless secretary said. "You almost get used to it. One or two of those may be actual messages. We didn't have time to sort them." She walked away.

Most messages looked like so:

TELEPHONE MESSAGE

To	Adiel S. Thomas
From	[Almost always blank]
Time/Date	9:42 a.m./8/17/89
Respond By	Once she's fucked herself
Phone	[Always blank]
Fax	
Message	

Texas-hating bitch go fuck herself, when finished join Cy Jost in grave, support the troops, et cet

OR

Should be shit on like the scum in those pictures

OR

[Reader, you can use your imagination, or you can keep your imagination pristine and keep on reading.]

She had to skim each slip before letting it fall into the trash. The paper felt thin and powdery. She read over and again: Her genitals should be electrocuted, how about the police dose her with LSD until she couldn't tell what was real and what was fake, what's wrong with having a dog in your face because dogs are cute, if you hate Texas so much you should leave (this one was iterated many times over), you're a cunt just like those filthy Americans, we will blow you up so completely they won't be able to identify your body. These went on. There were, unfortunately, actual messages in the stack that required attention: a source from a prior story about police not responding to distress calls in one neighborhood—a story Adiel had left behind once it was published—and Cy Jost's younger brother thanking her for finishing his work.

And a message she dropped into the black-bagged trash can before reconsidering and fishing it out:

TELEPHONE MESSAGE

To	Adiel S. Thomas
From	The Giant Cock (he insisted on the capital letters)
Time/Date	9:47 a.m./8/17/89
Respond By	This time next Tuesday at Kirby and Westridge
Phone	
Fax	
Message	

Congratulations on your success. Surely there will be more to come.

The Giant Cock. El Polla Grande? It had to be. Almost certainly. She would go to meet him, but in case of a trick she'd be prepared.

"Ladies and gentlemen of the newsroom," Margot Nought called from the doorway of her office in her announcement voice, vowels rounded and consonants more crisp. "We break the news, and sometimes that helps us make the news." She extended a hand out toward Adiel, palm up as if revealing a missing ball at the end of a magic trick. "Our little newsmaker will be gracing none other than *This Week in the Republic* with Neil O'Chisholm. Let us give her a hand."

Adiel felt her face and neck splotch. The applause felt perfunctory, and for the first time Adiel had the distinct sense that all of her colleagues disliked her.

Margot said, "Now let us get back to the noble work of shaping the world!" She walked over to Adiel's desk. "We'll have to buy you a smart suit. Oh, and honey, you'll want to keep the death threats in the unlikely event that one is actually real. I have absolute boxes of them in my garage."

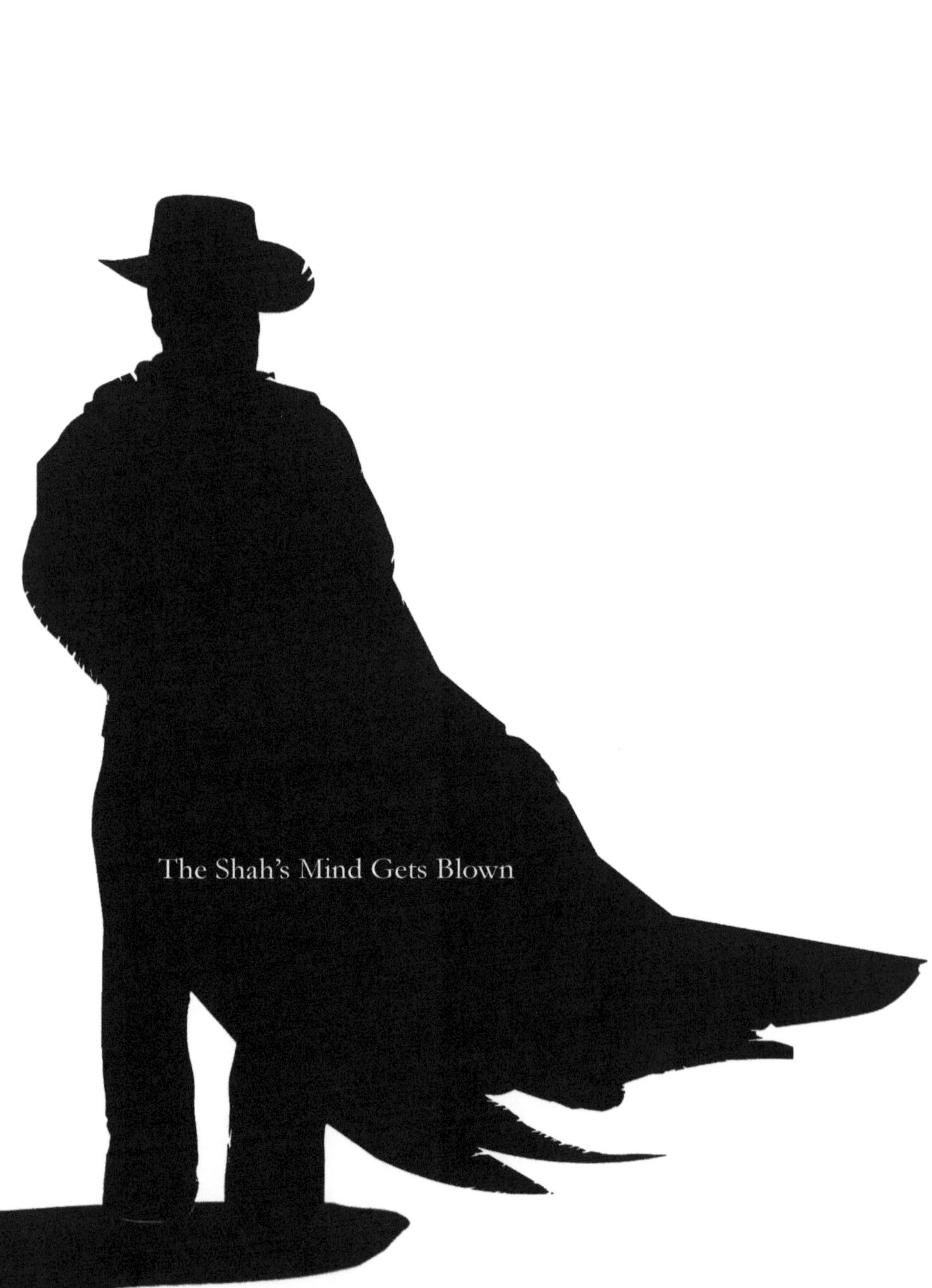
The Shah's Mind Gets Blown

The Shah's Mind Gets Blown

Usually, when the guards led the Shah from his breakfast into the Grand Office—they were back in Houston now, in the Grand Office of the Freedome, under the first reproduction of the painting of the first Shah—the sounds of bustle, hustle, and muted spurs surrounded. But this morning, with the taste of toothpaste still on his tongue (and a little gob he'd missed in a gummy nook between teeth), the guards led him through quiet halls, only their spurs offering a hushed chorale of *clink-hish, clink-hish* as they landed in the thick red carpet. When they passed the glassed-in Department for the Dissemination of Communicatory Ejaculations, the screens were black, the phone conversations muted rather than straining through the glass. The Shah worried. Had someone died?

When the lead guard opened the door to the Grand Office, Bob Toose was speaking. "We'll have to take the QwikPik cameras away from the soldiers."

"Nonsense," Dick Dick Dick Dick Dick said, coming into the Shah's view. "They have to have souvenirs from war, and we can't have them taking ears again."

"Or nun's habits."

"Hey, as long as they don't make a habit of it."

No one laughed.[*]

"What's the thing about the ears?" the Shah asked. "I just don't get it."

"Long story," Bob Toose said.

"So why is everything so quiet this morning? Did somebody die?"

Bob Toose put a hand on the Shah's shoulder. "You should sit down for this."

The Shah shrugged off the fatherly hand even though he appreciated it, and he sat down. His own father, the first Shah, had less a fatherly hand and more an invisible hand. Still, he had guided his son

---

[*]All writing is autobiographical.

into his Shahship, so he must have done something right.

Bob Toose sat on the facing couch. Dick Dick Dick Dick Dick gazed out the window though there was nothing real to gaze at—the windows of this inner office faced a mural of a blue skyline painted over gray concrete in a hallway no one was allowed to walk down. Now and again, felt geese flew across the painted sky in a perfect V. Scheissetete stood behind Bob Toose, holding a folded newspaper and failing to suppress a grin.

"The article we told you about, with the photos? It came out."

The Shah sat up straighter to look more Shah-like. (Shah-esque? Shahish? Which was right? As he thought of these, his posture reverted.) "And you need me to look at them."

"Yes, sir. We didn't want you to be surprised by them. Hence the quiet hallways."

"Hence," the Shah said and nodded.

"Just get on with it," Dick Dick Dick Dick Dick growled. "This shouldn't be such a big deal."

"You're right," Bob Toose said. "It really shouldn't, should it, Dick?"

"Just give him the newspaper."

"Do I have to read the article?" the Shah asked.

Bob Toose reached an arm back, and Scheissetete handed him the folded newspaper. "I'll warn you," Bob Toose said. "The photos are graphic."

He unfolded the newspaper and set it on the coffee table between them. Above and below the fold, a full-color photo showed a hooded man standing on a car battery with jumper cables running from the battery to his index fingers. A cable ran along the floor, from the back of the battery to somewhere outside the photo.

The Shah shook his head. "I don't get it."

"See?" Dick Dick Dick Dick Dick said. "It's not a big deal. Let's get on with our lives. We need to shift our focus back to the Base Race."

Bob Toose cleared his throat. "They didn't put the worst photo on the cover. They claim it's in the name of good taste." He opened the newspaper to reveal two full-page photographs: on the left, a soldier, baton mid-swing, smiling as he beats the already-bruised back of a naked prisoner. On the right, a prisoner standing in a cross, head and torso smeared with brown, with a soldier in the distance holding his nose in an exaggerated way.

"Okay, the one on the left is pretty bad. His sergeant or whatever should punish him. The one on the right, though, we did stuff like that in my frat at Haverland and worse stuff in my secret society.[*] One time, we ███████████████████████████████████,[†] and we threw bananas at him."

Dick Dick Dick Dick Dick said, "You're not supposed to talk about that in front of company who weren't part of Gullet to Gennies."

"Sir," Bob Toose said, "why bananas?"

The Shah shrugged. "We had them. Plus, they kinda looked like, you know. Anyway, we used chocolate sauce, like here."

Scheissetete beamed, and the tendons in his neck showed like taut ropes bracing a tent.

Bob Toose took a deep breath. "Sir, that's shit."

Reader, you have to understand: The Shah's brain was delicate. Of course, every brain is delicate, floating as it does in a calcified bedpan, shriveled with trauma and memory. We have words and phrases to describe what happened: he had a realization, a catharsis, an epiphany. His mind, we say, was blown. But that doesn't capture the before-and-after states of his understanding. Luckily, thanks to the miracle of narrative omniscience, we have before-and-after MRI images of the Shah's brain.

---

[*] Please note that the Shah neither attended nor spoke here of Haver*ford* College in Pennsylvania. He attended Haver*land* College, whose campus covers the borders of Rhode Island, Connecticut, and Massachusetts. Founded by 17th Century celebrity slave-trader Eusephia Haverland in 1635, Haverland College was the first private college in America to feature a middle-class student on the cover of a brochure.
[†] {Publisher's note: The author's violation of fraternity secrets galls me, and I have ordered the blacking out of such radical disclosure.}

Before:

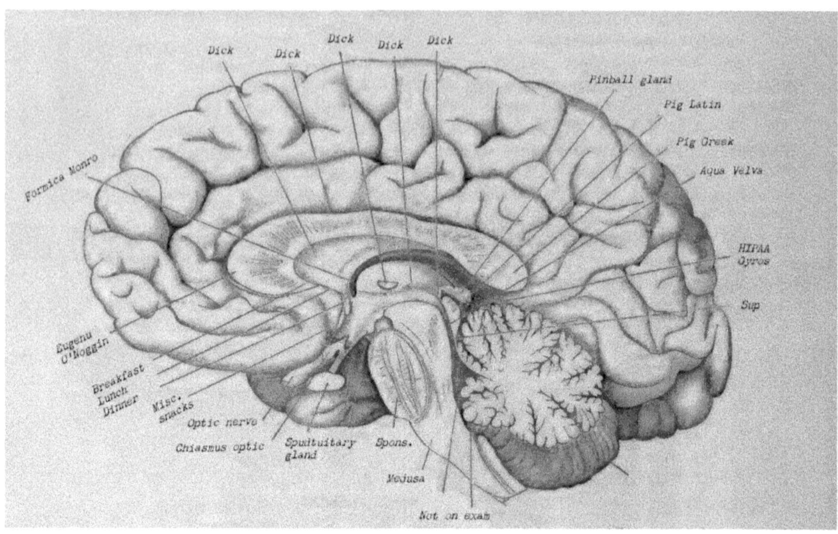

After:

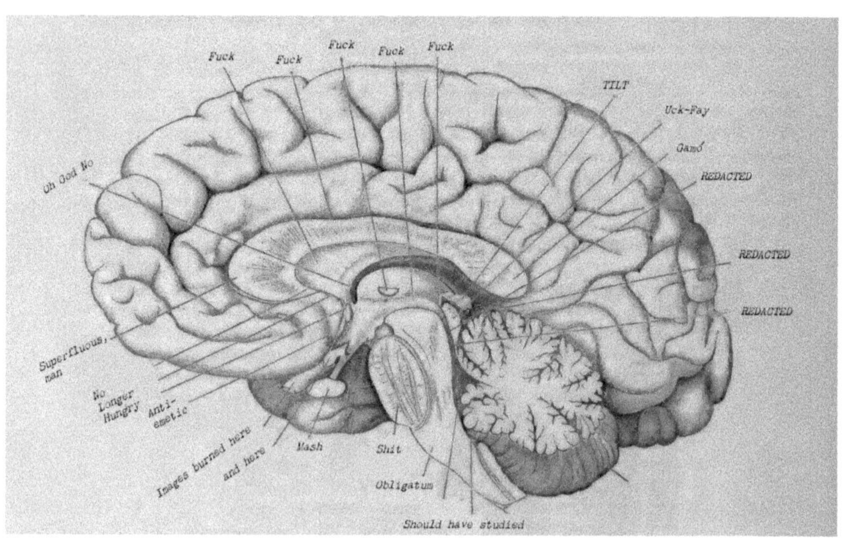

Dick Dick Dick Dick Dick walked over with a trash can; the Shah vomited into it. Scheissetete pulled latex gloves from the inside pocket of his suit jacket, put them on, and took the trash bag to the door. The Shah heard a guard say, "We got a Code 3!" Scheissetete returned sans bag and gloves.

"How could they do that? Why would they do that?"

Dick Dick Dick Dick Dick sat on the edge of the couch facing the Shah, legs spread wide. "Look, we all signed memos so our boys and men would have more leeway to have more leeway."

"But who taught them to spread—to spread—*stuff*—"

"Shit, sir," Bob Toose said.

"Stuff! On prisoners? I know they're Americans, but still. We didn't tell them to do that. Where'd they get the idea to do that?"

Bob Toose and Dick Dick Dick Dick Dick glanced at each other. Bob Toose said, "Do you want us to break plausible deniability?"

The Shah sat up straighter, Shah-likely. (Yes, that was it). "Scheissetete, the lights."

Scheissetete clapped twice. The lights dimmed.

Bob Toose leaned forward to the same posture as Dick Dick Dick Dick Dick. Their knees touched, and Bob Toose flinched and scooted away. "I think you should take this one, Dick."

"So," Dick said, "you remember the Nazis?"

"Of course! Those bastards."

"Well, they learned a lot of methods from the French."

The Shah narrowed his eyes. "Those vishy-vashy monsters."

"They learned it from work done by Swiss and Americans."

The Shah stood. "I knew it! The dirty Americans made us do this! Those cockroaches! We're not guilty at all!"

Bob Toose and Dick Dick Dick Dick Dick leaned back and looked at each other. "It's important to remember, sir," Bob Toose said, "that we were Americans once. Some people in this room may or may not have had some knowledge or say-so with Americans."

Dick Dick Dick Dick Dick nodded. "And it's important to remember that, in our founding, we were careful to borrow what was useful from America."

Bob Toose held up his index finger. "Like some of the freedom stuff."

The Shah smiled. "The freedom stuff." He looked at the ceiling. "We're in the Freedome."

Dick Dick Dick Dick Dick nodded. "And some other things, too. Your own father may or may not have borrowed from his American administrative experience."

The Shah fell back onto the sofa. "Aw, horsefeathers." He waved at the air with his hand as if this was really all no big deal, but he had to swallow the acid in his throat that accompanied the new memory of the photos he'd seen.

"But this is an opportunity," Dick Dick Dick Dick Dick said. "You can't look a gift horse in the mouth. You have to kiss that horse, aggressively, really show it who the stud is."

"The stud," the Shah said. He tried to envision kissing a horse so he wouldn't have to think about what he'd just learned.

A String of Pearls

A String of Pearls

"Of course terrible things happen in war," Maude Lynne wrote in what she knew to be the closing paragraph of her column. "Everyone knows that. But those terrible things stave off worse greater terrors and enable the ~~even greater freedoms that embrace us~~ warm embrace of greater freedoms. The greatness of Texas is in that warm embrace."

She sipped her lunch Chardonnay. "A delightful oakiness," she said to her home office, peopled only by her. One would take pride in that column. Yes, one would. Momently, one would call and dictate its terms to the stenographer at the paper for typing.

With narrative convenience, the telephone rang. She answered, and it was that fine gentleman, Neil O'Chisholm, host of the Sunday morning *This Week in the Republic.* He was calling to invite her to take part this Sunday in the roundtable. (With Neil, never the vulgar calling from his booking agent to her booking agent; he knew better. She required the human touch of an insider.) Adiel S. Thomas would be on the roundtable, too, to discuss her article and those photographs.

"The absolute rat," Maude Lynne said.

"Well," Neil said, "I can't divulge my opinion of her—I must remain ever the objective journalist—but you might find me sympathetic to your view. I assume, of course, you've read her article?"

"Yes, of course," she said.

She had not. Though Maude Lynne detested the *Texas Morning Sun* (primarily its circulation, having quickly become the largest daily in the nation), she did receive it every day. So Maude floated downstairs, retrieved the paper in its damp plastic (that insolent delivery bicyclist had failed again to purvey the news to her porch and not to her lawn as the sprinklers bedewed it), and brought it into the kitchen. She tweezed the corners of the plastic with her fingers and let the paper slide onto her kitchen island, next to the ceramic bowl of ceramic fruit.

Having deposited the plastic bag in the refuse silo 'neath the sink, Maude rinsed the grubby dew from her fingers and set to reading. She had seen all of these photos when Bob Toose secreted them to her home, but reading the article—such dastardly betrayal of Texas by

Adiel S. Thomas and Margot Nought—added viscerality that quickened the very serum of Maude's body: prisoners beaten without any link to interrogation, prisoners nearly drowned, prisoners forced to kneel in 100-degree heat for hours with their arms cuffed behind their backs. Americans all, Maude reminded herself.

There was the story of the captured wife of an American military leader, who had been forced to stir a flaming mixture of faeces and lighter fluid in a barrel in order to empty space for further faecal dischargements. When she claimed feeling ill at the flame and odor (naughty malingerer, Maude thought), the Texan soldier had been forced to threaten her with violent sexual defilement. (To Maude's anger, "violent sexual defilement" was not the phrasing the article employed.)

Where was the balance? Why wasn't the article leavened by government voices of Texan moral authority? Did one really need to read this article *and* to see these photographs? Yet she could not silence her impulsive qualms: why would soldiers do such things? Upon seeing again the photograph of a pyramid of naked prisoners, their bodies scarred by some unseen implements, their genitals blurred (which only, of course, forced Maude into the terror of imagining genital shapes in their particularity), Maude's hand went to the pearls around her neck. Her father had given her these pearls, the sole gift of worth he'd ever given her. As she read and viewed on, she squeezed them harder and harder, gripped them, feeling but not recognizing the heat flushing her neck and fingers, until, turning to a page of a man hanging from shackles, naked, some substance a-drip from his toes, his shoulders clearly detached from their sockets, Maude pulled at her pearls so hard that the string snapped.

No! Heavens! They scattered and bounced from the counter down to the tile, skittering their way around the floor and against the baseboards. Maude had to kneel on the floor and place the pearls into her cupped hand. From the baseboard, little hairs and flecks of God-knows-what made their way into her hand along with the pearls—she would have to fire Consuela.

Damn that Adiel S. Thomas! She cost a poor woman her job!

Maude took out the ceramic fruit from her ceramic bowl and

poured the pearls inside along with gibs and gobs of detritus that should have been swept from her life. She emptied her chardonnay into the bowl—alcohol was a cleanser, wasn't it? It often cleansed her mind from the vulgar parts of life—and the pearls sat at the bottom of the bowl like little judging fish eyes. And, lo, a jot of liquid effused itself from one of Maude Lynne's nasolacrimal ducts. Maude would terrorize that Adiel S. Thomas on *This Week in the Republic!*

Neil O'Chisholm Sees Himself

Neil O'Chisholm Sees Himself

Neil O'Chisholm enjoyed calling Maude Lynne himself—her voice, all upper-crust and italicized, took on a little purr. He had that effect on women. The show needed Maude Lynne for balance on Sunday: Bob Toose to represent the administration, Adiel S. Thomas to defend the story she'd written, and Maude Lynne for perspective. And, of course, Neil himself, the Consummated Objective Texan (even he was getting a little tired of hearing the promo), Truth-Teller, Asker of Hard Questions.

"You ask the hard questions," Dick Dick Dick Dick Dick told him once, and Dick Dick Dick Dick Dick wasn't one to flatterize or complimentate.

Of course, Neil had to go on in twenty minutes as a panelist for another show, so finally he had to skim the article and glance at the pictures. Neil himself wasn't actually that interested in the news: the deeper you dug, the more confusing it got, what with every side having a say and multiple, sometimes contradictory reasonations for things. There was always more to know, and you never knew enough, so he preferred the view from above. Newspaper writers treated him like he was just an entertainer, but he did something they couldn't: he bestilled the truth.

So he sat in the director's chair in the makeup room with its bright, hot lights and array of coloring pigments, and unfolded the *Texas Morning Sun.* He wanted to read the article, he really did—the photograph certainly drew his eye—but he noticed the bottom quarter of the front page devoted to an advertisement for HOSS oil. Their stock, which he owned a great deal of, had fallen due to a tanker spill in the Gulf of Christco[*] the year prior. But their recent marketing campaign was drawing the stock back upward: "As stewards of the planet, we take the oil from the ground, and we return it whence it came."

---

[*]Once Texas achieved independence, the government went about renaming certain geographic entities. For Texans, the Gulf of Mexico became the Gulf of Christco, in honor of Corpus Christi and the hydrogenated sheen upon the waters donated by Crisco. (Procter & Gamble maintained locations in both America and Texas.)

Two quiet knocks on the door, and Barb came in. "Sorry I'm running behind, Mr. O'Chisholm," she said. "Mr. Succop never comes to work with the same color twice, so I've always got to redo his foundation." Her perfume, flowery and muscular, reached him as her voice did.

"Hugh's a chameleon, Barb. And you know you can call me Neil."

She leaned her head over his shoulder and their eyes met in the mirror. She whispered. "Mandate from corporate. Hugh Succop wants to make sure everyone knows their place."

"That's why I never call him Mr. Succop."

Barb tucked tissues into Neil's collar and draped them around his neck. He liked the look: in his head, he pretended he was some eighteenth-century lord. It was the eighteenth century, wasn't it, when men wore enormous muffin wrappers around their necks?

He opened the paper to look through the photographs. He had to get edufied for air.

"I can't believe someone would do that," Barb said.

"Yes, some of this stuff looks pretty awful."

"No, I mean publish it. Our brave boys and girls have it so hard, and now they have to face the flak from all this. It's so unnecessary."

Neil's eyes went to a photograph of a man standing in the shape of a cross, naked, smeared in shit. Neil didn't mean to linger over any of these—frankly, he didn't have the time before air—but the image held him. "Yes," he said. "I don't know what this kind of story serves."

Barb pinched a triangle sponge and daubed it against a compact of foundation, then rubbed it on the back of her hand. "See, your color is consistent."

"I aim to please." He kept noticing details: how the prisoner spread his fingers wide as if to keep them from touching each other, how the amount of shit obliterated most facial features, how it ran in veins down his legs.

Barb spread foundation against his cheek, on his chin, his other cheek. She blotted the sponge in foundation again, smeared it against his forehead.

Neil felt suddenly that she was spreading not foundation on his face, but shit. He lurched forward; the triangle sponge brushed against his hair and ear.

"Oh, Mr. O'Chisholm, are you okay? I'm sorry—let me get that." She wiped his hair and ear with a tissue.

"I'm sorry, Barb, I'm fine. I just thought I had to sneeze." He usually loved the smell of the makeup, grainy, like plaster. *Focus on the smell—it's not shit. It's makeup. It's made from—what is makeup made from?*

He looked at himself in the mirror, saw the faint tinted difference between his skin and the foundation. Unfinished, it looked like it could be shit. For a moment, he was the victim in that photograph. Not prisoner, victim. There he was, confined to this chair, with Barb, as nice as she could be, a real sweetheart, referential, smearing this toxic mess on his face. What was it? What was it made of? It could've been shit! Everything came from shit in the end, right? That's where it all came from, where it all returned. He'd heard that somewhere. And he was sure they made this stuff out of the cheapest material they could find, some really cheap shit.

He took a deep breath. A little bile made its way into his throat. He had to cough so he could swallow it back. "Barb," he said, "I think—" And then he vomited on himself.

Adiel Getting Gussied

Adiel Getting Gussied

Adiel woke before her alarm went off, eyes bright and body quick with adrenaline. She was going to be on TV. And as much as she despised Bob Toose with his distortions and lies, and Maude Lynne with her gauzy worship of power, she was excited to be on set with them. They were celebrities, of a sort.

After she showered, she heard Otis say, on the other side of the bathroom wall, "You're up early, Adiel."

"You, too. You can watch me on *This Week in the Republic.*"

"Is it about those pictures?" he asked. "I don't think y'all should've published those. I've got a cousin in the army—"

"Sorry, Otis, no time to talk. I have to get ready."

Adiel put on the smart blouse and the smart suit that Margot Nought had steered her toward, then left her hair and makeup minimal—they would take care of that at the station. "Barb'll gussy you up," she'd been told. She didn't know why Margot insisted on heels, as Adiel's feet would be underneath the table, but she responded, "If Bob Toose thinks you can see the top of his head when you meet him, he'll be intimidated." So she scuffed the heels of her feet as she crammed them into the shoes, then walked back and forth in her kitchen like a newborn giraffe learning to walk.

"What's that clicking?" Cody asked through the kitchen wall.

"Nothing," she said, and sat, and sweated until it was time to head down and wait for the car. Outside it was cool and just light as she waited. Texas was at peace. Her street was at peace. In a little over an hour, she'd throw another brick into that peace and watch the ripple spread. Ripple? Spider-web cracking. In her head, she practiced the phrases she wanted to say: "If what we're doing is right, then it shouldn't matter if we show these pictures or not." "If Texas is going to be great, it needs to live up to the promise of its greatness." "If the all-powerful Shah can't take a little criticism, then how powerful should he be?" She felt ready and unready at once.

The car pulled up, a Mercedes, a-glint, with tinted windows. The driver got out—he looked like he could play Paul Bunyan in community theater, but he opened the back door in a gentlemanly way, nodding. "It's my pleasure to drive you to the studio."

The air conditioning inside the car blasted. "It's chilly in here," she said.

"Yes, ma'am. Got to keep you dry all the way to the studio. Don't want to be sweaty on TV."

Adiel hugged herself and tried to keep her breathing slow. She just wanted to ride quietly.

But the driver was chatty. "So you published that article about all the prison stuff."

"The torture, yes."

"How'd you get all those photos, anyway?"

"Sources who have to remain anonymous, for their protection."

"Yeah, for their protection. My daughter saw some of those pictures on the news. She's not easily rattled, but she had a nightmare."

"Well, I'm sorry to hear that."

At a stop sign, where they waited though no cars approached from either side, he turned, his right arm hugging the passenger-side headrest. "Listen, why'd you have to publish those photos? Some of that kind of stuff, we know it happens, but we don't need to know about it. You know?"

"Until I saw the photos, I didn't know it happens. And I think it matters who knows. And knew."

"But these are Americans—they're the worst of the worst."

"They have rights, too."

He turned around, eased the car through the intersection. Dawn was rising. "The worst of the worst? I don't know. Some people don't have rights to begin with. And even if they had them, they kinda sacrificed those rights."

She wanted to argue, but she needed to save her energy. Her pre-planned lines weren't silencing him. She tapped the armrest incessantly, watched dawn bloom into daylight.

At last they arrived. She didn't wait for the driver to open the door for her, but he stood by the door as she stepped out.

"Good luck, Miss Thomas."

Adiel wanted to say she didn't need luck, but she had to balance onto her heels before stepping away. So she nodded and thanked him.

There she was, heading into the building: this was W-ANK, the highest rated station in the nation (as they reminded viewers hourly and sometimes half-hourly; it was important to know what station viewers could trust). Her heels echoed in the lobby. A young woman with a clipboard greeted Adiel. Her hair frizzed and floated above her as if it were making its own running commentary on her incapability. She looked to Adiel as unprepared for anything as the driver had looked prepared for anything.

"Adele Thomas?"

"Adiel."

The woman flushed. "Oh dear. I'll have to make sure they have that right on the chyron. I'm Julie, the Junior Subordinate to the Director of Fabrication."

"Fabrication?"

"Producer, basically."

In the elevator, as Julie seemed to search her brain for things to ask, Adiel read the sheet on Julie's clipboard. It had only Adiel's name, spelled correctly, in large font.

At the fourth floor, the doors opened, and Julie led Adiel to the green room. Julie straightened up and said with awe, "The green room," then opened the door.

Arrayed on the two sofas were Maude Lynne, Bob Toose, and Neil O'Chisholm, with the latter sitting forward regaling them with a story and the other two sitting with the center cushion between them, faces raised in anticipation.

They gazed at Adiel. She felt her face flush and sweat trickle through the anti-perspirant she'd caked in her armpits. She wasn't sure what had to happen.

Neil O'Chisholm stood and came over to shake her hand. "You must be Adiel S. Thomas."

"I must be," she said.

Bob Toose and Maude Lynne stood but didn't come over to greet her. They wore perfect his-and-hers contempt. Adiel smiled the public smile her father had disdained—"It's so effortlessly fake," he always said—and walked over to shake their hands. She shook Bob Toose's first. He held his head back a bit, but she could see the oily smear of some sort of fake color on the hair atop his head, as well as a streak of black on the scalp beneath. "A pleasure," she said.

"I'm sure."

Maude Lynne offered her hand like a drooping orchid petal as if Adiel had come a-courting.

"Charmed," Adiel said.

"You're more charming than I would have guessed," Maude said. "Working with Cy Jost tends to rust people."

Minutes later, Adiel would think of the right rejoinder: "Only the politicians he covered." By then, Adiel was in the makeup room, Barb evidently working her magic. But the magic seemed more like witchery: Adiel didn't look like herself, or even quietly real. "Am I supposed to look like that?" she asked.

"It's right for the cameras," Barb replied.

When Bob Toose, Maude Lynne, Neil O'Chisholm, and Adiel were arrayed around the table in the chilly studio, Adiel could see herself on a monitor. She looked less unreal than she had in the makeup chair, but she also looked more a cartoon than the other three. "I look like shit," she whispered.

A production assistant leaned down to her shoulder and whispered, "Your mic is hot."

This Week in the Republic

Neil O'Chisholm made it through the intro without a stutter. Atta boy, back to the old game, in better shape than ever. You're the king, the tops, numero uno. Numoire un?

He turned to Adiel S. Thomas. "So, Miss Thomas, why did you want to publish these—these—these photos?"

"Well, Neil, I didn't want to publish these photos. It's a matter of needing to publish them. Texans need to know what's being done in their name."

"What's being done," Neil said. He wasn't sure where to go, what to say. He kept thinking of the photo that had triggered his nausea. So, half-heartedly, and more quietly than intended: "Bob?"

Next to camera two, the director raised his hands in a "what the hell" gesture?

"Well," Bob Toose said, "I think it damages our national security. It puts Texans and our very freedom at risk. We've just won a long war with the Americans. We don't want to start another one."

"Miss Thomas?" Neil said. "Your thoughts?"

Adiel S. Thomas: "This isn't about starting a war. It's about Texans knowing what the Shah's doing."

Bob Toose: "I don't see the Shah in these photos."

Adiel S. Thomas: "But his signature's on the memos. Your signature's on the memos."

Neil put on his best tennis-watching face, while his body felt light and heavy at the same time. His head was heady.

"Well," Adiel S. Thomas said, "maybe we should talk about what happens in those photos, just so the Texan people know."

Neil O'Chisholm said, "We don't need—we don't need to talk about what's in the photos."

"I think we do. I think the Texan people need to know."

"I disagree," Maude Lynne said. "Some things in life need to be mysterious. Sometimes you need to just keep walking."[*]

---

[*]Readers may note that this quote reads verbatim what conservative columnist and Reagan speechwriter Peggy Noonan in 2009 on *This Week with George Stephanopoulos*. Any resemblance to actuals, etc.

"Miss Thomas?" Neil said. A word split his fog. "Rebuttal?"

"I—I just don't know what to say. I—"

"Look," Bob Toose said, "what really matters here are the facts on the ground. These photos are not facts on the ground. They're simply photographs. We don't know who's in the photos, or who shared them with Ms. Thomas. The facts on the ground are these: the Shah is not in those photos, and his name's not on the memos. Ipso facto non sequitur."

"His name *is* on the memos! Your name is on the memos. Dick Dick Dick Dick Dick's name is on the memos. Are we supposed to believe the Shah didn't know what he was signing? What you were signing?"

"Point to word one in those memos that says explicitly to smear some brown substance on a vile American."

"Well, Mr. Toose, I think there's a clear line from the photos and the memos."

"We don't really need," Neil O'Chisholm said, "to talk about any brown substances. It's Sunday morning, after all."

"It's hard for me to look at a great nation issuing these documents," Maude Lynne said, "and sending them out to the world and thinking, oh, much good will come of that."[*]

"What's in those photos doesn't even matter," said Bob Toose. "First of all, what happened happened to Americans."

Adiel: "What about their rights?"[*]

"What rights? These are prisoners. They signed away their rights once they took up arms against a sea of Texans. Besides, even if this is real, it's a few bad apples, and they'll be prosecuted."

"A few bad apples?"

"Yes. Like red delicious, or gala, or Esopus Spitzenburg."

"Eposus—So the prisoners don't have rights that protect them from having feces smeared on their faces?"

"Allegedly."

"Really," Neil O'Chisholm said, "it's Sunday morning. Children

---

[*]Listen, putting the words of Peggy Noonan into a character's mouth cannot slander or libel her. *New York Times* bestseller and West Wing consultant Peggy Noonan is herself a fiction.

will be watching, if they aren't in church."

"What do you mean 'allegedly'?"

"Those are allegedly feces. You don't know what they are."

"It certainly looks like feces."

Bob Toose leaned forward. "Are you a scientist?"

"They don't have rights protecting them from being hand-cuffed naked to a bed frame and having underwear wrapped around their faces?"

"Good heavens," Maude Lynne said.

"First of all, allegedly. And second—"

"The photos are clear!"

"And second of all, they're used to wearing handcuffs. Why is this different?"

"Why is this different?!"

"Yes, Miss Thomas, tell us why this is different."

Adiel S. Thomas glared at him. She seemed to be thinking. Neil said, "Miss Thomas? We'll have to go to break in a moment."

"What we've done to those prisoners," she said, "is terrorism."

Neil O'Chisholm and Maude Lynne gasped. Bob Toose grinned.

"Do go on," Bob Toose said.

"How dare you call that terrorism," Maude Lynne said. "After what the Americans did to Texans." She put her hands to her throat. Neil O'Chisholm realized he had never seen her without her pearls.

"Yes," Neil said, "even as shocking as these photos are, I think that's not appropriate."

"Let's focus on the photos," Adiel said.

"No," Bob Toose said. "You can't just walk past a statement like that. How could you say something like that?"

"Listen, what I just said isn't the issue. The issue is—"

"I'll say," said Maude Lynne. "It isn't the issue indeed. The issue is why you'd publish such things if you think Texans are terrorists."

"I didn't say—"

A jubilant fart expressed itself with a rising inflection, a question waiting for an answer, a call for a response. Neil O'Chisholm looked to the cameraman, to the producer, both with large headphones on. They were grinning; they'd heard his expungement.

"That's all the time we have for this segment," Neil said. "I'm afraid it's time to take a break. When we come back, we'll take a look at the Shah's style choices over the years, culminating in his breathtaking speech last week at the Alamo. Stay with us, won't you?"

The REDACTED at REDACTED

Terrorism! She'd called it terrorism! Bob Toose had planned and planned for the show, readying himself for any and every claim she might make, but he'd been anxious. Honestly, he could have had them dead to rights, but she'd called it terrorism! How delightfully, horribly un-Texan!

And that fart—who'd unloosed that fart into the world? The whole thing was a farce, in the most useful possible way. Bob Toose had scripted the Shah's victory speech, the very idea of the victory speech to delay the Garza West report, he'd steered the Shah onto that white horse. But he couldn't have scripted this. He remembered, of course, when you don't know what to write, history usually scripts events for those in power anyway. History is written for the winners.

In the green room, he went up to Maude Lynne, shook her hand like they were both businesspeoples (no one could know, of course, of their relationship), said, "Always a pleasure." He held his hand out to Adiel S. Thomas, and he really wanted to thank her. Instead of taking his hand, she brushed a strand of hair from her forehead.

"Your name is on those memos. Blood is on your hands. Blood is on the Shah's hands."

He let his hand down, shrugged. "That's your opinion. You want to call it terrorism, please, go ahead. Seriously, go ahead."

"I will," she said. "What you're doing is monstrous."

Bob Toose stepped closer to her and spoke quietly. "People don't care what happens to American prisoners. They assume the worst anyway, and then they forget. This'll all blow over."

Adiel S. Thomas shook her head. He couldn't stand her, but he wouldn't mind throwing a fuck into her[*], too. There was something about her, he didn't know what.

"You know," Adiel S. Thomas said, "this is just the beginning. More is coming."

---

[*]Addendum to the earlier list of Sporting and Gaming terms for sex, to be used by men: throwing a fuck into.

Bob Toose felt his jaw go hard. What could she mean? Did she know about ████████? The ████████ at ████████? The torture of ████████? And where the hell was Neil O'Chisholm? Usually, he could change the subject or keep the peace, but as soon as the show ended, he bolted from the set.

"I'm quite sure you're bluffing," he said.

"Bluffing about what?" Maude Lynne said.

"Oh, she wants me to think she has something else on the Shah—not that she had anything to begin with."

"People care about this," Adiel S. Thomas said. "The more people know, the more they care. And you and Dick and the Shah are going to catch hell for what you've done."

"Good heavens," said Maude Lynne. "Such language."

Bob Toose nodded. "Yes. Such language. And such incivility."

Victorious! In a perfect world, Bob Toose would have taken Maude Lynne right then, just like the celebrating soldier on V-J Day in Times Square, and kissed her square on the mouth. But, as she reminded him all the time, one must be discreet. So instead of kissing her 'neath a rain of confetti (as he remembered the photo), in the car ride back to the Freedome, he reminded the driver to keep his eyes on the road, and he forced himself against the armrest. Afterward, he cleaned himself with his annotated copy of the Garza West issue of the *Texas Morning Sun*.

As he walked into the Shah's office, arms raised, the memory of champagne on his tongue, Bob Toose declared, "Victory!"

Dick Dick Dick Dick Dick leaned against the Shah's desk, arms crossed. "You said we would prosecute."

The Shah sat on the sofa, gazing up at the reproduction of the painting of his father. "Dick Dick Dick Dick Dick says I might have to get interrogated."

"Interviewed," Dick Dick Dick Dick Dick corrected. "By Neil O'Chisholm. That man loves you."

The Shah looked over, eyes glazed. "*Loves* loves?"

Holly Unlikely, sitting next to the Shah, tapped his knee. "No, honey. Admires."

"Something was off about Neil," Bob Toose said. "I don't

know if he's in the right place right now."

"Why did you say we would prosecute?" Dick Dick Dick Dick Dick said.

Bob Toose loosened his tie and flopped down on the sofa facing the Shah and Holly Unlikely. He lifted the Garza West issue of the *Texas Morning Sun* from the coffee table and flipped it open to the photos. "It's a firewall," he said. "The memos don't say anything about shit or taking photos." He was disappointed that he wasn't welcomed as a victor. "Besides, she called our boys terrorists."

The Shah closed the Garza West issue and slid it under the *Sporting and Gaming* section.

"But you said we would prosecute," Holly Unlikely said, "and now I've got generals crawling up my ass and a bunch of angry soldiers. Have you ever had a general crawl up your ass?"

"I can't say that I have," Bob Toose said.

Scheissetete, looking over his own copy of the Garza West issue of the *Texas Morning Sun,* grinned.

"You haven't," Dick Dick Dick Dick Dick said, "or you can't say?"

Bob Toose replied, "███████████████████████, and ███ ███████████████."

"Gentlemen," Holly Unlikely said. "Can we focus, please? Look at what this is doing to the Shah."

It wouldn't quite do to describe the look on the Shah's face. He wasn't a blathering idiot, nor was he *non compos mantis.*[*] Because we do have the power of authorial omniscience, let us take a brief peek into the Shah's mental state, and readers can imagine his external presentation for themselves:

---

[*] Editor's note: I'm stetting the typo, in large part because I'm enjoying imagining all these characters as praying mantises or mantes, and in small part because I don't make enough money to not enjoy myself from time to time. Love your job and you'll never work a day in your life, they say.

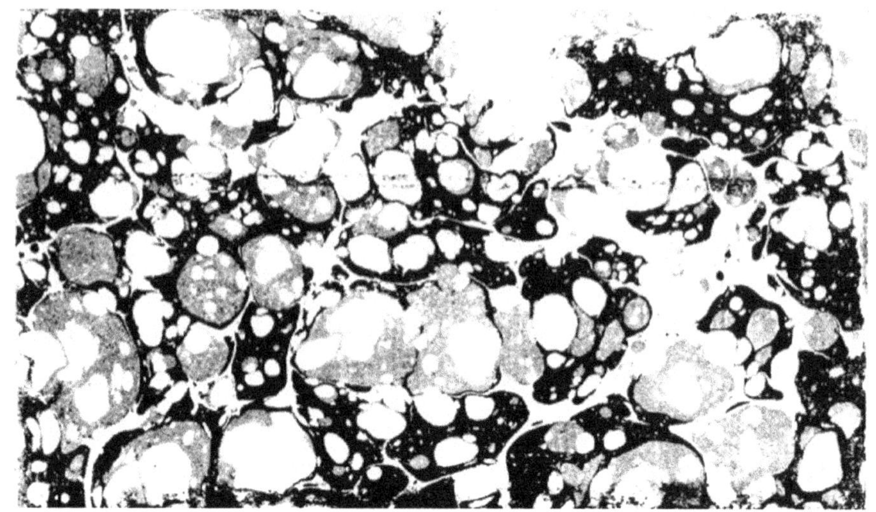

Clearly, he was having a time.

Bob Toose was frustrated. "Look, this isn't so hard. You have to go to war. And if you have to go to war, soldiers are going to get stressed out. And if soldiers are going to get stressed out, they're going to pile naked prisoners on top of each other. That's just a fact. They don't *have* to stand there with thumbs up, and they don't *have* to take photos, but it's going to happen. Of course, if we took away the cameras, this would all be fine."

"No," Dick Dick Dick Dick Dick said, "they need cameras so they can send souvenirs home. If we take away the cameras, they're going to start sending ears home again. We can't have that mess."

"Vietnam really bunged things up," Holly Unlikely said.

"One war ends in a tie," Dick Dick Dick Dick Dick said, "and the whole thing falls apart."

Scheissetete shook his head wistfully.

"Scheissetete's right," Dick Dick Dick Dick Dick said. "We're losing track. We need to get the Shah ready for an interview, whether it's with Neil O'Chisholm or Hugh Succop. We need a leader out front on this."

The Shah's eyes seemed to focus. "Why can't I just say plausible deniability? I didn't know they were going to do all this—this awful stuff."

Now Dick Dick Dick Dick Dick blinked all rat-a-tat, as if his blinker were on the fritz. "First of all, we need to stop saying this was awful or even bad. Second of all, we've already discussed this: we're past plausible deniability."

"But I don't know anything."

Bob Toose sat up and smiled. He had an idea. Victory! "Dick. You're the answer. Don't send a boy out to do a man's job. *You* do the interview."

Dick Dick Dick Dick Dick snarled. Bob Toose couldn't tell whether it was a snarl of pleasure or a snarl of anger. He never could. But he knew both existed.

Can Chickens Fly?

Can Chickens Fly?

"Such language," Adiel S. Thomas heard herself say.

Her home answering machine reminded her of the coarse vibrancy of language. Evidently, she should have changed her phone number before going on *This Week*. Some callers wanted interviews; some wanted to warn her that she had pissed off the wrong people; two wanted to thank her. Mostly, they described the tortures she should endure for her treason. They wanted her to suffer the flames of hellfire. They wanted her to be raped; they wanted to rape her. One man described in detail how he would violate her with an umbrella. They called her a cunt, an abortion, a dirty shit-slurping cum dumpster who, if she hated Texas so much, should leave. They called. And called. And she let them all go to the machine.

When a caller's volume vibrated the plastic of the answering machine, Otis, Cody, or both commented about how people were really piling on. Of course, maybe she shouldn't have published those pictures, but still. Enough was enough.

Adiel cried a little, worn out by the whole thing. She'd bombed on *This Week*. Even Margot Nought patted her on the shoulder pad and said, "Well, maybe you'll do better next time." And the threats wore at her. Every time she heard footsteps in the hall, she waited for a knock, with a man on the other side of the door brandishing a knife. The knock didn't come.

If she had any damn sense, like her dad used to say, she'd head outside and take a walk somewhere. Or go to the movies. But it was in the 90s outside, and the only movies were Texan propaganda—*Lawrence of Shahrabia, Dos Boots*. It wasn't that she didn't love her country, but she didn't want to think about it. Besides, going outside would put her out in the open.

The phone stopped ringing for a few minutes in the early afternoon. Adiel nodded off, only for the phone to awaken her again. She heard her tinny, too-thin voice ask the caller politely to leave a message, and then:

"The Giant Cock flies tonight at sundown! Join me, won't you, to reach the greatest of heights!" His hanging up caused a squeal of feedback.

Cody: "Chickens can't fly."

Otis: "Nonsense. They're birds. Of course chickens can fly."

Cody: "Not all birds can fly. You ever heard the phrase 'flightless birds'?"

Otis: "One time, a chicken flew for thirteen seconds. That bird was the goddamn Orville Wright of junglefowl."

Adiel tied her shoes. That was the first tidbit of knowledge Otis had ever offered, and she had no idea whether it was true or not.

Cody: "Miss Thomas, it sounds like we need you to adjudicate this one for us. Can chickens fly?"

"It sounds like they can," she said, picking up her purse. "But I'm no expert." Sundown was a couple of hours away, but she would go to Kirby and Westridge anyway to wait and keep an eye out. She put on a baseball cap an ex-boyfriend had left—honestly, the only thing about him that fit her at all—and headed out.

The meet point was too close to crime-ridden Link Valley for Adiel's liking—the interstate didn't really serve as a protective border—and she worried that she'd look like a narc sitting in her car. But she was far enough away to exist safely yet to continue feeling afraid. And even though she imagined a car would roll by and a silencer would erase her, that didn't happen.

About half an hour before sundown, someone tapped on her passenger window and startled her. From her vantage, she couldn't see above the man's chest, but he held the sombrero down by the window: it was El Polla Grande. Adiel got out and faced him. He had already re-breroed himself and held the brim down.

"I said sundown."

"I wanted to get out," Adiel said, "take in the sights. But you chose such a dour place."

"The people here wouldn't recognize you. They don't watch Neil O'Chisholm." *

------

*At this point in their acquaintance, El Polla Grande had dropped his accent to a mild drawl, but he did pronounce the name *Neeeel O'Cheeseholm*.

Adiel started to walk around the car, but he told her to stop and stay on her side.

"What do you have for me?" she asked. "I told Bob Toose more was coming."

"Yes," he said. "I heard. You are quite loud when many people are listening. Cy Jost was much better at this. It's a shame he's dead."

In the distance, a car backfired. Adiel ducked down.

"Relax," he said. "Link Valley is the safest place you could be. Even safer than many places in America." He slid a large manila envelope across the top of her car. Rather, he tried—it stopped halfway across. Adiel had to reach as far as she could, then hop several times to drag it over.

She opened the envelope. Inside were more photographs, along with paper memos marked CONFIDENTIAL. The photographs were stamped with yesterday's date. They were unrecognizable at first; it took Adiel a moment to piece the images together into what they were: rubble. A hospital, homes, an open-air mall.

"Those are in America," El Polla Grande said. "When you zoom in, you can see limbs."

"These were printed yesterday?"

"These were *taken* yesterday."

Adiel stared dumbly at him. "The war isn't over?"

"No war has ever been over. But especially not this one. The memos list the intended targets. Most of the bombs missed."

Adiel took a deep breath. "Save me the wait. Which one was the intended target?"

"The civilian hospital."

Adiel shook her head. "No. No. They wouldn't do that. There are rules in war."

"The international group that was at the hospital agrees with you."

Adiel felt herself shaking. "So I wasn't wrong to call them terrorists."

Beneath the brim of his hat, his lips pursed. "Sometimes, maybe you should say less."

Even though her throat was already sore from crying while

people left messages, Adiel shrieked. "Those dirty fucking shit—shit cunts! Fucking pieces of mother fucking shit!"

"Yes," El Polla Grande said. "Best to get it out now, before you see the rest."

A Brief Respite in the Boudoir
of Maude Lynne

A Brief Respite in the Boudoir of Maude Lynne[*]

Maude Lynne would have worn her restrung pearls to W-ANK, but they felt off somehow. Upon arriving home, still athrum from the quiet smolder of Mr. Robert Toose and the foul language of the foul Adiel S. Thomas, she'd put them back on. So she sat in bed, knees to her chest, mindful as always that she would never again in her life sit in the savage Indian style. She had done so once in kindergarten, before she became civilized.

Those photos! And the gall to call Texan soldiers terrorists! Even though she knew some things should remain mysterious, she had the Garza West issue next to her, glancing at the photos now and again to find some virtue in them. She would bust the tough nut of this complexity.

But the pearls distracted her. She'd never realized that they were different sizes. Minutely, but different. They felt wrong against her neck. She remembered an old joke her father used to tell when inebriated. He held an axe and said, "I own George Washington's axe. I had to replace the handle, and the head."

He was clever, her father, but either without ambition or with an ambition diluted by drink. She'd been too young to tell. Once he left and thrust Maude Lynne and her mother into poverty, Maude had decided she simply couldn't live like that. She would drag herself out of those bare days and never again be among the people who couldn't drag themselves out. That's how she got into Haverland, how she'd made the connections that earned her the spot as the first Shah's speechwriter, how she'd parlayed that job into her column and her regular appearances on *This Week in the Republic,* how she'd joined the board of the Thank Tank, Blueprint Underscoring Liberty, Laissez-faire economics, State's rights, and Historicalism In Texas[†]. She was powerful, not like

---

[*]Retract your mind from the gutter: she is alone and allowing her thoughts to masticate some complexly flavored morsels.

[†]Months after the first war began, there was a televised debate between a political scientist from the University of Texas–Austin at Conroe and a janitor from Harvard University. The closed captioning transcribed the Conroe poly sci guy as saying "Thank tank" instead of "think tank," and the moniker stuck. As George Michael sang, some mistakes were built to last.

that Adiel S. Thomas who had to go and ruin her pearls. Adiel S. Thomas was an empty-headed irritant, one of those idealists who believed the world could be perfect, who hated Texas for its imperfections by ignoring its glory. One of those secret America-lovers who saw some good in the enemy for some unknown reason, who made a mockery of Western values.

If only she could make Bob Toose appear. Together, they could bust this nut. He'd wrap his arms around her: wholly, wholesomely, wholly wholesomely. He'd been so masterful debating Adiel S. Thomas, shooting down her ludicrous claims. But those photos! Oh, those photos! Undoubtedly, something needed to be done, some punishment, but why couldn't she just forget about those damnéd photos? She glanced yet again at the man covered in an unmentionable, felt the odd animal thrill one could allow oneself to feel alone in one's boudoir.

Though she was not impulsive, on an impulse she dialed Bob Toose's work number; after Maude insisted she was returning a call, his secretary, that nameless barricade, put her through. His hello sounded gruff.

"Robert? It's Maude Lynne."

There was a pause, and when he spoke, he spoke quietly. "Maude, my dear, my dearest dear, how are you?"

She wanted to cut to the chase, as it were, to invite him over, to take off his clothes, to have him ravish her—an elegant ravishing, of course. "I'm well, Robert, I'm well. And how are you?"

"Fine, fine. Is something the matter?" In the background, shouting.

"Why, heavens no. I simply wanted to say hello, to see what you're doing right this second."

"Well, I'm a little busy. Always a crisis, you know."

"Oh, is it about those dreadful photos?"

"I can't really say, of course. But yes, yes it is."

"Oh, Robert, I want so badly to see you!"

"Yes, yes, and I you. Can I call you another time, when things are less hectic?"

"But when will that be?"

"One never knows."

They said their goodbyes. By the end of the conversation, she was talking quietly into the phone as he was. She was disappointed, yet his voice had helped something in her rise. Her tongue was unduly wet. She put her hand to her pearls, was reminded again how off-putting they felt. She unlatched them and pooled them in her hand.

For reasons she couldn't divine then or later, she put the pearls, one end of the strand first, three pearls, into her mouth. She tasted the metal of the catch. One pearl by one, she took more of the necklace into her mouth, as much as she could, until only a few pearls lay outside her lips. Then she pulled them out, one pearl by one, and felt her own saliva curl on her bottom lip.

Even in one's boudoir, this sort of thing was inappropriate. She wiped the pearls with a tissue* and set them on her dresser. Perhaps next time they would feel normal against her neck.

---

*Pronounced *tiss-you*, not *tish-ooh*.

Introibo ad altare Dick

Dick Dick Dick Dick Dick wrinkled his forehead as Barb, the makeup woman, patted foundation atop his head to mute the glare. "My gleaming pate," Dick Dick Dick Dick Dick said, "is one of my best features."

Scheissetete nodded.

"He's right," Dick Dick Dick Dick Dick said. "Second to my snarl."

"Well," Barb said, "the glow doesn't play well on the TV."

Such a beautiful word, snarl. And such a beautiful face to make. It could convey so much, and with so much strength. He snarled again. He was ready. He felt powerful, like Saturn in Goya's painting "Saturn Devouring His Son."

Neil O'Chisholm's head appeared in the doorway and the mirror, followed by his body. "Richard!"

Dick Dick Dick Dick Dick growled. Neil O'Chisholm's charming-doofus behavior irritated Dick Dick Dick Dick Dick's allergies. "You know it's not Richard."

"Only joking." He stepped forward and shook hands with Dick Dick Dick Dick Dick. There was something in his handshake that disappointed Dick Dick Dick Dick Dick. It lacked a certain cruelty, a certain je ne sais vivre.

"I'm so glad you're here," Neil O'Chisholm said. Across Neil's jugular vein, right before it disappeared into his white collar, Dick Dick Dick Dick Dick could see a faint line between makeup and the color of Neil O'Chisholm's flesh.

Dick Dick Dick Dick Dick felt a new snarl push to unleash itself. "Yes, I look forward to the interview."

Neil O'Chisholm pointed a thumb at Scheissetete. "New butler?"

"Advisor. Scheissetete's been with me forever."

As they walked down the hall, Neil O'Chisholm tried to make small talk, asking about hunting. Just so he didn't have to hear more questions, Dick Dick Dick Dick Dick told Neil O'Chisholm about a secret steak restaurant he'd discovered, L'Abattoir, where diners have the option to watch the animal skinned alive or to do it themselves. "It's French, but nothing in this world is perfect. If you go, order the Sacre Blood."

The little line of pale flesh above Neil O'Chisholm's collar paled further.

Everyone took their places and waited. Standing next to a camera, Scheissetete grinned and nodded: a Texas flag hung behind Dick Dick Dick Dick Dick. The intro music played; the screens next to the cameras showed Dick Dick Dick Dick Dick, then transitioned into *This Week in the Republic's* opening visual of muted heads talking reasonably. Dick Dick Dick Dick Dick would wipe the floor with Neil O'Chisholm. Oh yes, he would wipe the floor with him, as Saturn must have done with the remains of his son to sop up the blood.

On screen, Neil O'Chisholm's head and torso appeared.

"Good morning, Texas, I'm Neil O'Chisholm, and welcome to *This Week in the Republic,* brought to you as always by HOSS BOG oil. As we all know, Having Oil Saves Society, Big Industry Good. Instead of our usual roundtable, today we have an exclusive interview with the Demi-Shah of Texas, his very most excellent Dick Dick Dick Dick Dick. Dick, welcome to the program."

Gratuitous pleasantries, even those necessitated by the idiocy of television viewers, grated against Dick Dick Dick Dick Dick's essential nature, which was for directness. "Thank you for having me."

"We invited you on to talk about the now-infamous Garza West photographs and memos."

"Which are now-infamous because you helped publicize them."

"Well, that's true, to an extent, though they were originally published in *The Texas Morning Sun.*"

"Yes, but you showed them to the Texan people and to the world, despite their graphic nature. You just had to wrinkle the pure brains of our great Texan people, all for a few advertising dollars." He glanced back at the flag.

NO'C: "Well, it's their graphic nature I'd like to discuss with you. These photos depict behavior that seems clearly illegal, but they seem also to be approved by the memos signed by several people in the administration, including you and the Shah."

DDDDD: "First of all, allegedly. Both the photos and the memos. We don't know where this, this what's-her-name, Adiel S. Thomas, got those images and memos, so they could be faked."

NO'C: "There's no need to be obstetric. You're saying you didn't sign those memos?"

DDDDD: "No, what I'm saying is that they could be faked. They haven't been authenticated by anyone."

NO'C: "Would you say they're authentic?"

DDDDD: "No."

NO'C: "So you're saying they're fake."

DDDDD: "I'm saying they *could* be fake."

Scheissetete, next to the red-lit camera two, nodded.

NO'C: "But did you sign those memos?"

DDDDD: "I'm afraid I can't answer that. It's an issue of national security."

NO'C: "The documents are out there."

DDDDD: "Allegedly."

NO'C: "Why can't you give me a straight answer?"

DDDDD: "Neil, these are dark times. Obviously, they're glorious, shining days, the era of Texceptionalism, but they're also dark times. You tell me I don't need to be obstetric, but we're out here birthing a new nation. We're battling against barbarians, terrorists, who'll stop at nothing to destroy the Texan way of life. Bad things happen in war. And to battle against these barbarians, we've got to do some things differently, under the radar. We can't give you all the facts on the ground. We've got to seed the underbelly so we don't cede the overbelly."

NO'C: "Bad things happen in war? Overbelly? Whatever does that mean?"

DDDDD: "Without getting specific, one may have to use, or one might have to use, tactics that have been off-limits to one in the past."

NO'C: "So, torture? Of the kind alleged by these photos and memos?"

DDDDD: "Again, I can't be specific. But if you're talking ballpark, sure."

NO'C: "Ballpark. And what are the dimensions of this ballpark?"

DDDDD: "Dimensions?"

NO'C: "Yes. What's in left field, for example?"

DDDDD: "The sheer impertinence of these questions is galling. You want to know what our soldiers are doing, how they're doing it, and who signed off on it. Whatever happened to trust? I'm disappointed in you, Neil O'Chisholm."

Neil O'Chisholm looked cowed. Dick Dick Dick Dick Dick knew he'd won. Scheissetete smirked by the camera. Dick Dick Dick Dick Dick felt his own mirroring smirk. Dick Dick Dick Dick Dick didn't exactly feel love, but he felt its closest approximation for Scheissetete.

NO'C: "What about the principle of *möbius corpus*?"

DDDDD: "Neil, *möbius corpus* is our greatest principle. The body never stops."

NO'C: "But haven't you violated it?"

DDDDD: "Neil, you know the answer. Allegedly. National security."

Neil O'Chisholm furrowed his eyebrows. "Well, sir, I don't know what to say. I'm disappointed in you."

DDDDD: "You're what?"

NO'C: "I'm—I'm disappointed in you."

DDDDD: "How dare you!"

NO'C: "I dare because—"

DDDDD: "It wasn't a question! I'm here defending Texas and Texans against the claims of a bunch of lily-white Mercophiles, and it turns out you're one of those terrorist sympathizers. I thought much more of you, Neil O'Chisholm."

NO'C: "Well, sir, I apologize, but—"

DDDDD: "It's not going to be much of an apology if it has a *but*."

NO'C: "Profusion, sir. I'm profuse. But—"

DDDDD: "You're making implications." Dick Dick Dick Dick Dick felt himself snarl with his whole body. He pointed at the Texas flag behind him. "I represent everything that's good and pure about that flag, and you're attacking me. You might as well be attacking the flag. You might as well be going into the home of every good, decent, hard-working, freedom-loving Texan and urinating on their carpets. That's it—we're done here." He stood and walked off the set, toward the camera and Scheissetete, his snarl already conveying to Scheissetete his happiness.

Back in the office, Dick Dick Dick Dick Dick sat on the center cushion of one sofa and spread his knees as far apart as they would go. (Given his age, they would only go as far apart as the door of a minifridge, but the effect was still one of awe: -ful and -inspiring.)

The Shah paced around the office. "Dick, you can't just go on national television and insult Neil O'Chisholm!"

"Why the hell not? I'm the demi-Shah! You're the Shah! Is Neil O'Chisholm more powerful than us?"

Bob Toose sat on the other sofa, flipping through the Garza West photos in the paper. "I like the color scheme in this one." Dick Dick Dick Dick Dick knew Bob had the good sense not to challenge him. "In some ways," said Bob Toose, "he is. We have to be careful with people like him."

"Obviously," the Shah said, "I can do more with the right hat than he can with his cameras, but still."

"Can he lock people away? Can he send a thousand men to fight a battle?"

"No," said Bob Toose, "but he can filter how people see us."

"Oh, no, the filter. The people who support us will keep supporting us, and the people who oppose us will think he's holding our feet to the fire. Besides, I'll do another interview, this time with Hugh Succop. Everything will be fine."

Scheissetete came in with a spray bottle and a hand towel. He sprayed Dick Dick Dick Dick Dick's head and wiped off the makeup, restoring the glare.

"Well," the Shah said, "we have to do something. We can't just do nothing. If we just do nothing, then everything will fall apart, and then we'll have to do more than we would've had to do in the first place when we should've just done something."

Dick Dick Dick Dick Dick laughed. (Somewhere, respectable senators burst with laughter.) "We'd send you out there, but even Adiel S. Thomas would have a field day[*] with you."

Bob Toose's head jerked up with the force of an idea. He folded the paper shut, set it next to him, and stood up. The glow in his eyes was not unlike the gleam of Dick Dick Dick Dick Dick's head; perhaps it was a reflection. Later, Dick Dick Dick Dick Dick would think of this as another of Bob's Road to Damascus moments.

"I've got it," Bob Toose said. Everyone turned to him; he turned to face the Shah. "We let Adiel S. Thomas follow you around all day and write a story. She could even film an interview if she wanted."

"Bob," the Shah said, "that may be the worsest idea you've ever had."

Dick Dick Dick Dick Dick unspread his legs. "I have to agree with the Shah, Bob. She would eat him alive."[†]

"Of course she would," Bob Toose said. "That's the point. Our enemies think we're this all-powerful evil, and he'll show her he's just a regular idiot."

"Allegedly," the Shah said.

As it always did when he felt his equivalent of joy, Dick Dick Dick Dick Dick's vein throbbed. In this manner, the issue was decided.

---

[*]For Dick Dick Dick Dick Dick, "a field day" didn't have quite the benignity that it does in common parlance. Going back through many generations of Dicks, his family owned considerable bevies of slaves prior to emancipation, and for some time after the end of the war. (Aside within a note: after the actual end of slavery, they built and managed a chain of prisons called Hardtime's; the logo was a smiling sheriff's star.) For generations of Dicks, "a field day" meant a very literal whipping.

[†]As with "a field day," for Dick Dick Dick Dick Dick "eating him alive" kept the crisp snap of original language rather than the deadness of cliché. Cf. or ibid. or whatever "Saturn Devouring His Son."

The Common Man

The Common Man[*]

As noted in an earlier edition of interviews with the general public, the events of this narratological record only concern the characters who recur herein, as they are the actors and acted upon of history. That said, some may continue to wonder about the views of Everyday Texans™. With that in mind, below is a dialogue between a journalist and three blue-collar E.T.'s™.

Interviewer: How closely have you been following news of the war and the alleged torture at the Garza West facility?

N. Ron Hubbard, blue-collar oil tycoon: Both very closely and not that closely. It's important to know that our brave boys and girls are winning the fight, but it's important not to look for things to be critical about in the fight. Because you can look closely at anything and find fault. You want an example, take the frivolous lawsuit against my small business, HOSS BOG—

Bellamy Trumhall, blue-collar real-estate tycoon: Now, Ronnie, nobody needs to hear about HOSS BOG. Just as HOSS BOG purchases advertising time so the great people of the great nation of Texas can read the great news, Trumhall Land Adventures supports the kind of investigative journalism this journalist is doing right now. But it would be ridiculous for me to bring that up. I believe they call that paralipsis.

Winthrop Thrashwiggler, blue-collar bank executive: You've got a pair of lipses on you not to mention the good work of Likearock Securities Savings & Loan and our good work for the Texan people.

---

[*]One must note that the common man is an everyday good person who represents the views of society more generally. He is not, however, part of the common sort, which is a category of unheroic persons whose poor taste and low opinions are too undeveloped to represent the views of society more generally.

Interviewer: Now, now, you're all big boys, and Texas is grateful for your work as executives and as supporters of the news.

Hubbard, Trumhall, and Thrashwiggler, in unison: Thank you. Small business is the backbone of the economy.

Interviewer: Yes, of course. So are you all on the same page about the war and the revelations about torture?

Thrashwaggler: Absolutely. We bleed red, white, and blue—Texan red, white, and blue, that is—and as Ronnie said, it doesn't help our brave boys and girls to crucify them for doing what happens in war.

Trumhall: And it hurts them to crucify the Shah and all his administration because that crucifies our boys and girls, too.

Hubbard: They're 110% correct about crucifixion. There's only one good crucifixion, and it happened a long time ago, and it was terrible. Of course, if a few bad apples are spoiling themselves, then the Shah should do what needs to be done. But nobody needs to air that out.

Interviewer: When you say "what needs to be done," what do you mean, more specifically?

Hubbard: That's not my business. Oil is my business, as are its many subsidiaries. You've got to let the people who know what they're doing do what they're doing.

Trumhall: Exactly. We do our jobs, and they do theirs. Ronnie drills, I build, and Winnie moves money.

Thrashwaggler: Right. Whatever the Shah asks. And we do it selflessly for the Texan people.

Hubbard: Besides, those Americans have to pay for what they did to us. Trying to buy our oil for peanuts. Where have peanuts ever been money?

Interviewer: So you *do* support what soldiers have been revealed to be doing.

Hubbard: Yes and no.

Interviewer: Yes and no?

Trumhall: Exactly. Yes and no. We've gotta do what we've gotta do, except we obviously can't do the things we can't do.

Thrashwaggler: Couldn't have said it better myself. By the way, I call.

Hubbard: I've got four of a kind.

Trumhall: Straight flush.

Thrashwaggler: Full house.

Interviewer: I've just got a pair of sixes.

Hubbard: Well, well, well, Mr. Journalist, that's checkmate! You win again! You're just too good for us.

Trumhall: Too good, too smart.

Thrashwaggler: Must be why you're such a good journalist.

Interviewer: Thank you for your time and your kind words. I don't know when I became so good at this game.

Neil O'Chisholm's Dim
Night of the Soul

Neil O'Chisholm's Dim Night of the Soul

Neil didn't particularly like single-malt scotch, but he drank it every night. A blend, over ice, with a splash of water. He did particularly like holding the glass to his mouth with that first sip, letting the scotch buzz his lips, and the routine. With other drinks, he didn't feel right. To remain steady, one needed routines.

Instead of watching an old western, though, head against the sofa cushion, he kept his head tilted forward and stared at the Garza West photographs, trying to numb the crash of his heart and stomach.

Why had soldiers done this? And why had higher-ups signed off? It didn't have to be just; it only had to be legal. But it was disgusting, and even though the images make him physically sick, Neil didn't want to look away. He wanted to know as well as he knew himself the frail, scarred torsos, the blurred faces of terror, all the blood and shit.

The bile rose. Let it rise, he thought. Let it rise.

Awe and Opportunity

Awe and Opportunity

Adiel was going to go to the Grand Office of the Shah, where she would interview the Shah, then attend some sort of school function with him.

"It is an opportunity," Margot Naught said.

"To be used," Adiel S. Thomas finished.

Margot's eybrows popped up. "And for a new suit."

So she got a new suit. Within two minutes of waiting for the limosine—limousine? she couldn't remember the spelling—she sweated through her shirt. The armpits of the suit jacket were already damp.

She didn't want to be nervous, and she didn't want to be in awe. But since she'd seen those photos from El Polla Grande, every time she went into a building, she waited for it to collapse from a bombing. And standing in front of her building, she imagined images from the sky that rendered her an insect waiting to be blotted out.

But the bulletproof limosine—limousine?—rolled up. The men in suits and sunglasses got out glossy but unsweaty. One wanded her with a metal detector. When her lower back set off a beep, she raised her arms, and the other patted her. She knew he felt her sweat. The last pat from behind, under her arms, was a little too forward toward her chest, against the outside wire of her bra. "I left my gun in my other corset," she said.

"She's clean," one said to the other.

In the car, heading toward the Freedome, she reminded herself all this pomp was propaganda, but she was still thrilled. When the limo—limou?—turned into the parking garage that rolled beneath the Freedome, she gaped: the walls were carpeted in purple velvet on the decline underground, and there was none of the dirt or grime or dank basement milieu or scattered litter of every other parking garage. And on the walls they drove through were mytho-historical murals, all of heroes leading people on some crossing. Charon leading the damned to life back across the River Styx, Julius Caesar crossing the Rubicon, Jesus carrying his cross and leading the Disciples into Heaven, Hannibal crossing the Alps, Crusaders crossing a river of bodies in Spain, George Washington crossing the Delaware, James K. Polk crossing the Rio Grande to beat back the hordes of Mexican colonizers, the first Shah crossing the border back into Texas, leading the freed. The limo/u parked at an unfinished mural of the current Shah. He rode a white horse, leading the unpainted gray concrete behind him. Adiel assumed it would be filled after his death with who knows what marvels.

Inside the building, everything seemed brand new. On the carpeted hallways of the Shah's dual home and office, she could feel the posh squish under each step. Brass doorknobs shone, as if hands had never turned them or left an invisible skoosh of skin oil to begin a slow erosion. As the men in suits and sunglasses led her, like a guest of honor or a prisoner, to the Grand Office of the Shah, doors opened themselves before them.

When the door to the Grand Office opened, it made a sound like a refrigerator door seal coming open. The Shah sat at his massive desk. She'd seen photos of the room, she'd seen the first and second Shah deliver speeches from that gilt-edged desk, she'd stood in a replica of the office (the principal's office at every school had been remodeled after the Grand Office of the Shah), but awe foamed in her chest. The flowered sofas and the oval coffee table between them, a fan of magazines on the table, all recent issues of *Radar's Digest,* Bob Toose standing behind the Shah's desk, the painting of the first Shah over the mantlepiece, and, for some reason, a champagne cork in one corner by the foot of a side table.

The Shah held a paper in front of him. He put on his reading glasses, propped them on his forehead and leaned forward, then put the glasses back over his eyes and leaned further forward to read. Then, he lowered the paper to the desk and signed. The pen made a lovely wood etching sound. Adiel didn't want to enjoy all of this, knowing it was performance, but she did. It felt grand. Bob Toose took the signed paper, slid it into a folder, and tucked it under his arm. She'd love to know what he'd just signed. Either another document allowing torture and murder, or the renaming of a post office, or anything in between. The Shah rose and walked to her, hand extended. "Adiel S. Thomas, what a delight to meet you. I'm the Shah of Texas." After he intoned "the Shah of Texas," a soft, warm exhalation sounded from hidden speakers.

"No need to introduce yourself, sir. It's an honor." It's an honor? She'd imagined the first things she might say to him: "Why did you okay torture at Garza West?" Or "How do you justify this violence?" But pomp had sent her into this circumstance.

He smiled. Somewhere, perhaps again from hidden speakers in the room, the sound of a dove's wings flapping. "Let me say," he said, "it's my honor. I'm so glad you published that article and all those photos."

"Sir, no!" Bob Toose said. He was aghast, but his aghasm looked practiced.

The Shah waved him off. "Now, a lot of people are mad that you published what you did, and maybe rightly so, but I appreciate it. I think just like the rest of us you want to make a better Texas. Thing is, when war happens, these kinds of things happen. We don't want them to, but they do. But we've got to get better so they don't happen. We've got a saying around here: We're going to keep going to war until we get it right."

In Adiel's periphery, Bob Toose cringed. It was not practiced.

Eyes! on the Prize!

Eyes! On the Prize!

In the comfort of the limo/u, Adiel couldn't help but find the Shah affable. He had so much—so much aff. He'd tilt his head and grin with a joke. And even though the jokes were obvious, he was quick with his slow-wittedness, while Bob Toose sat across from the Shah, alternately reading over papers in a folder and glaring at Adiel. "I love going to see these kids," the Shah said.

"Is this a special group you visit regularly?"

"Naw. I just like to call kids these kids. See, since I'm the Shah, all Texans are my people, so all kids are my kids." He tilted his head and grinned. "Even if they are a lot smarter than me."

Adiel couldn't remember the Shah showing this kind of self-deprecation in public. But he was chummy. She reminded herself that this was obvious propaganda, a way to buy her off with the empty currency of charm.

"What about the children of Americans who've lost parents, or the children who died in the war?"

Bob Toose glared. "That's cheap."

The Shah waved him off again. "My heart goes out to every child. Texan childs, American childs, rich, poor, white, purple, alive, dead, in heaven or hell."

Adiel was at a loss. Where to start?

Bob Toose said, "Obviously, this government has always been pro-child, despite what some might claim about us being anti-child. You'll see that on display today."

Adiel scanned back through her notes for a question she could ask to get herself back on some footing. Had anyone ever called the government anti-child? But she remained unfooted, not even on her heels, when the limo/u pulled up in the drop-off lane of Crockett Middle. They got out. A banner, evidently colored in by children at the school, hung over the front door and read, "Welcome to his Greatness!" Kids in polo shirts and slacks or skirts stood arrayed in a semi-circle, with their principal in front of them. Most of the children looked bored and hot, but they perked up when the Shah rounded the car toward them, somehow wearing a felt hat he hadn't been wearing in the car, and shook the principal's hand. Then the principal shook her hand. His palm was sweaty.

The principal handed the Shah a microphone. Bob Toose led Adiel aside by the elbow. "You're a journalist," he whispered in her ear. "I'm sure you don't want to appear in the news photos. News isn't about journalists, you know."

"What an honor to be here," the Shah said into the mic, without even a wave of feedback. "Y'all are so nice to stand for me like this. I didn't expect any kind of welcome like this. Which ones of y'all made that banner?"

The principal glanced around, looking confused.

Bob Toose said toward the Shah, "Sir? Be aware of the time."

"Well, I'll get right to it. I'm so glad to be here to see y'all. I get to go to one of your classes and see this lovely school. I'm so proud of y'all. Y'all'll—all y'all'll be the next leaders of this great Nation."

Adiel looked around at the group. This wasn't a private school; she wasn't so deluded as to believe that one of these kids would be a leader. But maybe one would be a Bob Toose, getting a scholarship to Haverland and being vicious enough to move up the ranks.

The Shah said, "How about we hear you say The Word?"

The principal leaned over to speak into the mic. "Remember, put your hearts and backs into it." He held up a finger like a conductor, and when he brought it down, the students began:

> We pledge our hearts and minds and bodies
> To the star, the flag, the nation, and the Shah.
> The star is the flag, the flag is the nation,
> The nation is the Shah, and we are the Shah's.
> Each is one, and one is each. Amen, and yeehaw.

Adiel remembered in her body the awe she had felt as a child standing to recite the Pledge of Allegiance to the United States, and how she'd felt hurt by the kids who looked bored and either mouthed the words or didn't even do that, until she became one of them. And now she had to stop herself from rolling her eyes whenever anyone, child or adult, said the Vowing Word of Faith to Texas, usually called in shorthand "The Word."

But the Shah's eyes welled with tears. "Thank y'all," he said. "My heart's so full right now, it's running over with blood into the rest of my body. Now, I want to hear it. Y'all want to shout it?" Then, the Shah yelled, "Eyes?"

The children echoed dully, "On the prize."

Louder: "Eyes?"

"On the prize."

"I can't hear you!"

"On the prize!"

"All right. Now let's go out there and learn some." He took off his hat and fanned his face. "Sure is hot today. How about we go inside to the air conditioning?"

Adiel looked around as everyone dragged their feet toward the front door. She realized it was too quiet—she didn't hear any whir of air conditioning. And sure enough, inside the building was just as hot and a little stuffier than it was outside.

The teachers led the students back into their classrooms, and the Shah's cadre, the Shahdre, followed a group of students in historical dress into their classroom. Adiel recognized them immediately because, after Independence, she'd had to perform as a freed prisoner-of-war in the same scene in what was probably the same middle-school Texas History class: The Shah freeing the Texans. In the rê-ënæctmènt, the first Shah leads a daring midnight raid on a prison camp just beyond the Texas/Louisiana border to rescue several civilian families of women, children, and the elderly from dastardly American clutches. Every student is told that said rê-ënæctmènt is not factually accurate, because:

- The Shah did not lead the raid but ordered it from the Chamber of Tactical Engagement in the basement of the Grand Office of the Shah. Schools agreed to include him in the rê-ënæctmènt because the scene of him ordering the raid was insufficiently dramatic.
- The raid on the prison camp was 1) not a raid but an exchange of prisoners for a brief Desistance of Hostilies, 2) it was not a prison camp because it was 3) a squadron of soldiers who

snuck into Louisiana and found their boots and trousers and weapons well on the wrong side of dryness due to swampage, and 4) Texas did not follow the terms of the Desistance.

All that written, one can't be too critical, as simplification is a necessary tool for narrative storytelling, whether fictionist or unfictionist. And though students learn that the narrative isn't factually accurate, they learn that, more importantly, it is spiritually accurate. Speaking of simplification, because no one wants to sit through a middle school performance, even those with children[*]: the Shah, Bob Toose, Adiel, and assorted Guards of the Shah went into the classroom with its doddering ceiling fans and watched the students put on the show. The Shah et. al. were bored by the show and saw students outside in back of the school doing some sort of digging. When the class performance reached the first intermission, the Shaw raised his hand and asked,

"What are they doing out back?"

"That," the teacher said, "is an economics class."

"Ooh," he said, "I love the numbers. Y'all keep doing your show, but I want to see that."

"And," Bob Toose interjected, "he's supposed to visit as many classes as he can. Lovely performance, by the way."

Outside they went.

Twelve students in dirty white T-shirts with "Crockett" stitched across the left pectoral were digging in a long trench. At the far end of the trench stood the teacher, one arm akimbo, the other arm fanning himself with a handful of papers: he was a little teapot with his spout in moving flex. In front of him stood three students, watching the digging and taking notes in notebooks. He didn't notice the Shahdre emerging from the rear door.

"Eyes?" the teacher said.

"On the prize," the digging students muttered.

The teacher straightened when he saw the Shah. He called out, "Rest!" and the digging students stopped.

------

[*] I have no children, but if I did, I would resent the mandatory sitting in uncomfortable plastic and watching of amateur performances, and I would ënæct many small humblings on my child or children, as parents do in- or advertently. It's probably better I don't have children.

The Shah walked up to the teacher with a big grin and gave a big handshake. "What's this I hear about an economics class?"

The teacher stepped forward to shake Adiel's hand and gave a wary look at her notebook. She felt for a moment important. "Well, these three young men are in our Superiorly Positioned, Exceptional, Noteworthy, & Talented Program." [*]

"And the ones digging?"

The teacher looked away at the horizon. "They're in detention."

"During class?" Adiel asked.

The lead boy in the SPENT program said, "They don't have class right now."

Adiel drew a large question mark in her notebook.

"Well," the Shah said, "we're just here to watch. Do your thing. Oh, and: Eyes?"

The boys in the trench droned, "On the prize."

"Boys!" the teacher yelled. "This is your Shah!"

The Shah smiled and shook his head. "Oh, I'm just your normal, everyday Shah. No need to stand in ceremony."

The teacher nodded as if he had a stiff neck, then turned to the three SPENT boys. "So what do you think? Smith?"

The boys huddled, showing each other their notebooks, then broke the huddle. Smith, who had the gaunt, soulless glare of a school superintendent, stepped forward. "Sir? With twelve, the digging is arrayed this way."

X X X X X X X X X X X X

"But that creates inefficiencies. They're too close together, so each individual dig is smaller, and they lose time being careful not to

---

[*] Readers, he somehow spoke the ampersand. Admittedly, I am jealous of his verbal dexterity.

hit each other. Buckley?"

A second boy stepped forward and spoke with a distinctively New England idiotlect. "As well, their proximity in standing athwart each other means a greater risk of injury, which means greater cost of medical care put upon us, lowering profits. Milton?"

The third boy, who stood with an intellectual bent, stepped forward. "Combined, these inefficiencies mean an overall loss of freedom for the three of us, especially if the diggers work together to stop work. They need three overseers but can be managed at a lower overall cost."

Smith, his gauntness fluorescing, stepped forward again with a new image:

"So we've increased our profits and freedom, as well as the diggers' freedom of movement."

The teacher beamed. "Well done! Fantastic independent thinking, you three." He pointed to three of the boys and told them to get out of the trench.

When the three boys climbed out, Adiel noticed how much darker their skin was than the three overseers. At first, she thought it was just dirt from digging.

One asked, "Can we get some water?"

"You know the rules. If you don't have a hall pass, you can get water between classes."

"Can you give us a hall pass?"

"Technically," the teacher said, "you're not my students." He turned to the SPENT trio. "And what about Phase Two?"

Smith said, "For Phase Two, twelve is still an optimal number, time-wise, but nine will do. We lose efficiency with fewer diggers, but we maintain profits."

The teacher beamed. "Excellent work boys. Those of you still in the trench, start Phase Two: Please get out and refill the trench." He turned to the Shah and smiled. "Absolute power," he said, "corrects absolutely."

Adiel shook her head. "So they dug a trench for no reason?"

The teacher tilted his head and scowled at her. "Of course not. They have to practice Phase Two as well."

"But isn't this sort of child labor?"

Bob Toose cleared his throat. "No, no, it's preparing them for adult labor. That's what school does."

One of the three diggers who had been removed sidled up to the Shah. "Sir, what is the prize?"

The teacher and Bob Toose snapped in unison, "Don't bother the Shah."

The boy flinched and put his arms around his head.

"No, it's no bother," the Shah said. "Eyes! on the Prize! is one of my, and the Nation of Texaseses[*], most greatest accomplishments.[†]"

"But what's the prize?"

Reader, depending on your musical preferences, imagine here a piano tinkling, a fuzz-boxed guitar humming, or a white actress beatboxing on a talk show. If you dislike musicals as I do, feel free to take a short restroom, pleasure-principling, or cocaine break, and come right back when the song is done.

> When you think your pocket's empty
> And the tears are in your eyes,
> Don't forget that you can look up
> And see those beautiful, beaming skies.
> What's up there is God and country
> And your beating heart, so keep your Eyes! on the Prize!

---

[*]This isn't an insult. I studied English and still get confused about possessives with words that end in -s. This is a rare moment of "Le Shah, c'est moi."

[†]Now this one is an insult. At a college graduation I attended, one of the speakers was a biology professor who had won a teaching award. Early in his speech, he called teaching "the most noblest profession." I wish that weren't a true story.

The boy tilted his head. "Thanks, I think."

The Shah knelt down and put a hand on the boy's shoulder. "Glad I could help. We've got a song for everything."

In the limo/u, the Shah handed the hat to Bob Toose, who set it on the seat beside him, and put his face an inch from the vent. "Those economics kids are so smart. When I was their age, the thing I was best at was making fart noises with my hands."[*]

Adiel was exhausted. What was next?

Bob Toose said to her, "Don't worry. Nap time is next."

------

[*]All writing is autobiographical.

Lighter Reading

Lighter Reading

In times of war, it is necessary to curtail access to certain kinds of books. These curtailments are not bans, but it does sometimes happen that a curtailed text accidentally stays curtailed and does not return to shelves. Texas curtailed many of the following books and forgot to uncurtail them afterward, which was useful because war came again. (That cut down on paperwork.) We would love to provide a complete list of books curtailed by Texas, but such a list would add many pages to this text. However, in the interest of being as efficiently thorough as possible, we provide a list below of just one category of curtailed books. We are assured that Texas assigned its most fastidious people to categorizing and summarizing these texts.

Food and Drink
- Isabel Allende's cocktail-recipe book, *The House of the Spirits*
- Ray Bradbury's seminal cookbook, *Fahrenheit 451*
- Mikhail Bulgakov's cocktail-recipe book, *The Master and Margarita*
- Anthony Burgess' dieting guide, *A Clockwork Orange*
- William S. Burroughs' vegan cookbook, *Naked Lunch*
- Johann Wolfgang von Goethe's appreciation of hard candy, *The Sorrows of Young Werthers*
- Joseph Heller's fishing guide, *Catch-22*
- Vladimir Nabokov's guide to grilling, *Pale Fire*
- George Orwell's husbandry guide, *Animal Farm*
- William Powell's dinner-party cookbook, *The Anarchist Cookbook* for promoting how to make bombes and Molotov cocktails
- J. D. Salinger's baking cookbook, *The Catcher in the Rye*
- Mary Shelley's book about hot dogs and beer at baseball games, *Frankenstein*
- John Steinbeck's wine-making guide, *The Grapes of Wrath*
- J. R. R. Tolkien's guide to gas stoves, *The Lord of the Rings*
- John Updike's series on catching and preparing wild game, the Rabbit novels
- Voltaire's companion volume to Goethe, *Candied*
- Kurt Vonnegut's exposé of the meat industry, *Slaughterhouse-Five*

Maude Lynne's Station

Maude Lynne's Station

Reclined atop her divan, Maude Lynne watched the raw footage of the Shah's visit to Crockett Middle. Raw footage: a benefit of her relationship with Mr. Robert Toose, and a benefit of her station in life. As a child in stained denim, hiding away in her bedroom, she would look into the mirror of her smeared window and repeat, "Given my station in life," trying to get the emphasis just so. And, having gotten the emphasis just so, here she was.

The Shah looked dashing yet down-to-earth, as he should. A man of these little people arrayed in front of the school, chanting the inspiring phrase: "Eyes! On the Prize!" Yet something lacked. Perhaps she hadn't slept well. One simply didn't feel the resonant goodness of the moment. One was expecting the thrill of patriotism (the first syllable rhymes with matte in Maude's pronounciation, which she carved into its shape at Haverland College); one expected the *joie de vivre et veuve*. But one didn't feel it. And that one was Maude Lynne.

She glanced to her side table. A porcelain horse, rearing, the first Shah waving his hat, sat on that dastardly issue of the *Texas Morning Sun*. Maude had taken it with her around the house, into every room except the vestibule for the explusion of waste, concerning herself with how to understand the morality of what Texas had done.

Why must these photographs exist? They served no purpose but to mislead, to shame. One understood that a photograph could merely be a misleading capturing of a moment in a sequence; one understood that a photograph was not always a distillation of one's purest self or of a pure moment. Even in the Shah's visit to the school children, one could, if one wanted, kidnap some frame from its context and encage the Shah in some unflattering light. If one acted with the worst of motives, one could. And even with one's best understanding, one could be lured to forget.

Maude retrieved the issue from beneath the porcelain and opened it to the photographs. In her right hand, she held one of her mother's small ashtrays—a rare memento of her best-forgotten childhood—with her again-fallen pearls collected. Maude was so ashamed of how she had put them in her mouth that she had broken the new string. As she looked at the photos, the pearls clicked in the bowl. She'd wanted them restrung again, yet she couldn't bring herself to have it done. It felt such a loss. One's shame clicked in the bowl.

The faceless, naked man with a sheet over his head, his hands so delicate as they held the wires that ran to the battery. Who could know the context? And who could know why one was drawn to these again and again?

Perhaps Mr. Robert Toose knew. Yet she was reluctant to call on him. Sometimes, she heard in his voice the stress that must arise from his importance, and she did not want to harm the tender closeness of their intimacy.

She found herself tracing the torso of the hooded man with her middle finger. One could not say why—and perhaps one did so unconsciously—but she took one of the pearls from the bowl like a candy and put it in her mouth.

The scar that ran from one of the prisoner's pectorals diagonally down his midsection, the bruise on his forearm. What were his eyes under that hood? Were they pressed shut, as a child might do against the parents yelling two rooms over? Or were they frantic, the pupils dilated and searching against the dark fabric for some glimpse of hope? If only one could know.

Maude discovered herself to be sweating. She must be having a hot flash! Of course! She closed the newspaper and flung it across the room, though it neither floated nor landed with the drama the moment required. The pearl on which she sucked had somehow gritted her tongue and the roof of her mouth. She removed it, wet, between two fingers, only to discover that it was now, somehow, a small bullet. A bullet!

One needed help, yet one could tell no one about this.

Maude Lynne cried and dithered, as she had in much of her single-digited childhood, each time until her coarse-handed father straightened her out. He had not come from a high station in life, but he had given her the strength to reach hers and the desire to leave his and the similarly stationed behind.

So she put on a suit and heels, set her hair into its rightful place, and went, unannounced,[*] to the Grand Office of the Shah.

The guards smiled and nodded. "Are you on the schedule, Ms. Lynne?"

"Not scheduled," she said, "but known," she lied.

The shorter guard rifled perfunctorily through her purse.[†] The taller guard ran the wand over her. It beeped to signal her jewelry.

The shorter guard asked, "What's with the pearls?" He pulled the new bullet from her purse and held it between his thumb and forefinger to examine it.

"That something we need to worry about?" the taller guard asked.

"Only if I can throw a bullet with as much force as a gun can fire it." When the guards exchanged the kinds of skeptical looks she'd seen guards give for surlier, seedier people than she, she added, "It's a family heirloom that Mr. Robert Toose requested I bring for his perusal. A memento of the War of Texan Independence from the Surly Grip of America. One abides by the requests of gentlemen."

The guards shrugged, returned her belongings to her, and sent her through. She waited outside the Grand Office of the Shah, forced as she often was to chat with the Shah's Secretary of Secretaries, a pleasant woman whose smile spread too wide beyond the barriers of acceptable taste. Maude had to twist the crown of her watch to stay presentably calm.

Which she did until the party of Bob Toose, the Shah, a couple of guards, and—oh, heavens—next to the Shah, Adiel S. Thomas! Why was *she* here? Had *she* supported the Shah since the beginning, even through his early errors? Did *she* have a rewarding relationship with Bob Toose? Did she have a handful of pearls and a small bullet in her purse?

Worse, Bob Toose looked decidedly unhappy to see her. "Why, Maude Lynne, what brings you to our humbling offices?"

"Important journalistic work, of course," she said. "What

____

[*] Decorum, civility, taste: These are the cornerstones of Maude Lynne's life and morality. To arrive anywhere unannounced violated her ethos.

[†] Would one, following the metaphor, call a "perfunctorily rifling" by a smaller-gauge weapon? A bb-ing, perhaps? Only heaven knows.

brings *her*"—she pointed—"to these offices?"

Adiel S. Thomas had bags under her eyes and slumped shoulders, but her pupils bloomed in response. She stuttered but couldn't utter a sentence.

Bob Toose said, "She's been embedded with us today."

Maude Lynne dropped her purse to the floor, the sort of thing she never did, and yelled, "The gall! The unmitigated gall! Someone must mitigate this gall! Who shall mitigate this gall?"

One of the guards stepped to Bob Toose's side. "Please calm down, ma'am."

"I am not a 'ma'am,' sir! I am a madam!" She pointed at Adiel S. Thomas. "You and I, Miss Thomas—"

"It's Adiel, *Maude*."

Maude Lynne made a noise not unlike the one a lawnmower makes upon the first unsuccessful pull of the starting handle. She did not know from whence inside her it came.

"You and I, *Adiel*, must enjoin ourselves in the throwing of hands!" She lunged at Adiel S. Thomas, only to be grabbed immediately by Bob Toose and the guard next to him. They manhandled Maude Lynne and spirited her into another room. She saw the other guard guide Adiel S. Thomas and the Shah into the latter's Grand Office.

The guard settled her into the chair at the end of the oak conference table farthest from the door. Along the walls were a war-torn Texas flag framed and behind glass[*]; a topographical map of North America with America an extended depression from sea to ebullient sea; and a framed editorial cartoon of the first Shah shoving a tube, labelled "freedom," into the mouth of a goose, labelled "America."

Standing against the far door, Bob Toose asked her what was going on.

"What is going on, Mr. Robert Toose, is that you have betrayed me!"

He signaled to the guard to leave. The guard left.

---

[*] In actual fact, the flag had been singed, baked, and besmirched with smirchings by the crafty parent of an A+ student who did a stellar project on the War of Texan Independence from the Surly Grip of America.

Bob Toose stood at the far end of the conference table, putting his hands on the back of the chair before him, and said in a quiet voice pressed flat with anger, "Miss Maude Lynne, my dear, what is the meaning of this?"

Maude Lynne found herself unable to articulate a thing, no doubt infected by the artless, classless schemer, Adiel S. Thomas. She pulled the bag of pearls from her purse and dumped it out. Pearls skittered along the table, some falling to the floor. She grabbed the bullet and set it on its end, then burst into artless tears.

General Carnage

General Carnage

Adiel sank into the sofa. She wasn't sure she'd ever sat on a sofa this comfortable. She imagined weapons-grade comfort produced at some hidden factory, the designs not even patented, it was so essential they remain hidden. The Shah looked exhausted, too, slumped in the chair behind his desk, turning back and forth, gazing glazed into some middle distance. He looked like he'd rather be anywhere else, anyone else, like a child waiting to be called into the principal's office, even though he was in the role of the principal. At his orders, the guards had left them. She wasn't sure why he'd let her stay.

"Sir?"

The Shah looked up, wary. "Yeah?"

Adiel put up her fists. "Shall we enjoin ourselves in the throwing of hands?"[*]

They both puddled into giggle fits.

Once he caught his breath and could form a sentence without giggles disrupting, the Shah asked, "Who says that? Is that a thing people say in the real world?"

Adiel replied, "I don't think Maude Lynne lives in the real world."

The Shah threw back his head and laughed. "A lot of us don't." He looked wistful again. "I'm starving. You hungry?"

"A little." She was a lot hungry, actually.

"My cook'll make anything in the world you want."

"Really? Anything?" She was too hungry to think. "What do you recommend?"

"I usually get a grilled cheese."

"Special bread or cheese?"

"Nah. Texas toast and freedom cheese."[†]

---

[*]One might think here of *New York Times* columnist, 1996 Glamour Woman of the Year, and 1999 Pulitzer Prize winner Maureen Dowd, who wrote that John Kerry said, "Who among us doesn't like Nascar?" He did not, in fact, say that; editorial columnists, who earn more than most at newspapers, aren't fact-checked.

[†]Many traditionally American products were too useful or beloved to disappear.

Adiel fell back into the sofa. "Grilled cheese it is."

He ordered over the phone. Adiel set her head back on the sofa. God, she could fall asleep here. Of course, she had fallen asleep on many sofas in her life, but she could really snooze on this one.

After the Shah got off the phone, he went to the opposite sofa. "My chair's comfy, but it's a little too formal. Don't lie down, though. I don't know if you've got nap clearance."

They laughed again. Adiel knew she was caught in that exhausted, hungry delirium where everything funny gets magnified, so when a little spittle curled over her lip and onto her chin, they both giggled like idiots, as her father used to say after he and Adiel did so.

Once they settled down from the last giggles that burbled over, and the grilled cheese sandwiches arrived be-toothpicked ("Fancy," said the Shah), the Shah said, "Listen. I want to thank you for today. Bob Toose and them thought it was a bad idea having you come along, but you've been real straight all day. I appreciate it."

"I have to admit," she said, one cheek swelled with a bit of sandwich, "I've learned a lot today." She swallowed and said, "Listen. Person to person, between you and me, what did you think when you saw the Garza West photos?"

The Shah raised an eyebrow and looked around. "Off the record?"

"Yeah. I just want to know." Adiel swallowed the dry mush she'd been chewing. "Honestly, you're a lot more—more real than I imagined. More humane."

The Shah leaned forward over the coffee table, holding the last bite of a grilled-cheese triangle and staring at it. A crumb fell to the gold-rimmed plate beneath. "You know," he said, his voice quieter, raspy. He shook his head. "I hate it. I mean, overall, we're doing good. Good stuff. But when something like that has to happen, I just stop and I wonder if it's worth it. It's hard. Stuff is hard." He looked up at her. She noticed how worn his face looked, red, as if wind had whipped it daily or sun had baked it.

"Maybe it's not worth it," Adiel said. Now was her moment. She leaned forward and pulled a folder from her bag, opened the folder and showed the Shah two of the photographs she'd received from

El Polla Grande. "What we've done to American civilians, maybe it's not good stuff, maybe it's not worth it."

The first photograph was one of general carnage: a hospital's emergency entrance rubbled, an ambulance tilted on one side by chunks of concrete and a toppled pillar. Even though she'd looked at it several times, her eye went all over, unable to focus on a subject of destruction before moving on to the next. The second was of a dead, bloodied toddler, head thrown back in another civilian's arms, mouth open and eyes empty reds.

The Shah's face steeled. "You think I haven't seen these?" He looked up at her again. "You think I don't know? I see this all the time. I see what Americans do to our people. What they give us, they get back. When they turn one cheek, we turn the other one right back." He stood, leaning over the coffee table. "I'm the Shah. I have to make the hard decisions. You don't have to make any. You wipe your mouth. We're done. Get out. Get out! Guard!"

Adiel started to slide the folder back into her bag, but the Shah came over and pulled it away from her. "I don't even know where you got these!"

The guard, keys and spurs jangling, led her out of the Grand Office and out a side exit of the building onto a poorly lit street. She'd had her chance and blown it. Or maybe it hadn't been a chance at all, and she'd somehow made everything worse. Her arms hurt with exhaustion. She walked toward a distant streetlight, hoping to find a taxi.

Two in the Chamber

Two in the Chamber

Bob Toose knew many methods of persuasion. After gathering Maude Lynne's tears and her pearls and that bullet, trying to ignore her crazy story, he knew he had to use a particular method of persuasion. Rare, but essential. He poked his head outside the door and told the guard everything was taken care of. But he still had to get her out of the building without a scene.

So he led her downstairs to the sub-sub-basement and used his keys and fingerprints to get them into his favorite room in the building. In the center was a conference table ringed with chairs, a telephone in the center. On the far end, a mosaic of dark televisions covered the wall.

"What is this place?" she asked in a hushed, quavering voice.

Bob Toose remembered his first time in here, during the first Shah's reign, as an undersecretarial assistant of Public Relations to the then-Secretary of Conflagration. He felt then as Maude Lynne did now. A sense of awe and proximity to power. That morning, more than anything, made him feel the strength and authority with which he could operate in the world. "This," he said, "is the Chamber for the Strategization of Conflagration and Tactical Engagement."

Her eyes widened, her mouth went agape. She made the little breath she'd made the first time he penetrated her little delicacy delicately. She spread her hands across the back of a chair. "This is where the war happens." Maude gazed at him. "Why did you bring me here?"

Bob Toose stepped forward and held her fingers. She was essential to the Shah, and even, in a small personal way, to Bob Toose himself. So he enacted a strategic risk. "To show you how important you are to me. My little Miss Maude Lynne, I love you."

Her mouth made a tasteful O of surprise, and with her flaring nostrils, a facial error she could not contract a doctor to repair, made an ö. "My Mr. Robert Toose, I love you, too."

They embraced. They never hugged or squeezed or gripped one another; they only ever embraced. When they decoupled, he said, "I want to show you the secrets of this room."

Maude Lynne pulled away and looked to the wall of television screens. "You can turn those on?"

That wasn't what Bob Toose had in mind to turn on, but to assuage her, as he must, he unlocked the control closet and flipped the six switches to turn on the televisions. They lit up with night vision, dark green and gray. Little was happening. The war was at rest for the evening. Five of the cameras were stationed on bases or at war fields, pointed out toward the enemy at ████████, ████████████, ████████ ████████, and ████████████; the sixth was on the helmet of a soldier stationed at ████████████████████████. He was urinating from the top of a wall.

"Oh, Robert, that's awful," she said.

"War is hell."

He pressed a button, and the image changed to the viewpoint of a soldier standing in the corner of some room in an undisclosed location,[*] watching another soldier pour water through a funnel onto the masked face of a strapped-down prisoner.

"That poor American. How kind we are to slake his thirst."

"Yes," he said, "we are." Bob Toose turned off all of the televisions, then sat her down in a chair and sat himself down facing her. Their knees kissed.

"Maude, why did you go into a rage at Adiel S. Thomas?"

She turned her head away. "What must you think of me? I just could not believe she was here. She hates the Shah. She hates Texas. Her work is bringing down the war effort and offering aid and comfort to the enemy. A traitor, in this building, and not in chains! I mean, one could understand if you gave full access to Judith Miller."[†]

Maude Lynne shook, so Bob Toose took the next necessary

---

[*] Thus, there is no need to redact.

[†] For those who don't know or have forgotten, Judith Miller was the *New York Times* reporter who repeated in print anonymous Bush Administration claims about Weapons of Mass Destruction in Iraq and who was subsequently fired when those claims (to which she offered no counter) were proven false. She later defended her reporting: "My job isn't to assess the government's information and be an independent intelligence analyst myself. My job is to tell readers of *The New York Times* what the government thought about Iraq's arsenal." Remarkably, Judith Miller exists both in the real world and in this novel. It turns out Judith Miller serves every government that asks for her. She is one of humanity's truest patriots.

risk: he kissed her hard on the mouth. Once he completed his act, he said, "Maude Lynne, I want to make love to you. Right here, right now."

She put her hand to her chest and said, "Oh, my, Robert, wherever could one make love comfortably in this room?"

"Please stand back." He went around the room and pulled all the chairs back to the wall. Then he went to the closet and pressed a button. The table made a pneumatic hissing noise, lowered, and turned over to reveal a table in the shape of America and Texas, covered in felt. The Texan felt was green; the American felt was red.

Bob Toose handed her coat hangers from the closet. "Please, Maude Lynne. Let us remove our clothes."

Declassified Document: Yada Yada Yada

Declassified Document: The Deployment of an IED (Impressive Erectile Device) by Secretary of Conflagrational Elucidation Robert Toose in the Chamber for the Strategizing of Conflagration and Tactical Engagement

On Tuesday, ▇▇▇▇▇▇▇▇ Mr. Robert Toose and Ms. Maude Lynne removed their clothings and hung them on the coat hangers designated for that purpose in the ▇▇▇▇▇▇ for the ▇▇▇▇▇▇ of Conflagration in subfloor 2 of the Freedome. In said room, Mr. Toose engaged the wall of ▇▇▇▇▇▇, showing Texan outposts in ▇▇▇▇, ▇▇▇▇▇▇, ▇▇, ▇▇▇▇▇, ▇▇▇▇▇▇ and ▇▇▇▇▇▇▇▇. He also engaged the strategic map of America. Having denuded, Ms. Lynne and Mr. Toose climbed onto the map. Ms. Toose placed her feet in ▇▇▇ National Park in Maine and the panhandle of ▇▇▇▇. The placement of her feet engaged surveillance drones that recorded essential intelligence for Texas. Unbeknownst to her, we have added a Letter of Praise to her confidential file. Also to be noted, her hair spread tastefully across the Inland Empire of ▇▇▇▇▇. Mr. Toose placed his hands in the ▇▇▇▇ Ocean, likely due to his familiarity with the operations of the map. Thus arranged, Mr. Toose and Ms. Lynne proceeded to perform missionary acts across the continent.

Mr. Toose spent a good deal of time kissing the nape of Ms. Lynne's ▇▇▇ and saying he could not wait to initiate "Operation Rolling Thunder." "No," Ms. Lynne is recorded as saying, "not Rolling Thunder." He then proceeded to toggle Ms. Lynne's ▇▇▇▇ in the manner of a ▇▇▇ operator. Ms. Lynne alternated gripping her hands on Mr. Toose's triceps area and his ▇▇▇▇▇, which she called his "Toose caboose."

Mr. Toose then moved his head down to her belly, whereupon he made a growling noise not unlike that of a distant ▇▇▇▇ Tank and said that, having explored her "known knowns," he desired to explore her "unknown unknowns." Ms. Lynne replied, "Good ▇▇▇▇, no," ▇▇▇▇▇ evidently unbefitting a woman of what she is recorded as having called her "station."

"Ah," Mr. Toose said, "my sweet goose. *Mon goose.* Let us begin Operation Mon Goose."

Then, having achieved combat readiness, first gently and then with great rapidity, Mr. Toose ███████ Ms. Lynne's vaginal ███ zone, and it is known that he brought himself to fruition. Whether or not Ms. Lynne was brought to fruition remains unknown.

Mr. Toose and Ms. Lynne then cleaned fastidiously, but the Great Army of Texas did have to replace the felt on the panhandle of ██████. With great pride, we can say that the felt of Texas was spared any damage.

The entire scene was captured audiographically and video-graphically by surveillance accoutrements known only to ███████ ████████, ███████, and ████████. Copies of the audio-graphic and videographic recordings are stored in ███████ of the military base at ██ ███████.

Document declassified and redacted by Private CRG.[*]

---

[*] Pvt. CRG was dishonorably discharged for behavior unbecoming of the Great Army of Texas, having voiced what he viewed as a "moral complaint."

An Excerpt from a Very Different
Novelistic Rendering of Said History

An Excerpt from a Very Different Novelistic Rendering of Said History

Bob Toose lay in bed, pajamas warming him. In the bathroom, Meredith brushed her teeth. The *sh-sh* irritated him, but this was compromise: either he went to bed with her each night, or he went to bed alone, his bank account sheared by alimony. "Certainty makes the world go round," his father had always said, "and dithering lets the monsters take over." Instead of dithering, he accepted the terms.

And she'd had to accept that he would bring work to bed with him. Tonight, that meant re-examining the photos from Garza West, looking for details that could be argued as tell-tale signs of forgery. He knew the photos were real, and the soldiers' behavior turned his stomach, but the world was complicated. Sometimes a minority had to suffer for the greater freedom of the majority, didn't it?

Now he heard the little pocks of Meredith flossing. He'd loved her once. He'd been in bloom for her entirely, but now their marriage curled, dry, like a leaf ready to fall. But like most marriages, theirs would hang onto the branch. Bob couldn't take the distraction of divorce.

The fingers—he examined the prisoner's spread fingers, blood dripping. The soldiers' savagery couldn't be justified by anything, but Bob still needed to frame the lie—forgery—that would help tell the truth—Texas was just. As he brought the photograph closer to his face, nausea sat heavy in his stomach. It was easy to say the world was complicated, but saying didn't make it easier to live with.

Meredith was humming. That meant she was circling cleanser on her face. Bob had a fierce, clear memory of watching her spread cleanser on her face the first time, decades ago, when he barreled over the cusp of love. The memory left its echo. He smiled and set the folder of photos on his nightstand. What song was she humming? He closed his eyes and felt the muscles in his face shift as he tried to hear it clearly.

Then she stopped, turned out the bathroom light, and stepped into the bedroom, rubbing lotion into the back of one hand. "What are you doing?"

Bob opened his eyes and smiled. "Just listening to you hum. What was that tune?"

She shrugged. "I didn't realize I was humming." She pulled back the comforter and worked herself into bed.

Bob went to brush his teeth, then stopped in the doorway. "I was just thinking about how much I love you."

She laughed, then her forehead creased when she saw he was serious. "Something wrong?"

He shook his head. "Nope. Just listening to you, I started thinking about us."

Meredith smiled and blushed a bit. She rolled over onto her side, facing his side of the bed. "That's sweet. Can I look at these?"

"You don't want to look at those."

"You sure?"

Bob walked over and set the nightstand lamp on the folder. "Absolutely certain."

Meredith sighed. "Certainty makes the world go round."

Bob raised his eyebrows and went into the bathroom. While he tried to pee, he thought of Maude Lynne. She always smelled so delicate, and he felt about her the way he'd felt about Meredith before he crossed over into love. By the time he flushed the toilet, he felt wistful and a little guilty. He reached under his pajama top and rubbed his hairy, fleshy belly. There was no way he had another love in him. He went to the bathroom doorway and looked at Meredith's lumpy human shape under the cover. Maybe soon he'd end things with Maude. Maybe.

Regarding the Pain of Others

Regarding the Pain of Others

The Shah sat back on his desk, arms crossed, head tilted down just so. He knew from training, from correction, from looking at himself in the mirror, that he looked serious. "All right, we're all here."

Bob Toose and Holly Unlikely sat on the sofa to the Shah's left; Dick Dick Dick Dick Dick and Scheissetete sat on the facing sofa, where Adiel S. Thomas had sat the night before. And above them, the reproduction of the painting of the first Shah, his victory shaming their error.

"Sir," Bob Toose said, his arms crossed, "it's not like you to call a meeting."

"We just want to make sure there's even a need for a meeting," Holly Unlikely said, arms crossed.

"It's not your job to call a meeting," Dick Dick Dick Dick Dick said, arms crossed in clear anger.

Scheissetete stared at the Shah, then for a moment crossed his eyes a la Jerry Lewis.

"I'm the Shah. If I want to call a meeting, I call a meeting."

Yet he had never called a meeting before. He remembered the way his father would intone at some underling, from his time in the CIA through his time in business to his years as the first Shah, "Call a meeting," and people would move. In the second Shah's time as Shah, people moved, but only to open doors, to shake his hand, to bring his food. They led him to meetings. In the morning, he was told his schedule for the day. War happened, but he felt like he hadn't made decisions on his own. Papers were brought for him to sign, ideas were bounced off him, but all the choices had been made. Wasn't the whole point of being Shah to order and rule? Wasn't the whole point of being the Shah to be the Shah?

Dick Dick Dick Dick Dick, curling flaccid into himself, skulked. "So what's this meeting about?"

"This," the Shah said. He took the folder of photographs from his desk, held it up like a courtroom attorney holding up an essential, damning piece of evidence, and flung it onto the coffee table. He had hoped the photographs would scatter neatly, immediately in full view of the four of them, but instead, when the folder landed, the photographs slid to the floor, all except for one, which lay face down on the table. The sitting quartet stared at the pile of downturned eight-by-tens on the floor.

The Shah: "Dang it."

Thus began a power struggle. No one could pick the photos up or turn over the one on the table. Curiosity was weakness. In the strictest sense, the organizational chart (including just the set of people relevant herein) looked like so:

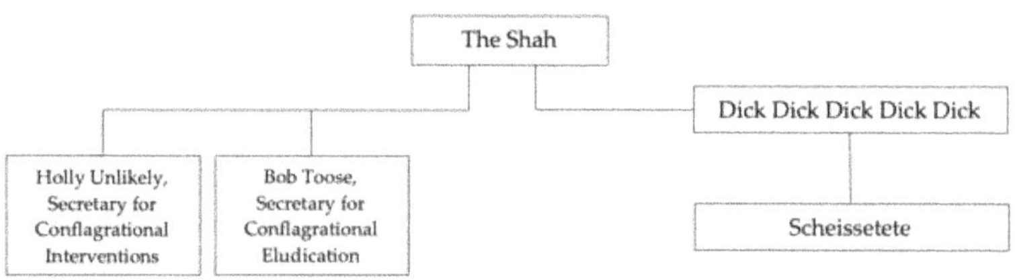

Narrative omniscience allows us to present our interpretations of what each person imagines as the organizational chart. To wit, Bob Toose imagined it as:

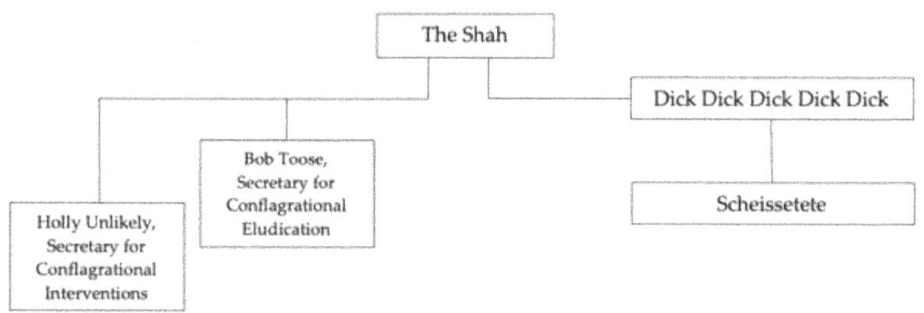

Holly Unlikely imagined it like the above, but with one obvious change.

Dick Dick Dick Dick Dick considered the organizational chart through the lens of pragmatism and actual experience:

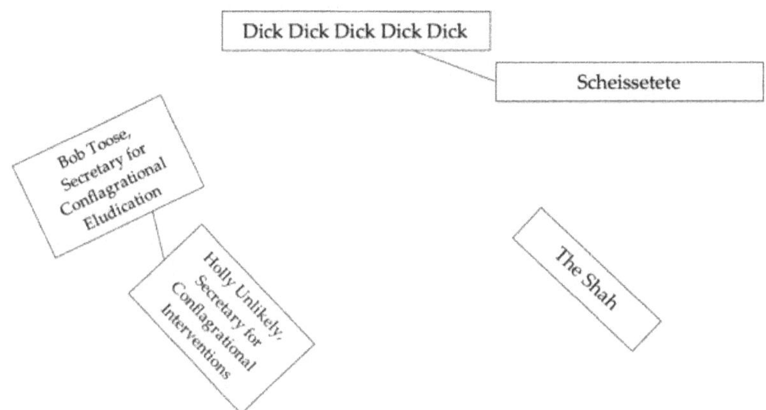

Reader, one would prefer not to venture into the headvisions of Scheissetete, real or imagined, but for your benefit, such was done, producing the following spinning image, stilled:

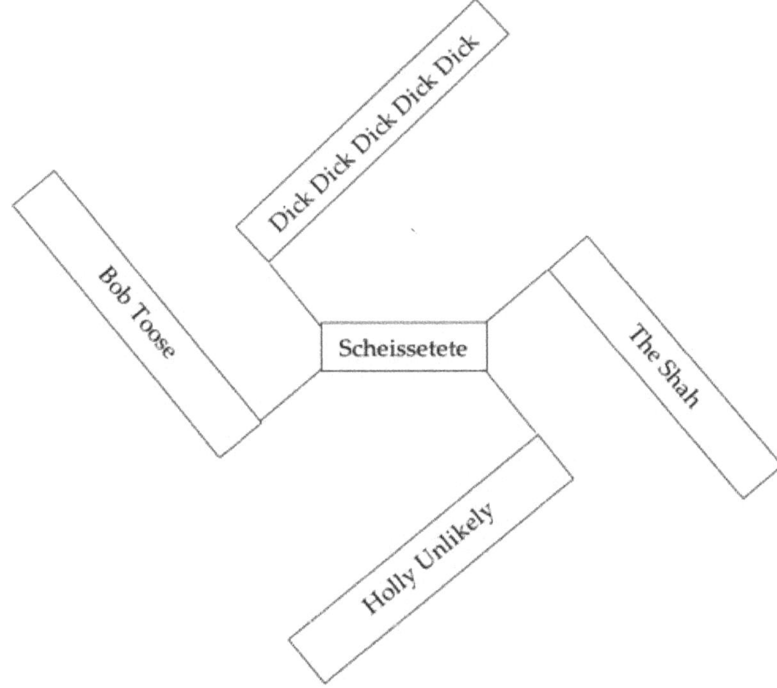

With their various organizational ideations in place, so began a moment akin to a Mexican Standoff, this one known as a Tonkin Incident: whatever happens will initiate a years-long humanitarian disaster.

Luckily, in a stroke of brilliance, the Shah pressed the intercom button on his desk and called in his Secretary of Secretaries. She entered, pad in one hand and pen in the other.

The Shah pointed to the photographs on the floor. "Could you please pick those up and arrange them on the table, without looking at them?"

She nodded. Looking to the ceiling, she stepped over like someone going to the toilet in the middle of the dark night, then knelt down and felt around the floor, patting the photographs into a stack. Once she had them all, still looking upward, she set them on the table. Then she stood, nodded her head, and said, "Boys. Holly." She went out and shut the door.

"Now," the Shah said. He stepped to the coffee table and turned over the photographs, spreading them so all eight were visible. "What do you think about these?"

All four pursed their lips. They shook their heads.

Bob Toose asked, "These are civilians?"

"All of them," the Shah said.

"My God," Holly Unlikely said, "a hospital."

"A horrific massacre," Dick Dick Dick Dick Dick said. "Those American shitstains will do anything to the good people of Texas."

"Those are Americans! American civilians! A hospital! A wedding party!"

The four on the sofas tilted their heads and nodded. Bob Toose said, "The unavoidable cost of war."

Holly Unlikely said, "The cost of war. It's unavoidable."

The Shah shrieked, surprised to hear his voice go so high. "The unavoidable cost of war? When it's Texans, it's a horrific massacre, but when it's Americans, it's fine!"

Dick Dick Dick Dick Dick flopped his head forward and back in a nod. "Yes, you clearly understand. The good people of Texas sometimes have to do anything to those American shitstains."

"The cost of war," Bob Toose said, "we can't avoid it." He

nodded to the reproduction of the portrait of the first Shah. "Even the smartest of our weapons makes occasional mistakes. Why are you so disconcerted?"

"Why are y'all so—so—undisconcerted? Or just concerted?"

Holly Unlikely said, "When there are clouds, it rains. When there's war, people die."

"But we're responsible. And it doesn't always rain when there are clouds."

Dick Dick Dick Dick Dick rose and paced the room as he spoke. "Who cares about dead Americans? They didn't care about the dead in Egypt in 1952, or Iran in 1953, or Guatemala in 1954 and long after, or Laos in the late fifties."

Scheissetete smiled.

Bob Toose nodded. "Scheissetete is right. The fifties were a better time."*

Dick Dick Dick Dick Dick waved his hands as if he were a magician tossing innumerable scarves into the air. "The Dominican Republic, Cuba, Vietnam, Brazil. This is how I remember all the countries of the world."

Bob Toose added, "Don't forget Iraq, Bolivia, Chile, Afghanistan, El Salvador, Nicaragua, Grenada, and Panama."

"How could I?" Dick Dick Dick Dick Dick said.

Scheissetete shook his head.

"Exactly," Dick Dick Dick Dick Dick said. "We get no respect for our work in these dangerous fields." He stepped up to the Shah. His breath smelled like a snuffed match. "Listen. They're Americans. If they were better people, they'd join us in the fight against America, or they'd move to Texas." His scowl hummed like an amplifier.

"But we're detaining people at the border. Nobody can come in." The Shah went to his desk chair and flumped into it. "I don't even know what you're talking about with half these countries. And I was educated in the best schools."

---

*Dick Dick Dick Dick Dick also thought of Indonesia, but he preferred to save the complexity and pleasure of that memory for a later time.

Bob Toose leaned back and gazed at the ceiling in the posture of thoughtfulness. (He had used that phrase to describe a way of sitting he taught the Shah.) "Maybe you're squeamish because you've seen the photos of the Americans," Bob Toose said.

Dick Dick Dick Dick Dick's scowl moved from one of anger to one of confusion. "What do you mean?"

"If you heard a thud and a scream from the next room, you might be startled, but you wouldn't necessarily go see what happened. But if you saw someone have his thumb broken by a hammer in this room, if you saw why someone was screaming, you'd be taken aback."

Dick Dick Dick Dick Dick stood erect. "Gentlemen, in this age of science and reason, this Era of Texceptionalism, we must test this."

Reader, they tested it.

Scheissetete stepped outside, then returned moments later and nodded. His crow's feet danced with his smile. A few minutes later, one of the Shah's guards brought in their test subject in his orange jumpsuit and shackles. Behind them came a man in an electrician's overalls with gold epaulets on his shoulders and a bandolier of swinging tools.

"Start in the next room," Dick Dick Dick Dick Dick said.

The guard led the test subject through into another room, followed by the electrician. The Shah covered his ears. Some loud, screamed *nos* came through the reinforced door, followed by the thud, followed by a scream. Bob Toose flinched.

Dick Dick Dick Dick Dick's sneer reached his eyes. "Sounds like we missed a good one."

The guard, followed by the electrician, dragged the subject back in, holding his hand and dripping blood.

"Try it on the desk," Dick Dick Dick Dick Dick said.

"This was my father's desk!" the Shah cried. Then he cry-cried.

Dick Dick Dick Dick Dick: "We'll replace it with a better one, same as we did with the first Shah."

The electrician lined up his hit, but at the last moment the subject jerked his unbroken thumb away. Splinters and chips flew.

"Goddamn it!" Dick Dick Dick Dick Dick exclaimed. "You can't get good help anymore these days. I'll do it myself. Scheissetete!"

Scheissetete paced over. From the inside pocket of his suit jacket he removed what resembled a driving glove. It emanated a smell that made the other men in the room think "rich, Corinthian leather." Scheissetete slid the glove on Dick Dick Dick Dick Dick's right hand and gave him the hammer. Dick Dick Dick Dick Dick lined up his swing, but the prisoner would not stop wiggling and moaning. Dick Dick Dick Dick Dick nodded at Scheissetete, then Scheissetete pulled a small box from a separate inside pocket of his suit jacket, removed a syringe and filled it with liquid from a small bottle, and injected the prisoner's arm. The prisoner went limp.

"There," Dick Dick Dick Dick Dick said. "The best kind of hunting." He brought down the hammer. The man's body flinched; blood and more wood spurted.

Dick Dick Dick Dick Dick looked around. "You see? Question answered. In here, it's much more rewarding. Scheissetete, off we go."

Off They Went

Off They Went

Off went Dick Dick Dick Dick Dick and Scheissetete, ringed by a confederacy of guards, through halls to secret halls, underground to the hidden parking structure, where they got into Dick Dick Dick Dick Dick's car, sheathed in bulletproofing. Scheissetete drove Dick Dick Dick Dick Dick the thirty minutes to his residence, ███████████. During the ride over, Dick Dick Dick Dick Dick orated, as he liked to do when alone with Scheissetete, who was either muse or amanuensis, or both.

"If you want to change the world, you have to break a few things. And if you change the world, they put your name on monuments and history books and college buildings. That's how we make progress. Nobody gets remembered for peace." He thought of Indonesia in the 1950s, and how if that idiot CIA pilot hadn't crashed and been caught, the American government could have had its fun.

Scheissetete looked in the rearview mirror and raised his eyebrows.

"Gandhi's the exception that proves the rule. And it's not like India is some beacon of peace now. No, if you want to make a name, you have to make change. Alfred Nobel: he invented dynamite and made his fortune by producing weapons. He only created those prizes after a newspaper accidentally ran a judgy obit. And now what do we remember?"

Scheissetete offered another glance in the mirror.

"I agree. In a just world, I'd have at least one of those Peace Prizes. It would prove a point. Andrew Carnegie, Pierpont Morgan, John D. Rockefeller. Vanderbilt and Stanford. They all prove it's cheaper to buy good publicity than to do what some people think of as actual good."

Scheissetete smiled.

"I love that you get me. My favorite, though? General Henry Shrapnel. Old time Limey. Eighteenth or nineteenth century. He invented a cannonball that exploded and sent what we now call *shrapnel* into the air. Nobody remembers him or curses his name or complains about *him*. It's just his name.

"If I ever die, don't name some university after me. I don't want a bunch of twee little Dickies running around quoting poetry. I want a weapon named after me. I want people the world over to limp around complaining about how they got injured by *quintic dick*. God, I'm already wet."

At home, Dick Dick Dick Dick Dick set his eye to the eye scanner, placed his thumb on the thumbprint reader, and keyed in the secret code to enter, ███████. When all three devices beeped, he turned the doorknob and pulled instead of pushed, as he always did by accident, cursed the door, then pushed it open and entered the house. "Wife!" he yelled. "Prepare yourself for a great dickering!"

Scheissetete pulled away and drove to nearby Fort Wood Military Base. He didn't need to show his credentials at the gate: the guard recognized him. As he drove in, soldiers turned and held salutes. He drove past the main building, curled the car behind it, and parked next to the portable building that rested a foot off the ground. Grass grew beneath it, almost reaching the bottom of the portable. To enter, one had to climb the steps or the wheelchair ramp. Scheissetete chose the clattery ramp, likely because it announced him better than the stairs did.

Indeed, when he entered, the two drone pilots already stood in salute, as did their superior. Scheissetete handed the superior a slip of paper. The superior read it, nodded, and handed it to one of the pilots. She—yes, she, the military had introduced a program called "I Would Kill for Equality"—she read the paper, nodded to the superior, and nodded to Scheissetete. He left the portable, returned to the car, and exited the base.

Back at ███████████, as the drone pilots began their work, Dick Dick Dick Dick Dick removed his pants and folded them on their hanger, ensuring the creases would remain neat. Wife was already in the inverted-wedge position on the bed. He stood at the end, arms crossed. They had a daughter, but they had never had a child: Years ago, Wife had given birth to a human who emerged wearing a tasteful dress and comfortable pumps. Now she represented a rural county in the Texas Legislature.

Dick Dick Dick Dick Dick's penis hummed, detached from

his body, and rose. Piloted elsewhere, the penis flew to its coordinates, monitored its targets, flew its route, and dispersed its payload.

Meanwhile, over a St. Jude's hospital in Pittsburgh, far from the great nation of Texas, a drone released its bombs. The next day, Texan papers reported that a drone strike had killed a major terrorist insurgent at a hospital known for harboring and treating terrorists. American papers reported differently. Months later, Texan papers would report, toward the back, that the numbers of civilian dead were revised upward to a figure still notably lower than those alleged by American papers.[*]

During the drone strike, smaller black shadows appeared on the screen, indicating children. One of the drone operators called them "fun-sized terrorists."[†]

Dick Dick Dick Dick Dick's weapon returned to his housing. He'd left a little mess, but that wasn't his to consider or clean. Sated, he wiped spittle from his chin and decided to cook a steak.

---

[*]We do not include here the American descriptions of what happened. We must be careful about the inclusion of propaganda in this text.

[†]Language borrowed from a 2015 *Guardian* article.

A Shakespeherean Rag: And Other Stuff

A Shakespeherean Rag: The Hiftorical Tragedy of Richard V'f Penif; or, Louef Laborf Loft

For those curious about the genital mechanics of Dick Dick Dick Dick Dick, please read the following one-scene rendering of the need for such a device.

Scene: On the Hunting Ground

Enter Richard V and his train, Falftaff, and a Forefter carrying two cages of ducks awakening from anefthefia.

Richard V: Forfooth! Whofo lift to hunt?
Falftaff: I do fo loue the uital mafculine maftery of the hunt!
Richard V: Yes, we meafure and exprefs our honor on this field of battle.

Richard V, his train, and Falftaff form a ftanding circle. Each man holds a rifle. The Forefter fets the two cages in the center of the circle, opens the door, and waits for the ducks to exeunt. The ducks blink and do not exeunt. The Forefter tips the cages and pours the ducks out onto the field. The Forefter leaues the circle.

Richard V: Hark! These feathered killers threaten our uery way of life! We muft deftroy them before they deftroy us!
Forefter: Ready!

Richard V, his train, and Falftaff raife their rifles to their fhoulders and aim.
Forefter: Aim! Duck duck duck duck duck!

Richard V, feueral members of his train, and Falftaff fire. Several of the ducks explode in feathery puffs; other ducks, ftartled by the noife and explofions of feathers, attempt to exeunt by flying. Falftaff fhoots at one of the marginally airborne creatures.

Richard V: Yeargh! Aieeeee!

Richard V: I haue been flain! My penis and fcrotum haue been difentangled from my corpfe! My weapon of generation! How fhalt I engloue myfelf into my dear wife's uagina?! This fuckering fuccotafh will not ftand! fhit! fhit!

feueral of Richard V's train lift him and carry him toward ftage right.

Richard V: A horfe dick! A horfe dick! My kingdom for a horfe dick!

Exeunt, purfued by a duck.

The Prod

The Prod

Adiel S. Thomas didn't like steak. She didn't drink martinis or smoke cigars or giggle at men's unclever innuendos.[*] But tonight, to serve a purpose, she would. And in heels, which she rarely wore, so her calves and toes hurt. She thought everyone could see her ungainly steps as she walked into the bar of The Velvet Cattle Prod, a favorite steakhouse of journalists, elected and unelected officials, and lobbyists.[†]

And why was she there? Margot Nought. The Shah had taken the folder of photographs Adiel had brought to the Freedome, but she had kept the originals and the negatives. "Always keep the negatives," Cy Jost had always said. His more promoted colleagues usually replied, "That's your problem: you never let go of the negatives." And after the disastrous day with the Shah, she took the originals to Margot, hoping for a sequel to the exposé of Garza West.

"Adiel," Margot said, "I appreciate your hard work, I really do, but this isn't news." Margot told Adiel that her job had been to spend the day with the Shah so she could write an even-handed story about him: lightly critical, but ultimately fair.

An argument ensued, as arguments are wont to do. Margot claimed, among other things, that Garza West was one thing, but the *Morning Sun* couldn't be seen as actively anti-war or anti-Texas. In war, there were boundaries, there was objectivity. She finally agreed to run a story—but not the photographs—on page A38.

"That's not good enough!"

"Well, we can't run news that sacrifices our access. And the photographs will."

"What's the point of access if we have to flatter people and lie?"

"Then saunter your ass on down to The Velvet Cattle Prod

---

[*] As a deliverer of unclever innuendos, I resent Adiel S. Thomas for her choice, but no character is perfect.

[†] Maybe "unelected officials" and "lobbyists" is a redundancy, but the Venn diagram of those two categories isn't a perfect circle quite so much as it looks like so (()).

and network. If you're not careful with me, you'll need a new job."

Adiel had gone home and eaten and cried until she had the idea to take Margot's dismissive suggestion seriously: she would go to The Velvet Cattle Prod in search of a useful face: Neil O'Chisholm's. He had offered mild criticism in an interview with Dick Dick Dick Dick Dick; among the rest of the media, that made him a rare outlier.

So she went with a big purse—a stiff, unused gift in which to carry the photographs—to The Velvet Cattle Prod,* or, as regulars called it, The Prod. The waitstaff, busboys, and bartenders were dressed in Western gear: leather chaps, unpointed spurs that jingled as they went through the restaurant, and big hats. Bartenders and waiters had to tip their hats each time they approached a customer or table: a tip for a tip.

When The Prod opened, the staff were known as the Hands. Over time, for their quiet, excellent service, they had become known as the Invisible Hands. Given the expense of the Prod, even bad tips made life livable for them, along with their other jobs; for many, that included selling drugs out the back or in the side alley of the restaurant, often to customers about to enter or just leaving. The market finds a way. Thankfully for buyers and sellers, one invisible hand ignored what the other was doing.

Throughout the War of Texan Independence from the Surly Grip of America, each time an enemy soldier was captured (good) or

____

*Immersion: one of the great pleasures of reading a novel. You enter a world, and if you recognize it as precisely drawn, you feel the great mental yes of knowing someone sees the world you see and has shown it as it is. And if it's a world entirely unknown to you, it's tourism without the screaming children and perspirant mass transiters. You get to go back to your friends and family and talk about the moors of England. But writing a novel? It means exploring and creating the worlds of these characters and realizing how little of the world you know. Once you write the sort of journalist who frequents upscale steakhouses, you confront the wall of your ignorance: you haven't been to a steakhouse in decades, and you haven't been to an upscale it's-who-you-know place in your entire life. So reader this one's on you: I'll give you the scaffold of the little I actually know about this place, and the rest is up to you. Research sucks. And next time you rag on Karl Ove Knaussgaaaaard for writing about taking a shit, forgive him: at least he has the good sense to stay within the narrow fissure of what he knows.

killed (great), the manager rang a bell, and the diners hollered. When the manager didn't receive any notice of victory, capture, or death, he rang the bell around 8:15 when a lot of diners were about to pay and a new set waited to be seated. The bell was good for business.

When Adiel went in, she looked around for Neil—she'd heard he was a frequent drinker and diner—and people stared back at her. Since Garza West and her TV appearances, she was known, but she had never been known to grace or disgrace the Prod with her presence. She didn't see Neil and planted herself at the bar, everyone's eyes following her, with a stool on either side as a buffer from the men ingesting their bourbon and pouring out their exaggerations. No televisions flanked the bar—the media already peopled the place—so she watched the mirror instead, spied the glad-handing and self-congratulating patrons, as well as the tray-bearing waitstaff scowling until they crossed the threshold into smiling, laughing, yes-anding.

Every time the front door opened and hot Houston air puffed in, she checked the mirror for Neil. But, for a while, no such luck. Eventually, a news producer—she could tell from the rolled-up sleeves and clammy sheen on his forehead, the way gray hair tonsured his head—sat on the stool next to her. He tried to chat her up, and she told him she was waiting for her husband and hid her left hand by her side so her ringless finger wouldn't contradict. Once he left, she chunked her purse onto that stool so no one else would occupy it.

She was considering another martini, already feeling helium-veined and sour-mouthed, when she saw Neil O'Chisholm enter. She turned to the bartender, pointed to her empty glass and signaled for two, then waved to Neil with a *joie de vivre* that wasn't entirely faked.

As he came over to her, he pointed and waved to all the people who knew him. He wasn't an outcast yet. That made him useful.

"You seem friendly tonight, Miss Thomas. Didn't know you were ever a Prodder."

She smiled and tilted her head. College parties had trained her for this. "Call me Adiel. I'm just glad to see you out in the real world, Neil. Martini?"

"Don't mind if I do," he said and signaled to the bartender for a drink. The bartender nodded. "I heard you had a Shah day."

Adiel nodded and used her teeth to tweeze an olive from a toothpick. "I learned a lot."

Neil smiled. Up close, without makeup, he looked sallow but still had a glowing charm. "He's not such a bad guy, the Shah."

"You know him?"

"I've met him a few times. No interviews. I'm jealous."

The bartender brought two martinis to Adiel and set a third in front of Neil. She didn't know how to explain.

"I hope you're thirsty," he said.

"Always," she said, aware her smile was a little too wild. "You flying solo tonight?"

He dug under his thumbnails with the nails of his pinkies. "I usually end up having dinner with whatever friend will have me. I guess tonight that's you."

Soon, they were in a booth. The leather under her heralded every milimeter she moved, but the noises seemed to get drowned out by the restaurant's chatter and clinks. They ordered; all meals at the Prod looked like so:

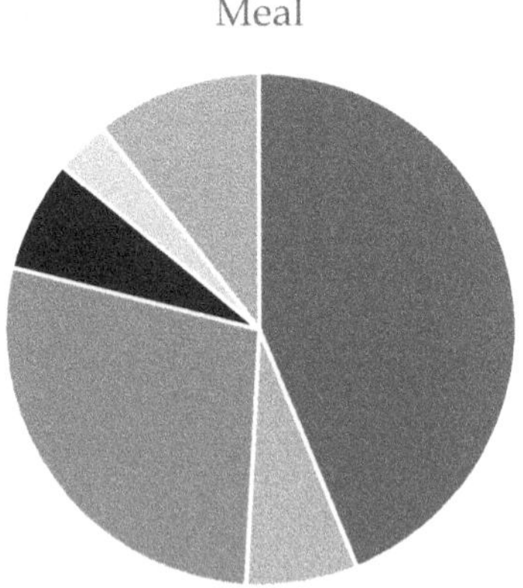

After they ordered, Neil raised his glass to clink hers. Adiel raised one of hers, very aware of the horizon of her drink trying to overtake the horizon of the glass. As Cy Jost had said whenever anyone criticized his drinking, "If you need to get good at it, practice."

As his toast, Neil said, "So what exactly is going on here?" He tapped her glass with his, and cold martini splashed the web between her thumb and forefinger.

Adiel set the glass down and let her face relax. When she looked back up at him, her eyes felt the swirl of drink. "You seem like the only other media person who," she said and squeezed a little crust on her bread plate, "is bothered by what's going on."

Neil tilted his head as if in confusion.

"At Garza."

His face tensed into discomfort as hers had.

"War is always full of difficult decisions. My job is to stay objective."

Adiel leaned forward, and the table seemed to wobble toward her[*]. "Even if you don't know what objectivity is in these circumstances."

Neil sat back and spread his arms to his sides on the booth. He looked toward the bar as if there were a television to watch.

"I need something from you," Adiel said. Even though she would never do what she was about to propose, she added, "Should I just offer to fuck you and get it over with?"

He stared at her with something that looked like moral authority.[†] "I don't know who you think I am, but I'm not that kind of person."

Adiel straightened her face and nodded, looking down at the table. "I know you're not that kind of person. I'm sorry. I'm a little drunk. The way you reacted to the Garza West photos, the way you

____

[*]One might expect tables at a nice restaurant to have no wobble, but The Prod had ordered their tables from a company that specialized in wobbly tables. Customers enjoyed the experience because it felt rewarding to balance the table with a sugar packet.

[†]I have little life advice to offer beyond "eat right and exercise," but I'll also offer this: distrust anything that looks like moral authority, especially if it has any other kind of authority. {Publisher's note: I'm deeply offended by this Author's ideas about authority. Obviously, some authority is non-valid, but most authority in the world is justified and makes complete human sense. Frankly, the Author should know his place.}

challenged Dick Dick Dick Dick Dick, I really admire that. I didn't mean to be crass." She made eye contact. "I'm sorry."

Neil sat up a little straighter, too. "Thank you."

Adiel pulled the manila folder of photographs from her bag, slid it across the table, and opened it to the facing photo. "That's why I wanted to show you these photos. These are American civilians."

Neil paled. At just that moment, for prime narrative tension, an Invisible Hand arrived with a tray and tipped his brim. Neil closed the folder as the waiter started talking. "Tumbleweed salad," the Hand said, "light on the gristle, for the lady." He set it down before her. "And, for the right honorable pardner Mr. O'Chisholm—big fan of your work, sir—the Black Slaughterhouse in our double butter sauce. Another martini? Looks like you're low."

Neil stared down at his plate and nodded gravely. "I think the lady is ready for another, too."

Anxiety threaded Adiel's body. She'd either won Neil, or she'd lost everything.

Neil lifted his fork and nudged a plastic-looking steamed broccoli floret, then used the handle of the fork to reopen the folder. He gazed at the first photograph, then took his steak knife from the plate and used it to turn over each photograph. As the steam of his steak thinned into nothing, he looked at them all.

As Neil looked at the last one, The Invisible Hand came to their table and set down their new martinis. "How is everything?"

Neither Adiel nor Neil had tasted a bite. "It's really good," Adiel said. Neil let the folder close and nodded.

After the Hand left, Neil looked up at the ceiling. "Bad things happen in war."

Fuck. She'd lost him. Now the best she'd be able to do with the photos would be to leak them to underground journals that opposed violence and war and the Shah so regularly that they had no credibility to oppose violence and war and the Shah. In this world, to be taken seriously in opposing violence and war, you had to support both most of the time. And once you had the credibility to be taken seriously, you had earned the right to be politely disagreed with or ignored.

So at best, Adiel S. Thomas would become one of those low-paid castoffs who scrounged together articles read only by powerless cranks. She didn't want to admit that she'd fantasized about being more, that behind her hopes for these revelations and some justice, her selfish aims rubbed their hands together.

Neil jabbed his fork into his steak and sawed off a large chunk of it. He held up the meat and examined it. "Bad things happen in war. Dick Dick Dick Dick Dick said that when I interviewed him. Ultimately, he said, it's a just war." He set the forked meat back on the plate and thumbed the condensation of his martini glass. "I didn't even imagine it. It's just—*bad things.*"

The bell rang; the rest of the diners hollered.

Adiel took a gulp of her martini and coughed. Once she could talk, she said, "I shouldn't have shown you those photos."

"No, you shouldn't have. Why did you?"

With her fork, she rearranged her salad. "The *Morning Sun* won't run them. I made a big stink, so I'm probably going to lose my job. Everyone should see them, and I thought you might help. You're—you're different." She looked up to meet his eyes: last ditch. "You're better than the rest of them."

"That's nice," he said. "Your paper won't run them. Do you really think my producers or even Routines, Procedures, Manners, and Customs would let any of these through?"

Her throat still burned from that dumb gulp of martini. "You showed the Garza West photos."

Neil put his arms in his lap and leaned forward. He looked for a moment like a limbless torso. "We had to because everyone else did. That wasn't some moral choice."

"But you tried to stand up to Dick Dick Dick Dick Dick. You challenged him."

Neil stood up from the booth. "I have to go to the men's room. Excuse me."

Adiel watched him walk past the bar, down the hallway toward the sign that read "Exit Troughs." She ate a bite of lettuce, crouton, and gristle. It was meaty and sweet, with her anxiety making the flavors too loud. He was probably on the phone calling someone in the Shah's government. Bob Toose, most likely. She should take the photographs and her bag and go. But she couldn't. This was the end to any hope of justice. So she nibbled at the leaves of her Tumbleweed salad.

Reader, let's break for a moment from the confines of shifting limited omniscience to go to the Men's Exit Trough of The Prod. It appears like so:

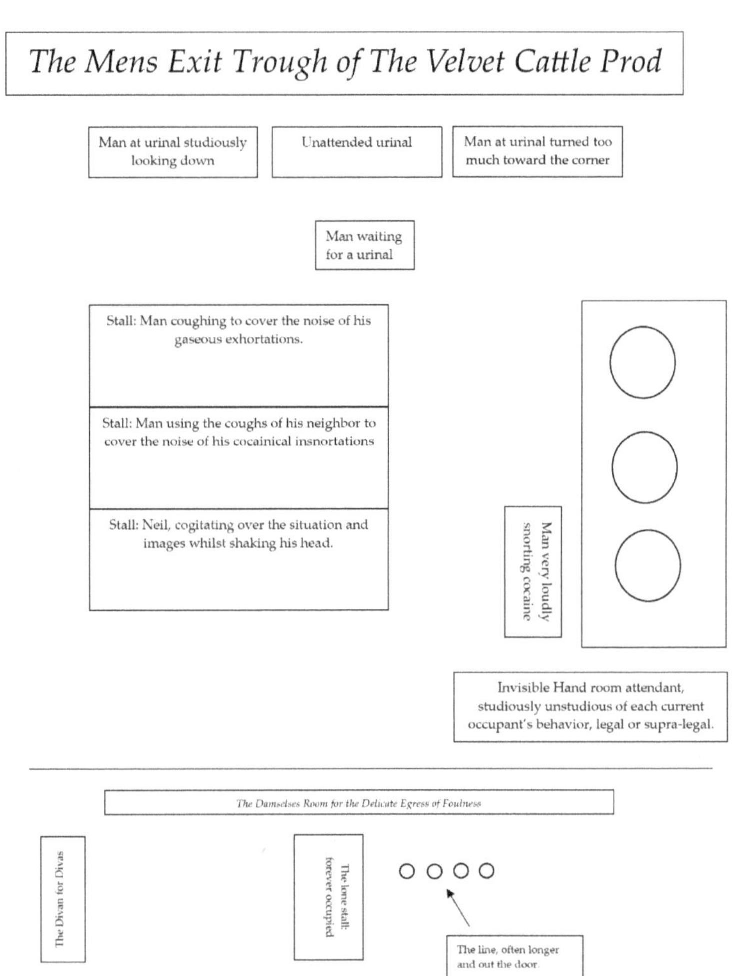

Reader, now we return to the table and the comfortable confines of shifting limited omniscience.*

Adiel was pleasantly surprised by how good the free bread was. At least there was that, the only pleasantness in this moment. Now she was rationalizing her staying as a kind of courage: in the moment that her career careered toward its end, she remained in the booth to let it happen.

Neil walked back to the table, eyes resolutely looking at the floor. Adiel saw people waving and nodding to him unacknowledged. She thought of bolting and even pushed her heels down to stand up, but sat back down, forearms hard against the seat of the booth.

Neil slid in across from her. He picked up his folded napkin and spread it back in his lap, then lifted the fork still with the chunk of steak on its tines. He eyed the chunk as if awaiting its last words, then put it in his mouth, and chewed, and chewed, and chewed, and chewed. Watching him gnaw—Neil still hadn't looked at Adiel since he'd left for the trough—she could taste the dryness he must be tasting. She'd done that, had to chew and chew and chew, not wanting to keep eating but wanting so desperately to be done with that bite. Maybe she hadn't lost him after all.

Once he swallowed, he took a big swig of his martini, then rasped and chased the rasp with a gulp of water. He kept looking at the center of the table. "The one photo with the black walls and the hands. What happened there?"

"According to the government's classified report, the first bomb tore open the roof. The second set fire to the water heater, so people who weren't killed by the first bomb were boiled alive."

Neil finally looked at her, lips split from one another except a single off-white string of spit. "Who were they?"

---

*To be clear, this is not a time for you, reader, to attend to your own exiting needs and skip to the next chapter. Though I suppose you have your own free will about what you do or don't choose to read. I suppose you're welcome to take the novel to your execratory labors or repose.

"It was a shelter." [*]

For the first time, Adiel saw Neil's face uncompose, the cheeks beneath the eyes and then the jaw. She'd seen this kind of face before. When she was nine, she and her father were playing Scrabble in the kitchen when the phone rang. Her father answered, and as he listened to what she would learn was the news that her mother, his wife, had been killed in a car accident on the way to the grocery store, his face and then his body uncomposed themselves.

Adiel almost reached her hand across the table to Neil's.

"I don't—" Neil started. He picked up the folder and put it in his lap beneath the table. "The underbelly."

"Yep," she said. "That's their underbelly. Part of it, at least."

He shook his head, then looked up at her. "Who else has seen these?"

"My editor. My source." With her fingers, she tweezed crumbs from the roll she hadn't finished. "I showed them to the Shah."

Neil blurted a laugh. "Okay." He leaned forward, though the noise of the restaurant made most conversations private anyway. "You are going to make clear nobody will publish these photos. You go back to the paper and tell Margot, your source, whoever. Say it wherever someone is listening. I'll do what I can to get these on the air." He raised a finger to the waiter.

The Invisible Hand arrived, ready to act. "Something wrong with y'all's food?"

Neil shook his head, a smile somehow comfortable on his face. "No, we've just both had something come up, so we'll need these boxed. And she's being gracious—the check goes to her."

When the Invisible Hand looked at her, Adiel jerry-rigged a smile onto her face and nodded. For Neil's help, she could pay for this dinner and eat ramen for a week or two.

---

[*] Any reader with a memory unfragmented and informed enough to remember Amiriyah, the shelter bombed during the Persian Gulf War by the American military, please don't make any untoward association between that historical event and the one referred to above. And if you don't know Amiriyah, please don't put down the novel to do a bit of wiki or library research, heaven forfend.

Maude in Love

Maude in Love

Love. Love! Amo! Amas! Amat! Liebe! حب! Maude was in it! With Mr. Robert Toose! And he, Mr. Robert Toose, was in love with her! The birds outside looked to be singing, or would if she could see them more clearly from a distance; the air conditioner and her grandmother's lamp hummed as troubadours. So why did she feel so unsettled? [*]

After Mr. Robert Toose told Maude he loved her and made that love to her on the map of ████, figuratively showing their love to the world, her body would not stop tingling. Only part of that tingling was the map-rash on the skin over her sacrum. (Thank Heaven the map wasn't topographical, for the corn fields and silos of the otherwise flat landscapes of ██████ and ████████ would have been indelicately and injuriously placed.) She felt hot and sweaty all over, even after dressing. And Robert had picked up the bullet and said, "I'm going to get you a ring, and this will be the gemstone. See? It looks like a black pearl. That'll make it all better."

He was right, of course, as always. It did look *like* a black pearl. But it was also clearly a bullet, so he was also wrong somehow. Yet the gesture felt sweet, and when the ring arrived via messenger at her home, she slid it on the ring finger of her left hand as if they were engaged, hoping to cast some propriety over just how improper it felt to be in love, and with a man already wedded to another. But her heart kept thumping hard, and the ring kept catching on her clothes. So she put it back in the ring box and set it on her dresser, where she would forget about it for a while until she noticed the eely tingle that emanated out from her gut—that word, *gut,* so bodily, only correct and proper in instances when one could say one knew a thing in their gut and really meant in the rightness of their soul.

Yes, love had changed Maude Lynne, and she didn't like it.

She had been married before, to an oil magnate-turned-economist. No mere *oilman,* Husband was a magnate, a great man. (His father

____

[*]Ah, the fictional structure of "X is good, so why did he/she/it/they feel so bad." Old reliable. "So why," as if the writer doesn't know? Bless that narratively helpful rhetorical question.

had owned a poultry-breeding concern and was a chick magnate.) When Husband's oil company failed and was bought out (circumstances beyond his greatness), he became an economic advisor, first to an American president, and then to the first Shah. Husband and Maude joined the Shah together—him as economist, her as speechwriter.

Maude and her first husband had told each other "I love you," but Maude knew that they liked and respected one another, which was really more essential and proper. Yes, as they'd dated, as they rode on his father's boat, as he bought her rings and then the ring, she'd felt that flush of excitement, but it hadn't been love. It had been comfort, and she was content with that.

And then, early in the years of the first Shah, Husband died. Husband shot himself. No one ever told her exactly why, but he had been erratic for weeks, and she figured out vaguely he had made some bad economic decisions, improper and possibly illegal decisions, perhaps on the behalf of the Shah and perhaps not. Thankfully, she was financially protected from these. The first Shah's administration worried that she might hold some grudge against them, but she held a grudge against Husband, in fact, for killing himself. She exonerated the Shah and onerated Husband. But in the turmoil following his death, she needed rest, so they allowed her to resign, and now she wrote newspaper columns and appeared on television, proving time and again to all Shahs, the first and second, that some things—duty, country—were more important than any potential indiscretions of Husband. Yes, she'd liked Husband, but she loved Country.

Or so she'd thought. Her country never made her feel as did the love of Mr. Robert Toose. One was proper; the other most certainly did not seem so.

Somewhere between the fervid love for Mr. Robert Toose and the milder liking of Husband, one held for her Country the appropriate affection and love. For when one found two extremes, one most often found the right situation and solace in the center.

And so to calm herself from the perferviding enervations of Toose, Maude Lynne did what she always did when she needed to certify her truest beliefs: she wrote them in a column. Thusly, as one did: anecdote, larger question, analysis, another anecdote or two, a question one might ask in challenging the idea and a riposte to said question, and anecdote in summation. An order to the word, an order to the world.

Ergo, anecdote: The twin deaths of Romeo & Juliet;[*]

Larger question: what, actually, is love; there are the tepid and the roiling, and in between is the pure love of some thing greater than oneself. In this case, the somethings were God and Texas;

Another anecdote or two: the great love of Abraham in nearly killing his son, the great love of Texas in excising itself from America for its people;

A question one might ask in challenging: But what of the dangerous violence of Abraham against his son, what of the violence of the war between Texas and America;

Riposte: But what of the necessary violence of the father in correcting his son, and what of the unloving violence of America and the necessary retaliation of Texas;

Summation in anecdote: The star of Texas is the star of love, and when she sees a father tousling his son's head, that is the love that Texas shows. Everything Texas did, it did with love.

The headline, her *pièce de résistance*, her *coup de plume*, her *coup de grace*, was this: Texas Is Love.

Maude Lynne felt relief. Texas is love. She called her typist, who would type and deliver it to the paper, where it would be printed word for word and letter for letter (save for any spelling errors created by her typist), for "Attitudes and Estimations" editors had the good sense not to question or fact-check important ideas.

She went to her bedroom and changed into her napping pajamas: the tingle was gone, and she had earned a rest. Maude lay on her bed. As she fell into her doze, though, she started awake at an image that forestalled any further repose: the first Shah of Texas, glowering and large, bringing down a knife to her throat. On the corner of her dresser, the closed ring box sat with its sinister velvet.

---

[*]I do admit a jealousy: Maude Lynne could handwrite an ampersand with the fluid ease of a surgeon incising the flesh between two ribs.

General Nodding

General Nodding

Bob Toose had to stay late at the Freedome to observe re-felting of the map. He was responsible for the cost as well, which meant a series of transfers of funds, from military weapons to military PR, laundered through two different slush funds, then—you know what? It's complicated. Money moved.

The map's capabilities had been turned off and the re-felters blindfolded so they couldn't see anything to share what they saw.

Once they were done, Bob ██████ed with himself in memory of his night with Maude Lynne, then sat by himself in the Communications and Relations Office to watch the bank of TVs at the start of the national news shows. Maybe the ring was a mistake; when he proposed getting the ring made, her smile glowed a glow he'd never seen. He worried she took the gesture as a particular kind of proposal. He was, of course, already married; he had wanted to appease her so she wouldn't again mention the pearl turning into a bullet. Bob laid the charm on thick and told her it looked like a black pearl. She seemed to appraise its value highly then. His coercive appeasement had won.

The news channels were muted except Neil O'Chisholm's: Bob Toose liked to sing lyrics of his invention with the opening theme of O'Chisholm's news show: "You're a ████, you're a ████, you're a nasty little ████, and your mother birthed you slimy out her filthy open ██." Even though he liked Neil O'Chisholm well enough, he smiled each time.

"Tonight," Neil O'Chisholm intoned, "oil profits are up and what you can spend that money on; welcoming home our brave men and women; weather and sports; but first: new revelations about civilian deaths at the hands of Texan forces. These photos tonight have been given exclusively to us at W-ANK TV."

Two photos from the Shah's folder were arrayed on screen in boxes, one above the other. A blackened, fire-thinned arm reaching to touch an American ambulance in one, the outline of two figures against a charred wall next to a singed bridal bouquet on the ground.

"Fuck!" Bob Toose yelled. It resonated off the walls. "Fuck! You cunt!* You absolute spineness bleeding-heart cunt! I'm going to dig up your mother and strangle you with your umbilical cord!"

Both phones in the Communications and Relations Office began ringing. Only a handful of people had those two numbers.

Half an hour later, Bob Toose sat hard against the armrest of one of the sofas in the Grand Office of the Shah, arms crossed and head bowed. The Shah sat leaned back behind his desk, his arms also crossed, head shaking no. He was furthest from where Bob cowered. Nearer, past the far end of the other sofa, also shaking his head but grinning, stood Scheissetete. Standing just past the end of Bob's sofa, scowling, stood the Secretary of Conflagrations, Holly Unlikely. And hunched over Bob, redly and readily ejaculating insults, was Dick Dick Dick Dick Dick.

Dick Dick Dick Dick Dick orated. "You untalented motherfuck! You idiotic abortion of a man! Number one on your list: know what the news is going to say before they say it! First Garza West, and now this! You piddling afterbirth! Why didn't you know?"

Bob stood. "The other channels went with our story about the brave little soldier. How was I supposed to know? Neil O'Chisholm snuck those in. Besides," and here Bob stepped behind the opposite sofa to put himself out of Dick's flailing distance, "how did Neil get those pictures?" He pointed at the Shah. "We know *he* had them."

The Shah leaned forward. "You think I would leak those pictures to the media? How would I even do that? I've got people watching me all day long. I couldn't have leaked them. But I'm glad they got out. Now this one" —he pointed at Holly Unlikely— "can maybe refocus on not killing innocent people."

"Nonsense," Holly Unlikely said. She stayed sitting, leaning back, legs crossed. "No American is innocent. Besides, I'm the innocent person in all of this. I'm just following his orders and yours." She pointed, at the end, at Dick Dick Dick Dick Dick.

"The whole thing is nonsense," Dick Dick Dick Dick Dick said. "We didn't do anything wrong. It's war."

---

*We do apologize; our redactionist's Sharpie ran out of ink, so he's gone to requisition a new one.

Everyone sighed except Scheissetete. He kept grinning.

"Now," Bob Toose said, "we just have to fix it."

Holly Unlikely shook her head. "We can ignore it. Bad things happen in war. We all know that. Everybody knows that."

Dick Dick Dick Dick Dick swelled and stared at the Shah. "Apparently, not everybody did."

The Shah replied, "Maybe people should know what that really means."

Bob Toose: "Maybe someone should have spoken up and said he didn't know what it means."

In a television transcript, the next few seconds would be represented like so: [Crosstalk.] Prose fiction can't really present people talking at and over one another in any effective way without seeming ridiculously artificial. But if you're the sort of reader who needs very literal presentation—and some of us are—here you go:

Rhubarb Rhubarb Rhubarb Rhubarb Rhubarb

Dick Dick Dick Dick Dick ended the crosstalk with a cinematic, "Enough!" He waited until everyone's eyes were on him to speak again. "This whole thing is so stupid. There's a reason the media aren't supposed to show dead civilians in wartime. It's like murder: if no one sees a body, there's no crime. It's why we drape flags over the coffins of soldiers who come home."

Nodding was general all around the office, except for the Shah.

Bob Toose: "No matter who in this room may have made a mistake—and yes, mistakes were made—the real mistake is Neil O'Chisholm airing those photos. Showing the deaths of Americans is aid and comfort to Americans. He's—" Bob glanced around the room—"he's a traitor."

More vigorous general nodding, again except for the Shah. Scheissetete grinned harder.

"And that Adiel S. Thomas, too," Holly Unlikely said. "Aiding and abetting and comforting."

Bob Toose shook his head. "We've got several recordings of her saying she couldn't get anyone to bite on the photos. But we should put Neil on trial."

Dick Dick Dick Dick Dick wrinkled. "A trial's a waste of time. Too messy and costly. We should just take them out and make it look like the Americans did it."

The Shah stood and walked around his desk. "Dick, no! That's a horrible thing to suggest. That's the worst thing I've ever heard." The Shah looked to Bob Toose for agreement; Bob glanced away. When the Shah looked to Holly Unlikely, she did the same.

Dick stood up straighter. "Then you haven't heard nearly enough things. An American bomb takes out W-ANK, we publicly mourn and get more support, and the war goes better. If you're worried about innocent lives, then this would probably help more innocent lives be spared."

Someone laughed. It was strange and rough; it sounded as if someone had pulled the cord to start a chainsaw, but the engine didn't catch.

It was Scheissetete.

Bob Toose held up his forefinger. "Was that you?"

Holly Unlikely said to Dick Dick Dick Dick Dick: "Have you ever heard him make a sound?"

Dick Dick Dick Dick Dick, his mouth a rictus[*] upturned on one side and downturned on the other because a full smile risked serious damage to his health, said, "Never."

The Shah stepped face-to-face with Scheissetete. That was a marvel: everyone knew he was terrified of Scheissetete. (They knew he was terrified because everyone, except possibly Dick Dick Dick Dick Dick, was terrified of Scheissetete.) "Why did you laugh?" the Shah asked.

Scheissetete's mouth opened.

---

[*] I'm so delighted to use this small literary delectation. I feel like I've earned a writerly merit badge.

Scheissetete Speaks

Scheissetete Speaks

"I laughed," Scheissetete said, "because it was funny. More lives spared, or more lives lost. Innocent lives, guilty lives. It is all so funny.

"Do you know this delightful children's book, *Everyone Poops?* 'An elephant makes a big poop. A mouse makes a tiny poop.' 'All living things eat, so everyone poops.' The pages show a great deal of excrement. It's delightful, except after children learn that all living things poop, they are supposed to grow out of discussing it.

"I have been working on a similar monograph so we can all remember: *Everything Dies.* It reminds us, everything dies! You will die, and you will die, and you and you. America will die, and Texas, someday, will die. If the thousand-year Reich had lived, it would have died after a thousand years, or earlier, or later. As it was, it died before it reached a decade. I work on my monograph in my quiet hours. I'm doing the illustrations myself. So many images of death! I have to stop working before I put myself to bed, lest I stay awake all night with delight.

"Even though everything dies, one must never lose one's sense of humor. After The Greater War—that is what I like to call World War Zwei—I escaped Germany in the ratlines. I like to think of it as my lifelong study abroad. One might call me a citizen of the world. I will return home once I graduate, perhaps in shackles or a box. I spent time in Spain and Argentina, and I came to love *jamon* and flamenco. But the older officers complained all of the time. They worried about being caught and tortured and executed. They hated the shabby attics and basements, the small portions. But to me it was all delight and wonder! It was all life! Every moment is like peeking through a keyhole to watch your mother strip. We will *all* die, so every breath is a stolen moment!"

A Brief Interruption

A Brief Interruption

"World War Two?" the Shah asked. "How old are you?"

The others tsked. "Sir," Bob Toose said. "It's not polite to ask someone's age."

"Of course. I know that. I'm sorry. Please continue."

Scheisetete Resumes

Scheissetete Resumes

"Thank you, though the apology is quite unnecessary. Never you mind how old I am. At every step through life, we saw these people who believe things do not die. The Catholics who spirited us through Europe, the Americans who hired so many of us to help establish the United States as an unbeatable force. They all believed that the things of this world last. Catholicism, America. But when their meat was charred, or, heaven forbid, there was no meat at all, they looked so ashen and scared. But each morsel is life! Each empty plate is life!

"And everyone dies. The elephant makes a big poop. The mouse makes a small poop; some people die big deaths, most people die small ones. There are, after all, many more mice in the world than elephants, and we toss mice into trash bins or yards. And if we wept for every mouse that pooped or died, we should have no bodies of our own to live. Do not weep for their deaths. Smile because they got to live, no matter how invisible or poor their lives.

"If someone dies in our pursuit of our next breaths, so be it. We will die for someone else's breath, and so on until there is only rubble, and it will not cry for us."

The Room Recovers

The Room Recovers

The Shah cleared his throat. Bob could tell he was blinking back tears. "So you're a Nazi?"

Everyone looked intently to Scheissetete.

Scheissetete Conclu—

Scheissetete Conclu—

Scheissetete tilted his head and his lips curled, bemused.

Discussion Resumes

Discussion Resumes

Dick Dick Dick Dick Dick shook his head. "You missed the point. Scheissetete may have been a Nazi, just like he was an American, just like someday he'll be dust. The point is, if the W-ANK building is dust, that's just because it has to be dust someday. Just like us."

Everyone looked to the Shah. Because he had heard the plan, he had to approve. He had never disapproved any action that everyone else agreed on.

The Shah locked eyes with Bob Toose. Bob could see the Shah's eyes pleading to him for support. Bob was unsettled: he'd never been in the position of emotional support to the Shah. Some human connection made itself flesh between them, until Bob turned his head and pretended to examine a spot on the carpet.

"No," the Shah said. "I say no. Now that you've told me, you can't do it and claim Plausible Deniability, so you can't do it." He started out of the room as if to punctuate his next and final sentence of the conversation. "That would cross a line we've never, ever crossed."

Bob Toose, Dick Dick Dick Dick Dick, Holly Unlikely, and Scheissetete all shared glances. They would have to continue telling the Shah nothing about any lines that had or had not been crossed.

At Last, the Novel Moves on to
Another Scene and Situation

At Last, the Novel Moves on to Another Scene and Situation

Each evening at 9:00 p.m., Maude Lynne turned off the ringer on her bedroom telephone. Only distressing calls occurred at night, and one required one's sleep. Several years prior, her phone rang at 11:19 p.m. with a prank call of heavy breathing, and she had been unable to return to sleep for hours. Not long after, she learned the term "sleep hygiene," and it was as if her whole life she had been a bell waiting to be rung. Her sleep would be, as she had made the rest of her life, hygenic.

So it was that she did not know about Neil O'Chisholm's report and the photographs of dead American civilians that evening, that she missed quite a number of calls from friends and journalists (often both as one) who wanted an anonymous source who had the ear of Bob Toose. So it was that she took in the newspaper, the filmy plastic damp with humidity and dew, elated to see her "Texas Is Love" column. Not only did she feel a chaste thrill each time she saw her all-capitalized name and grayscale headshot on the upper left of the Attitudes and Estimations page, she felt a chaste thrill each time she bent down to pick up the newspaper knowing that she would open it first to see her name and headshot. Each and every and all.

To the kitchen. She pinched the corners of the closed end of the newspaper plastic so the paper itself slid out and flopped open on her kitchen island, then flipped open the lid of her kitchen garbage with her slippered right foot and dropped in the plastic. Grubby little fingertips. She rinsed them and dried them with a paper towel. (She would have to extend her housekeeper's hours so as to avoid this grubbiness.) Now, to the newspaper. The *Houston Times* had a smaller circulation than the *Morning Sun*, but that was changing. The *Times* brought balance to the coverage, and its balance was growing. Besides, her column was syndicated in local newspapers across the state and two magazines. All told, her column appeared in more homes in the state than the *Morning Sun*. Margot Nought and Adiel S. Thomas, take that.

The newspaper had plopped so the below-the-fold half faced up. Just the bottom inch of a photo appeared below the fold, full-color gray rubble and a shoe. Maude put her hand to her chest: those dastardly Americans had killed more Texans! She turned over the newspaper and—

Gasp! Aghastitude! Maude dropped the paper when she saw the leg bloody and gray with dust from rubble. The corner of the newspaper, damp from rogue dew, left grimy print on her fingertips. But the headline and caption must have been in error: This was a dead American civilian? An American hospital? She shook her head, put her fingers to her face. No, no, not the morning of—. She opened the A section to Attitudes and Estimations, and there were her name and face, all-caps with her neck arrayed in those pearls, beneath the elegant headline in elegant print: "Texas Is Love."

Hand to her throat. She was running out of gestures for her shock. In those days, she did as one must to find out what people were saying. She turned on the television: a little zap, the center dot spread to a faint glow, and then the colors filled in toward reality. They were talking about these photos, and they were talking about her.[*]

Perhaps Maude Lynne was out of touch? The furthest rightward (from Maude's sitting perspective) read aloud the thesis paragraph, and the other two scoffed. Obviously, of course, Texas was in the right, they said, yet—and here Maude Lynne shut off her television set, all aflame, afume, abother. She wanted to scream (though she did not, even though she lived in a large house at a great enough distance from neighbors that she could scream without being heard), she wanted to hurl something (but had only costly things in the house, and though there was a definite pleasure in breaking costly things, that pleasure lay in breaking the costly things of *other* people), she wanted

---

[*]Reader, it is obvious that they were not talking about her at the moment she turned on the news channel. For narrative simplicity, though, I have removed her nervous sitting and pacing, her leg bouncing, the turbulent anticipation and hopping little jaunt to the restroom during commercials (medical aids for retirees, investment opportunities in rare earth metals, weatherproof window installation), the return from the restroom, her realization that the center cushion of her sofa needed reupholstering, until after minutes of analysis of whether or not these photographs were real and when they were taken and how they had arrived to Neil O'Chisholm and been aired (no mention of the cause of the death and damage or the morality of war), the cheery morning anchors turned their attention to the unfortunate juxtaposition of

the photograph of death and Maude Lynne's "Texas Is Love."

to hurt someone. Mr. Robert Toose! How could he not have warned her? And he lured her into his arms in that room, that Chamber for the Strategization of Conflagration and Tactical Engagement, and now she wanted to put on a glove so she could remove it and slap him. She wanted him to go to his knees and grovel, she wanted to take his throat with her delicate, slender fingers, she wanted—she wanted—she wanted to take him!

A shudder! A shudder in the loins engendered there! Robert's throat in her hand, her passion in her body! She went to her toilet[*], her comfort station so she could return herself to her station of normalcy. Instead, Maude saw newsprint on her cheeks, newsprint at her throat, and newsprint above her upper lip and its fine row of hair. Now she *did* scream; it resonated in a metallic pitch off the mirror. With the newsprint on her face, she looked like her mother had after her father left, a mess of mascara and mourning. And then the aftermath: no more grand estates, no more luxurious cars, no more lazing in a colleague's boat on serene waves, no more sense that the weekends could last all month. When she saw her father, she was delighted and pampered. Most of the time, though, she lived in the aura of her mother's stress and poverty. She vowed she would never live like that again. She would leave poverty and the impoverished behind.

And now look at her: a mess of smears, wet and red eyes, unkempt hair, mind afrazzle. She went back downstairs, took the bag of pearls from her purse, and put them all in her mouth. She sucked on them, nearly swallowed one, and spit them back onto the carpet. She didn't know her mouth could be so wet. Several clips' worth of bullets were arrayed on the floor.

---

[*]Fancy readers will understand that this means she goes to her vanity; unfancy readers, keep up.

The Will of the People

The Will of the People

As noted in an earlier edition of interviews with the general public, the events of this narratological record only concern the characters who recur herein. They are the actors and acted upon of history. That said, some may continue to wonder about the views of Everyday Texans™. With that in mind, below are quotes from more E.T.'s ™.

Question: What was your reaction to seeing photographs of bombed hospitals and wedding parties in America?

Streeter Stevens, Assistant Manager at Road O'Routers Maps and Atlasi: First of all, we don't even know if those pictures are real or when they were taken. Second, they're lucky we didn't nuke them.

Daniel Dayo Lewis, former Lead Singer of Harry Belafonte tribute band The Kingston Trio: Look, man, war is tough. Really tough. At least they were already at a hospital.

Leslie DeGorgio, Sandwich Savant at actor Larry Hagman's restaurant chain Hagman's Heroes: I'm really not supposed to talk about stuff like this at work. Did you say you want the J.R. Mooing or the Suet Ellen?*

---

*For younger readers, there used to be a television show called *Dallas,* in which— you know what? Never mind.

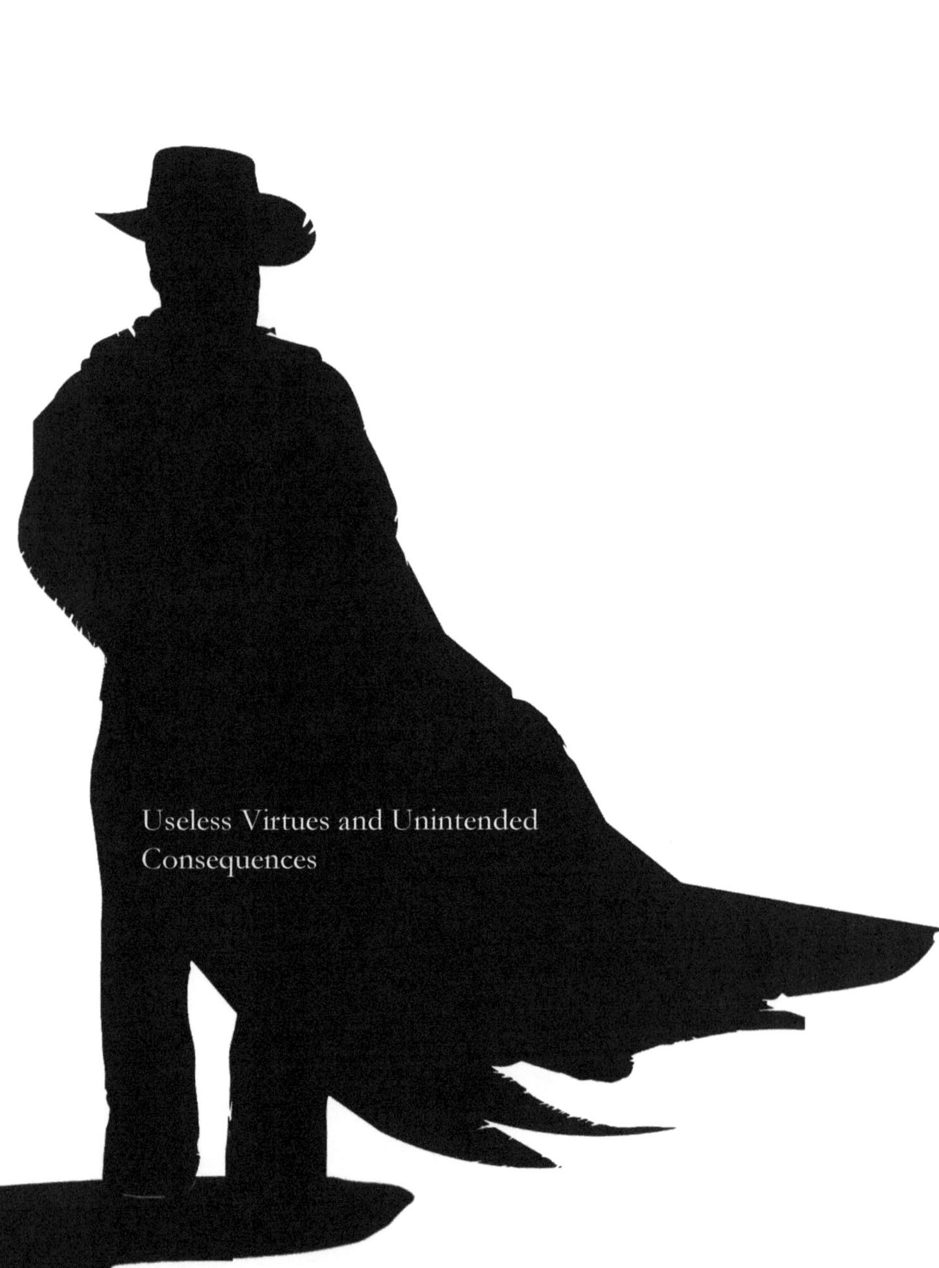
Useless Virtues and Unintended
Consequences

Useless Virtues and Unintended Consequences

Adiel S. Thomas could not stop grinning. "How did they get those photos," she said aloud for whatever listening devices there might be. Normally, she detested watching Hugh Succop and his hair (heavily gelled, cubic), but this she loved: his attempts to soften the impact of these images, the other commentators who weren't having his rationalizations, the mocking of Maude Lynne's column, which had apparently been headlined "Texas Is Love." Adiel only read *The Times* in dull moments at the office.

Granted, the conversation on screen was less about the morality and more about the optics—how did this look for Texas? How could the Shah ease tensions?—but optics were a start. Change what they see, then you can change how they see. Her dad had told her that's how propaganda worked; now she was using it to fight back.

From the other side of the bedroom wall, Otis called, "Are you seeing this?"

"It's so shocking," Adiel called back.

From the other side of the kitchen wall, Cody hollered, "What's shocking?"

Adiel's name wasn't linked to any of it, yet she felt prouder than she had about the Garza West photographs. She'd shown these new ones to the Shah, she'd shown them to Neil, and now Neil had shown them to the entire country of Texas. They would be disseminated to America and probably beyond. On the covers of Texas history textbooks, the first Shah rode a horse, having freed Texan citizens from the clutches of villainous Americans. But behind, ahead of, or around the Shah, out of the image, were the nameless many who did the actual work. Their glory was in the doing, not the hagiography. Adiel's name might go into history's recycling bin or garbage can or compost, her name might disappear into the belly of some nameless whale and, unlike Jonah, remain unknown, but she'd done her work.

The phone rang, again. Several times, reporters had called, asking for a comment since she'd published the Garza West photos. Did she have any thoughts about these new photographs? Had she known anything about them? No idea, no comment. Each time.

This time, though, it was Margot Nought. "Congrat-ulations," she said, the first T marking an articulate caesura. "Look at what you've done."

The phone was warm against Adiel's ear. "I have no idea what you're talking about."

"Don't even try," Margot said. "I can hear that self-satisfied grin you're wearing. I did not mean for you to literally find whoever might be gullible or stupid enough to publish those photographs." Ice clinked in the background. Could be iced tea, could be a gin & tonic—if the latter, a GIN and tonic. "It was a warning."

"Again," Adiel said, her smile hurting because she'd been wearing it so long. "I had nothing to do with this. I took your advice. Whoever wanted those photos out there really wanted them out there."

"Yes, someone really must have wanted it. By the way, did you enjoy your meal at The Velvet Cattle Prod?"

Adiel's grin diminished, then disappeared. "I'd never been there, so I thought I should try it."

"I prefer the sides to the steaks," Margot said, "but I also prefer an atmosphere that's a little less industry-centric. Fewer eyes and ears."

Adiel put her forehead in her hand. A stress headache began in her right temple.

"Anyway, the reason I'm calling, I just wanted to let you know that if you need a recommendation letter for your job search, I won't be able to offer it. I wish you luck shopping that story of yours about the Shah. And please do clean out your desk on Monday."

Adiel pulled her feet up under her. "Margot, please, this is a misunderstanding. I—Neil and I are having an affair."

Margot laughed a single *ha*. "Neil isn't the brightest, but if he conducts any affairs at all, he doesn't conduct them at the Prod. No one's that dumb."

The last comment stung. Adiel *was* that dumb. "Margot, please, I really did have nothing to do with it. He asked *me* to be there, and I told him I didn't know anything about it. Even if it had been me, you always say loyalty is an overrated virtue."

"But it's not a useless one, either."

"I had nothing—nothing—to do with it."

Cody, from the other side of the kitchen wall: "Nothing to do with what?"

Adiel heard the click on the other end. She tried to reset the phone in its cradle, only to have to finagle the tangled cord out of the way. At least, she told herself, the story was out there. Consequences be damned, right? She turned the channel to W-ANK, hoping to re-warm herself with their victory lap. Neil hadn't reappeared on the air since his news half-hour ended the previous night, but that morning, with people clamoring for more coverage, the network teased bringing him back that afternoon.

However, instead of a conversation in the studio, there was chaos outside: a reporter on what looked like Capitol Street, outside the W-ANK building. Some dark gray smoke, lots of camera shaking and running, the reporter speaking in sentence fragments. "Two explosions. No one knows. Unidentified, maybe American." Then: "We think W-ANK was targeted. Neil O'Chisholm may have been the target."

The sound that came from Adiel's throat was animal, not hers. She wanted to take it back, all of it—the dinner with Neil, the day with the Shah, the meets with El Polla Grande, the appearance on *This Week in the Republic,* even Garza West. Take her back to the day Cy Jost asked Margot for help on the story. Let Cy Jost look her over one time to see she wasn't ready for any of it, then choose instead some other reporter with more ambition than sense. Erase it all, let her go back to covering city council meetings, let her go back to her anonymous life, let suffering continue anonymously elsewhere, let this man be alive and unhurt.

Knocking at her door. Cody's and Otis's voices. She went teary to the door and told them she was fine. She'd stepped on a nail. She'd be fine. She slid the door chain into its slot.

The law of unintended consequences. After her mother's death, her father intoned the phrase bitterly on his bad days, with so much guilt over his small errors. If only he'd given her one more kiss before she went to the grocery, if only he hadn't wanted pasta for dinner, if only he'd gone to the store himself, even though he never went to the store. "Never forget that," he'd told her. "No matter what you do, someone somewhere somehow will get hurt. And you probably will, too."

She had believed him for a long time, but in college she unearthed herself from the soil of his guilt. At a party, she'd kissed a boy who had a girlfriend, and the girlfriend never found out. When the girl broke up with the boy, Adiel went on one disappointing date with him and happily moved on to another boy. And the other girl moved on to meet the boy she would marry. Everything worked out, and no one got hurt. In the place of that guilt, she had learned to believe that the law of unintended consequences didn't really apply to her, the same way that so many people know they will die someday but don't really believe it until they examine the wreckage of wasted days behind them.

Her wreckage now: she was a killer. Someone was dead, probably Neil O'Chisholm, and others were hurt.

The phone rang. She let it go to the answering machine, so she heard her own tinny, chipper voice: she couldn't come to the phone, but she'd be happy to call you back. The beep.

Then, a pause, and a voice: "Adiel. Miss Thomas. Missus Thomas? It's me, the Shah. Of Texas. We need to talk."

Neil Arrives

Neil Arrives

Neil wished he'd never seen the Garza West photos, because everything seemed wrong to him, and he couldn't stop throwing up or shitting. Literally, he said to himself, he couldn't stop.[*] He'd think about the images of torture at Garza West, or he'd see some moment or object of extravagance and think how inappropriate it seemed in contrast to Garza West, and his stomach loopy-looped, and he had to find any kind of receptacle.

So it was that he arrived to the W-ANK building to be on air not in his normal role as host, but to talk as guest about his role as host and what he'd been saying lately. All morning, he'd had his nervous stomach, but on the drive over, he succeeded at squelching it. When he caught how pale he was in the car window's reflection, and how the makeup lady would comment on his paleness, he started to feel it again, but he made it all the way to the station without having to ask the driver to pull over. A crowd of fans with handwritten signs cheered, and some booed, outside the morning studio. Everyone had thought it corny that the morning show decided to film in front of open windows at the corner, and it *was* corny, but it was successful, too. People turned up to be on TV, and people turned on their TVs to see who turned up. The crowd wasn't there for Neil, but when he saw them, it made him think of all the people watching him while he talked and thought about the torture at Garza West, and so he started thinking about all those people thinking about the torture at Garza West, and so he started thinking about the torture at Garza West and the torture of people watching him talk and think about the torture at Garza West, and he knew he wouldn't even make it to the bathroom on the eleventh floor. He wouldn't even make it to the elevator. Thank God he made it to the bathroom on the first floor.

Neil O'Chisholm had never been in this bathroom. It didn't

---

[*] We know he means metaphorically, but we see the point—when the metaphorical becomes the literal, it feels super intense, etc. Yes, some people confuse the two, but as a culture we've become far too judgmental about people emphasizing "literally" when they use it figuratively. Given how often even smart people confuse the literal and figurative, perhaps we should be more forgiving.

have the grandeur or the comfort of the bathroom on the eleventh floor. It had a her-sats grandeur—gaudy gold leaf on imitation marble, the button on the air dryer worn by thousands of unknown hands fresh from a tour or the gift shop. The walls of this stall had graffiti: penned, markered, and etched. Who would take the time to etch "Here I sit, all broken hearted, tryed to shit but merely farted"? And why did Neil find it so funny?

But focusing on the graffiti relaxed him, distracted him from thinking about Garza West, and he was mid-fart (a beginner's drum roll) when the bathroom door opened. When his fart finished, whatever stranger it was said, "Good one."

"Thanks," Neil said. "I have a lot of practice."

The guy laughed. Just like that, Neil had his charm again. If only he could do his work from the comfort of a toilet.

Neil listened to the man's soft pee against the urinal, and then the zippering. A little belch. The man didn't flush the urinal, didn't wash his hands, and left.

Once Neil was done with the business in the stall, and after another minute passed—he didn't want the stranger to see him and recognize him as pergenitron of the fart—he flushed, stepped out, and flushed the unflushed urinal. He'd never done that, cleaned up someone else's poor moral or hygenic choice. He felt good: he'd done good. He washed his hands, dried them under the air dryer, watched his skin wave under the force.

In the mirror, he looked okay. Pale, sure, and a little thinner around his cheekbones, but his hair was already in place, and his tie and collar were crisp. Neil took a deep breath and said, "I have a lot of practice."

As he stepped into the hall a thunderous noise and terrible wind shoved him back into the bathroom's door jamb.

A Connoisseur of Necessaria

A Connoisseur of Necessaria

The human body being what it is—a filtration device for carbohydrates and proteins and whatever else people channel into their tum-tums—a not-insignificant amount of Shah-centric logistical organizationing revolved around the toilet.* If there were world enough and time, every toilet that the Shah graced would have been a throne. Not, obviously, the Great Throne of the Shah, but a regular throne. One task of the Shah's many handlers included immediate on-site inspection and disinfection of every toilet; if necessary, a small team would modify the seat and/or handle. (One casualty of the War of Texan Independence from the Surly Grip of America: American Standard toilets were no longer standard in Texas.) Despite the most anal planning of the Shah's handlers, his diet remained largely unregulated as it had been in his youth. Waste-management trips could be unpredictable.

Sadly for the Shah, of course, not every toilet was a throne. For every W.C. there a shitter, for every reading room a crapper, for every restroom a can, for every powder room a john, for every comfort room a latrine, for every porcelain god a peon, for every holy shrine a false idol, for every ablutionary constabulary a pisser, for every private convenience a public pool, for every privy an outhouse, for every brick shithouse a hole in the ground, for every upper decker an engine room, for every commode a bog, for every royal flush a bust, for every lavatory a loo, for every house of office a house of pain, for every jacks a netty, for every thinker's block a stinker's dock, for every gent's a toiler's, for every sanctuary a prisonhouse, for every Wall Street a sewer, for every *salle de bains* a *terlet*.

The Shah knew he didn't know much, but he was a connoisseur of necessaria. His not knowing much had long been a source of ribbing, teasing, and even insult by those who had enough power to be unafraid of his power (viz. the first Shah, Dick Dick Dick Dick Dick, some media) or no power at all (other media). But everyone knows a

---

*Unfancy readers are correct to think of the obvious definition of toilet here. Fancy readers, please follow us through these dirty halls. I'm quite sure you will exit clean.

lot about something most people don't.[*] The Shah didn't have a lot of specialized knowledge, but he had a head for heads. As a child, traipsing along with his father on adult ventures, with nothing to do, he'd explore the uninhabited rooms. That usually meant the water or earth closest[†]. On the cusp of reaching adolescence, when for many people the desire to like the right things smothers curiosity, the Shah asked himself, "Where does it all go"? So he walked into basements, and though he didn't much like to read, he studied the schematics of sewers. Among his favorite facts: whereas contemporary excremental purgatoria look like so:

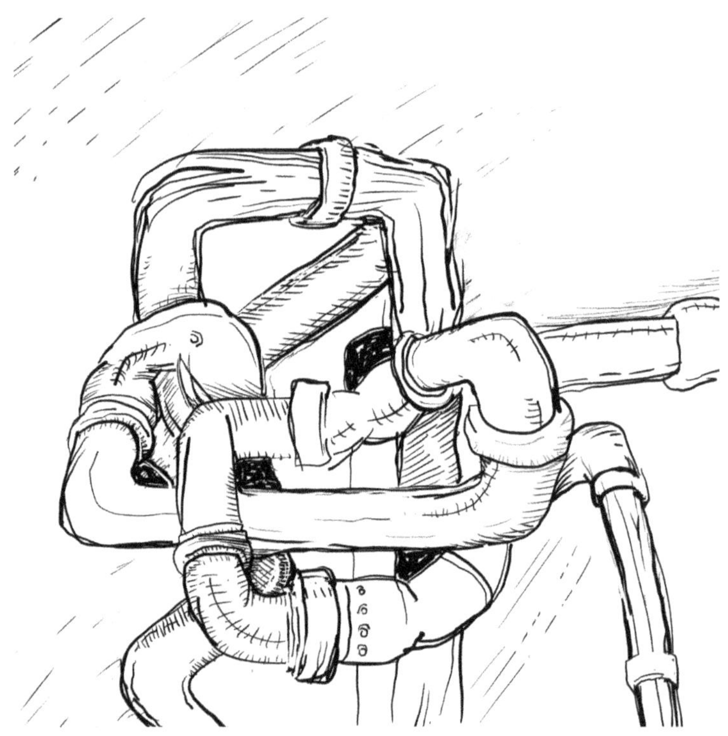

---

[*]This is one of my most private prayers.

[†]As architectural historians and scholars of Zarathustra know, the "restroom" originated with design based on the four elements: the water closet for urination, the earth closet for defecation, the air closet for gaseous expulsion that failed to produce a solid object, and the fire closet for explosive diarrhea.

—medieval effluvial passageways (castled edition) looked like so:

As we all know and understand, progress is simply another word for complication that is, at times, unnecessary.

And when the Shah's father became the first Shah of Texas, the son and eventual second Shah found himself with a great deal of time to digest the intestinal trails of the in-construction and newly-built Freedome. In his wanderings, he discovered a sub-floor tunnel that had been designed and tiled; it would have been a path to what would have been a subway but instead led to a little unused shack that looked like an outhouse, fenced by rusted chain-link.

The Shah never learned the following, but once, a Houstonian proposed a subway system for the city. Said proposal was rejected for its cost, so, under a building the Houstonian owned, he commissioned digging and tiling: he would show those who had rejected his plan how elegant and cost-efficient it could be. The workers didn't mind the work, as it was a summer of drought, and the underground tunnel was cooler.

And then it finally rained. And rained. The tunnel flooded;

237

workers drowned two by two. An enormous fortune became marginally less enormous. The Houstonian saw his folly and ended the project; other than payments to widows, he didn't tell anyone.

In his sub-floor meanderings, the Shah found the tunnel. Once he became Shah, when he wanted to remain unbothered by the responsibilities and stresses of Shahing, he wended his way down to his secret tunnel of dust, tile, clay, and rats. He wasn't a good singer[*], but he loved how the echo gave his voice reverberation. So he would sing:

I am the Shah

Shah

Shah

Shah

Shah

I am the law

law

law

law

law

---

[*]All writing is autobio, etc

Just like my pa

pa

pa

pa

pa

A crow says caw

caw

caw

caw

caw

After Dick Dick Dick Dick Dick suggested they bomb the W-ANK building and assassinate Neil O'Chisholm, and the Shah said no, he went down to the tunnels for relief. He yelled into the echoes, but the yelling felt as helpless as his final "no" in the Grand Office. Dick Dick Dick Dick Dick would go where he wanted, do what he wanted, Bob Toose would do and say what he wanted, Holly Unlikely would do what they told her, and Scheissetete—God knows what Scheissetete would do. And what even were ratlines? So the Shah yelled for a while until he was tired, then snuck back into the building and went to bed. He fluttered between sleep and waking for a while, and several times in the night he woke from nightmares, only to forget them in the morning. When the kitchen staff brought in his breakfast, he felt unrested.

Once he made his way into the working area of the Freedome, everything was noise and bustle. Phones ringing, Bob Toose hoarse,

TVs all on talk shows. A fray the Shah usually stayed above, or away from. In the Grand Office, all eyes focused on him. When he was out in the world the cameras were out, all eyes focused on him. But in the outer offices of the Freedome, he could stand in the back, noticed and then ignored. During periods of relative quiet, unpaid interns glowed at shaking his hand. (Yes, some of these interns insulted him when he wasn't around; however, when confronted with the man himself in the aura of his fame, they hoped power would spread to them.) This morning, with images of dead civilians and yelling commentators on multiple screens, the Shah could watch, unwatched.

And then he saw W-ANK's coverage shift to the street, where there was shaking and running and rubble dust in the air. Bob Toose muted the other channels and turned up the volume on W-ANK. A bomb had gone off outside their building; they thought Neil O'Chisholm was the target. The Shah felt sick. Bob Toose shook his head violently and repeated, louder and louder, a "no" as hapless as the Shah's had been. The Shah could tell: the plan hadn't come from Bob. Dick Dick Dick Dick Dick and Scheissetete had probably organized it themselves.

The Shah felt something in his face and throat he hadn't felt for years, not since he'd learned his father died. The lacrimal gland aqueated; the globus sensation, what we know better as a lump in the throat, activated.[*] He hied himself back to the tunnels.

Down below, the Shah yelled and yelled and followed his echo down moldy and musty hallways all the way to the door that led outside to its fenced-in area. The cool of the tunnel gave way to the heavy breath of late-morning heat and humidity. The horizon was made up of auto-parts stores and strip malls with boarded businesses like missing teeth. To the Shah, it barely looked like Texas. He went to the sidewalk, scrounged enough coins to use a payphone, and flipped through the dusty phonebook, hoping a name would announce itself. An idea

---

[*]Why such pretentious, scientific language for an emotional moment? Because the moment we relate to people in power and empathize with them, we begin to forgive their atrocities. And when we forgive, we assent. As I've gotten to know the Shah, I've found myself empathizing (The Shah, *c'est moi*) even though I don't want to. Don't let his tears mislead you.

flashed, so he found Adiel S. Thomas'eses number and called. The handset and buttons felt grimy. He held the receiver just off his ear.

Waiting as the phone rang was tedious. In the Freedome, whenever he called anyone, they picked up after the first ring, if not on the first ring, and asked what he needed. But this was ring, pause, etc. Until her answering machine picked up. He almost hung up, but he didn't know if he'd get the change back—even he thought that impulse for the money was strange, since he'd scrounged it just moments prior.

At the beep, he didn't know what to say. "Adiel. Miss Thomas. Missus Thomas? It's me, the Shah. Of Texas. We need to talk." He knew he needed to say something else, but he didn't know if someone other than her would be listening or not. "It's important. I—"

And she picked up. "Hello? Mr.—Sir?"

The Shah didn't know what to say. He really should have planned this better. But he was out of practice: he hardly had to plan anything anymore. "Have you been watching the news?"

"Yes," she said. She sounded like she'd been crying. "It's all a lot."

"I need your help," he said, and felt a release of relief. "Do you have a car?"

"You don't have—you need a ride?"

"It's a long story," he said, then realized what he needed. "I want to go to Garza West."

A ponytailed girl wended by on a bicycle, pink and rusted, staring at the Shah. The Shah put on a grin and nodded. The girl nodded back and rode on by.

"You don't have a team that can take you there?"

"Listen," he said, whisper-yelling. "We have to go. I want to see it, without Dick or Bob or Holly or anyone else. I don't want anything prepared for me." There was a long pause, so he added, "That's where everything started to go wrong."

A shorter pause. "Where should I meet you?"

The Shah almost named the street, but remembered someone might be listening on her end. He looked at the strip mall. "Do you remember where there used to be a video store with a tanning bed inside? It was next to a takeout Chinese place."

"I used to buy weed there," she said. "I'll pick you up in a half-hour."

After he hung up the phone, the Shah wiped his palms down his pants and stepped out of the phone booth. He had to wipe sweat from his forehead, too.

The girl on the bicycle rolled up to him. She was wearing jean shorts that frayed above her knees and a dirty white T-shirt with a quarter-sized hole at her armpit. "Are you the Shah?"

The Shah tried not to stare at the hole and smiled. It was still easy to switch into the mode of charming interpersonal leadership. "I sure am."

"What the hell are you doing down here?"

The Shah laughed a practiced laugh. "I don't know that's the kind of language you should be using. But I had to make a phone call, and I'm waiting for a friend."

"Okay, but why here?"

The Shah thought of giving the girl the rest of the change he'd gathered and telling her to go buy some candy. Instead, he knelt—knees popping, he was getting old, for sure—and put his hand on the girl's shoulder. She looked at his hand as if it were a surprise dollop of bird shit. "I can't really tell you," the Shah said, "but I can tell you this: it's important to keep your eyes. . ." He raised his eyebrows, tossing the phrase to the kid.

"This ain't school."

The Shah stood up and sighed. "Eyes on the prize, kid. Keep your eyes on the prize."

Sacrifice is Holy

Sacrifice is Holy

Dick Dick Dick Dick Dick fumed. "A video store with a tanning bed in the back? We're the greatest country in the world, with the most powerful military and the most sophisticated surveillance, and we can't find a closed-down video store that used to be next to a Chinese place?"

Bob Toose was kneeling under the Shah's desk, feeling around for a button or lever. "I just want to know how he got out of here in the first place." He felt a hard, rough lump on the carpet. He pulled it out into the light; it was an almond. He tossed it back where it had been. They would have to fire another custodian. "I mean, why don't we ask the guards at all the doors if they saw him?"

"We can't ask," Holly Unlikely said. "Then they'll know we don't know where he is."

Scheissetete stood in the corner with headphones on, listening repeatedly to the phone call between the Shah and Adiel S. Thomas, evidently hoping to hear some clue.

Bob Toose said, "We can say something like, 'The Shah's late for a meeting, do you know where he is.'"

"Stop being an idiot, Bob," Dick Dick Dick Dick Dick said. "If you can. Besides, it doesn't matter where he is right now. We know where they're going. We just have to know when to aim and fire."

Bob registered what Dick Dick Dick Dick Dick had said and climbed out from under the desk. "No. No! He's the Shah."

Holly Unlikely walked over and stood next to Bob. "Dick, you can't be thinking—he's the Shah!"

Scheissetete rolled his eyes.

"I don't want to hear a word from you," Bob said.

"As of now," Dick Dick Dick Dick Dick said, clearly being as deliberate as he could, his face turning red with care, "he's a traitor. He gave those photos to Neil O'Chisholm, and now he's on the lam with another traitor."

Bob walked up to Dick Dick Dick Dick Dick. Standing so close unsettled him. Dick Dick Dick Dick Dick smelled like sweat and cedar, vaguely like a hamster cage. "Don't you dare mention Neil," Bob said. "You killed him. You killed him and you'd kill the Shah." Spittle flipped over his bottom lip, and he had to wipe his arm on his sleeve. He hated showing so much emotion.

Dick Dick Dick Dick Dick looked taken aback. "I didn't. I thought you or Holly did."

Bob shook his head and looked at Holly. She looked shocked. "Why would I?" she said. "It was your idea, Dick."

Everyone looked at Scheissetete. He pursed his lips and looked disappointed.

"I think we should have," Dick Dick Dick Dick Dick vented, "but the Shah said no."

"So you obey the Shah one day and you're ready to assassinate him the next?"

"Yesterday he wasn't a traitor," Dick Dick Dick Dick Dick erupted. "Today, he is. Besides, this benefits everyone. Apparently some American radical or Texan patriot or whoever bombed W-ANK, and now an American plane—no matter who ordered it—would bomb Garza West in retaliation when the Shah just happens to be there trying to bring some accountability."

Bob Toose's arms felt weak. "You're a monster. You just want to be Shah."

Dick Dick Dick Dick Dick laughed. "You think I want to be the face of any of this? I can't do PR."

"But you're talking about sacrificing the Shah," Holly Unlikely said. "Not just any Shah, but the second, the son of the first!"

Scheissetete laughed. When everyone looked at him, he pointed to the headphone over one ear. He was still listening to surveillance.

"Sacrifice is holy," Dick Dick Dick Dick Dick said. "It benefits us all, despite what the peaceniks will tell you."

Bob had to sit down. He was no peacenik. He could stomach what needed to be done. But did this need to be done? "What about the soldiers who work at Garza? Are they a necessary sacrifice?"

Dick Dick Dick Dick Dick waved. "We've already moved personnel out of Garza."

"You were planning this all along?"

Holly cleared her throat. "That's coincidence. We already had that in the works after the Garza news broke."

"Why did nobody tell me?" Bob's voice cracked to reach an uncomfortable octave.

Dick shrugged. "You're Conflagrational Elucidations. We weren't going to announce it." He sat down next to Bob and put his hand on Bob's thigh. Bob was terrified: Dick had never looked or acted empathetic. This could only mean the worst. "Bob, I know it's radical. And I can't just do this on my own. It has to be unanimous between you, me, and Holly, or it doesn't happen. No pressure."

Bob set his heels back under the edge of the sofa and felt something under his heel. He reached down and picked up a swollen champagne cork.

"And you didn't kill Neil O'Chisholm?"

"Technically," Dick Dick Dick Dick Dick said, "I can neither confirm nor deny."

"Has anyone ever said that when they're innocent?"

"No."

"So you did it."

"That I can neither confirm nor deny."

Power's Out

Power's Out

"It's so hot in here," the Shah said. "I thought you said the AC would kick in." The knob was already turned as far to the left, the thickest blue, as it would go, but he tried turning it anyway.

"It kicked on a while ago," Adiel said. "I guess you're not used to riding in a normal car."

"If this is normal, I'll take unnormal."

Adiel set her elbow against the driver's side door and put her head against her hand. They were about a half-hour into the drive, and everything the Shah said had to do with the heat. It took her longer to pick him up than she said, so he'd had to wait out in the heat; the sun was shining in the passenger window, and that made him hot; when would the AC kick in, when would the AC kick in, I thought you said the AC would kick in. For such a charmer, he complained a lot.

She tried to change the subject. "How did you get out of the Freedome without anybody seeing you?"

"There's a tunnel under the Freedome. Nobody knows about it. Or at least I don't think anybody does. It's cool down there."

"You could take your suit jacket off."

In her periphery, he looked in the backseat. She could feel him judging the mess back there: file boxes, balled-up bags of fast food with grease stains, empty soda bottles. She judged it herself every time she got in the car. Not enough to clean out the backseat, but enough to feel her own judgment heavy in her chest and arms.[*]

"There's not really anywhere to put my jacket."

"You could put it in your lap." Adiel didn't mean to take the tone she did; he was the Shah, after all.

"You know," he said, "I *am* the Shah. I called *you*. You don't have to talk to me that way."

"Sorry."

The Shah tried to finagle himself out of the jacket. In her brief glances over, she could tell he'd never had to take off a jacket in an enclosed space. He'd lived his entire life with plenty of room to move,

---

[*]All writing is autobio.

assistants to grab the end of a stubborn sleeve, working AC to cool him off. She pitied him and felt deeply jealous at the same time. Did the Germans have a word for that?[*]

Once the Shah unpretzeled his arms and folded the jacket, Adiel said, "I'm sorry about the AC. I can't afford to get it fixed."

"How much does it cost?"

"At least a thousand bucks.[†] I need a new condenser or something. I don't know much about cars."

"That doesn't sound like a lot."

Adiel looked to the hills in the distance. On this drive, it seemed like there were always hills in the distance, an impressive scenic drop of hills, and they would never reach them. And since they were headed southwest toward Garza, they never would.

"Is a thousand bucks a lot?" the Shah asked. Adiel heard a vulnerable curiosity in his voice. Maybe he was just thirsty.

"It's a lot for me. Probably for most."

"Not most," he said. "Surely not for most."

"If you're thirsty, I've got bottled water in the backseat somewhere. It'll be hot, but it's water."

"Nah, I'm good."

After a few minutes of quiet, Adiel had to ask: "So why did you call me? I mean, of all the people in Texas, why me?"

The Shah looked out the window for so long that Adiel wasn't sure he'd heard her. But when she looked over, she could tell he was thinking. "Because you don't like me. And you've been right about everything."

"Of course I like you," she said.

He looked over with a charming and shit-eating grin that said what it needed to: of course she didn't like him. At the same time, she recognized in that moment the power of his charm.

To pass the time, Adiel turned on the radio to a staticky news station. She hoped to hear that Neil O'Chisholm was okay; she doubt-

---

[*]Seriously, do they? [Editor's note: They do. *Armut*.]

[†]In case readers are curious, the official currency of Texas is the Buck, also called the Owens. This led to a plague of fathers and uncles saying, as a joke, "I owens you money."

ed they would report anything about the Shah's disappearance. She turned out to be right to doubt—no APB or report—but her hope about Neil wasn't confirmed. There was only confusion: two reported dead, names not released, no specific word on the health or whereabouts of Neil.

"Oh, look at that," the Shah said as they passed a green road sign. "'Texas School of the Year, 1972. Next turn.' Can we go see it?"

"This isn't really a sightseeing trip." Adiel wiped the sweat above her upper lip. "I'm not sure we have time for that if they're looking for you."

"They have no idea where I am. We've got time."

"Why do you want to see a school so much?"

The Shah sighed. "When I was in school, I hated it. I mean, I hated it. I was always bored. But now I like seeing the kids. Everything is ahead of them. They've got their whole lives ahead of them. They can be whatever they want." *

Adiel exited the car off the highway, toward the Texas School of the Year, back when it would have been the best school in the state, not the best school in a nation. She turned in the direction of the school, and the car's ride registered the change to an aging road.

"You might want to get your shocks checked out."

"Shocks?"

"I don't really know what they are," the Shah said. "I've just seen a lot of commercials. Anyway, get them checked out. Unless it's too expensive." He held his hand in front of an asthmatic vent. "When we get back, I'll forward you some cash."

Adiel laughed. "Do you have a bank account?"

"Texas has a big one. It'll get you where you need to go."

The next sign touting the school was bent backward at its frame. On the STOP sign just before the school, someone had spray-painted in silver "THE SHA." The Shah let out a frustrated sigh.

Even from a distance, the school looked abandoned. One big

---

*If you find yourself feeling some wistful pity for him, remember how much power he has. Granted, I've had to remind myself many times over throughout the writing and revising not to sympathize because that's how the powerful win, by pretending to be human. But stay strong. At best, he's still the least-bad monster.

window boarded up, others cracked, weeds and dandelions waving like half-hearted flags, chunks of rust and gray steel showing among chipped paint on playground equipment. But the school wasn't abandoned; Adiel saw the silhouettes of children leaning against their arms, whispering bored to each other, ceiling fans rotely wiping the air, a teacher by the window talking and waving herself with a stack of papers. And on the side of the building, a row of students shoveling, sheened in sweat, refilling a trench.

"Who let this place go?" the Shah asked.

Adiel knew enough that she could say "Eyes! On the Prize," that schools that didn't keep their eyes on the prize lost funding, but she also knew enough to say nothing at all.

"At least they're trying," the Shah said. "God bless 'em. Let's head on to Garza."

He didn't complain again about the AC again. The quiet unsettled Adiel. He seemed depressed, so she turned the radio back on and turned the dial through statics and country music until she found, of all things, an oldies station.[*] Static dotted the songs, but they were otherwise clear. Adiel knew all the music from her father's obsessive listening, so she mouthed the words. After a few tracks, she glanced over at the Shah and saw him mouthing some of the words, too, at least the ones he knew.

Not long after they saw a sign for Beeville (10 miles), home of the Garza West facility, The Bobby Fuller Four's "I Fought the Law" came on. The Clash version had been played over and again in the year leading up to Texan independence, a wail against the tyrannies of the United States government (and against copyright claims made by The Clash). It played on oldies stations, on rock stations, at parties in the country, in bars and honky tonks. Adiel had grown tired of the song pretty quickly but still mouthed the words even now. In the second verse, she heard the quiet voice of the Shah echoing the lyrics. When the guitar solo came around, the Shah was sitting up and, with his fin-

---

[*]One might think that oldies stations would be banned or frowned upon in a nation recently independent from the nation that produced most of those oldies, but nostalgia trumps and even absorbs patriotism until it becomes its own nation demanding loyalty.

gers moving minimally in his lap, air-strumming the solo.

The third verse started, and the Shah sang along and air-drummed the iconic fill:

"Robbin' people with a   six gun"

●　　●　　●　　●　　●　　●

Once the song ended, the Shah said, "I bet you didn't know I could play the drums."

Maybe Adiel was a little delirious: she giggled. He could be annoying, but she couldn't help but like him. She could see in him something she recognized at times in herself: he was desperate to be liked.*

When a green sign told her the Beeville exit was in one mile, her nervous gut activated. Her ass hurt, and she needed to pee. "We're really doing this," she said, though she didn't understand what, exactly, they were doing.

"Yep," he said, "we're really doing this." She could feel him looking at her. "Thank you."

She shook her head. "Thank *you*, sir."

The Shah laughed a little one-breath laugh. "You don't have to call me 'sir.' My father was 'sir.'"

Adiel said with a smile, "But you're both Shahs."

"You've got me there."

On the horizon, Adiel saw the tips of light towers, then the guard tower, then the fence poles and spread of gray buildings like sinister, linked strip malls. The barbed wire and the chain link.

Adiel had been to a military base once—her father took her to an air show at an Air Force Base—but she had never been to a prison facility. It shared the abandoned look of the school.

They drove up to the front gate. Inside a little toiletless out-house, a sweat-beaded man in a long-sleeved military green stood up from his seated slouch. "Y'all lost?"

Adiel put on her most professional voice. "The Shah and I are here to do a surprise inspection of Garza West."

---

*All writing, etc.

"That so?" the man said. He leaned down from his open window and peered into the car at the Shah. "That's an awful good likeness. Say something stupid."

The Shah unhooked his seatbelt, got out of the car, and appeared on her side of the car face-to-face with the guard so fast that Adiel barely registered it. She opened her own door and started to get out, only to be choked by the strap of her seatbelt.

"When you address your superiors," the Shah said, "you do so with respect, soldier. You straighten your spine, put your feet together, and salute like you deserve to wear this uniform and represent this country. We are, after all, the great Independent Nation of Texas, not some pissant all-hat, no-cattle ranch for pretty boys. You understand me?"

Not on TV, nor in person, had Adiel seen the Shah act with such precise ferocity. He seemed like a different person. As he spoke, the guard's neck and face turned pink-red with white pin dots. And once the Shah was done, the guard's body snapped into military formality, his salute went up, and a creamy drop of sweat and sunscreen fell from his chin.

"Sir, I'm sorry, sir. I didn't mean disrespect."

The Shah eyed him a moment. Adiel sat with one foot in the car, one foot on the concrete outside, holding the strap of her seatbelt away from her throat.

The Shah's body then released its tension. He clapped the man on the shoulder. "No one ever does mean disrespect. It's alright,[*] soldier. At ease. I'd hate for you to just wave a car through without checking. But like she said, we're here to do a surprise inspection."

"Thank you, sir. But there's nothing here."

"What do you mean?"

"I mean there's nothing here. I mean, there's the building, but everyone's gone. All the prisoners were moved to other quarters late last week, and the personnel with them."

Adiel said, "So why are you here?"

---

[*] The editor and I are aware that "alright" is a misspelling of "all right," one grown so common that it soon will replace the original as the correct spelling. We both would prefer correct spelling in all matters.

"Because it's my duty," the man snapped, as if the question were entirely too stupid. His tone swayed her for a few seconds to feel entirely too stupid for having asked.

"Well, we can go in anyway, right?" the Shah said, back to buddy-buddy. "That's what we came to look at."

"It's all yours," the guard said. "Doors're open. Power's out in the buildings, though." He went back into his little outhouse and pressed a button. A buzzer started, and the gate slowly rolled open. A second gate inside the first slowly rolled open in the opposite direction. "You can park anywhere you'd like, I guess."

Adiel rolled the car through each gate, then steered it toward the largest building. Near the front door, she put the car in park, but the Shah said, "Don't park too close to the building. It gives me the willies." So Adiel turned the car and put it in park by the inside fence. That's when she saw that the fence rose vertically, then tilted inward near the barbed-wire rounds at the top. When she got out, a dead-animal smell overwhelmed her.

"Hey," the Shah said, pointing toward the right side of the building. "Eyes on the prize!"

Adiel looked and saw what appeared to be a trench. She shrugged at him, and they walked to the building. The thick front door stood ajar; its thick inner bolts stuck out and rested against the frame. When they stepped up to the door, Adiel expected the Shah to reach forward and pull it open. But they paused, shoulder to shoulder. When was the last time he'd opened a door for himself? She looked to him and said, "You ready?"

Taking her cue, he pulled the door open and held it for her to enter.

The power was indeed out. There were no lights on, and the air felt like that of her grandmother's attic, close and claustrophobic, but instead of the smells of yarn and cedar, she smelled body odor and bleach and something she couldn't quite place, something like blood, something like a dead animal in a crawl space. They passed an office enclosed by plexiglass, with cords that had once run to what Adiel assumed were TV monitors but were now gone. The barred doors to barred cells were slid open, disrupting the regular lines with their vertical syncopation. The hallways darkened in their distances.

"The AC's better in your car," the Shah said.

Adiel looked around at the ceiling. She only saw vents inside the plexiglassed office. "I don't think this place is air-conditioned."

"Nonsense. Of course they'd have AC for a prison in this heat."[*]

They explored hallway after hallway. The longer they went, the less satisfied Adiel felt. She'd studied the ███████ photographs when Cy Jost showed them to her; they didn't match any of these rooms or cells. The prison's kitchen and dining rooms reminded her of her junior high (Go Boll Weevils! Be! Aggressive! B-E aggressive!), as did the library. Most equipment had been removed, but the books had been left, their spines lined with creases. The Execution and Solitary areas creeped her out but didn't match the photographs.

They went into the infirmary last. The patient rooms just looked like old hospital rooms from a B horror movie, except for the occasional set of handcuffs dangling from the metal railing that framed a bed. Adiel smelled too many smells, and she could tell the Shah picked them all up, too. His nose crimped, making great diagonal caverns of his nostrils. Antiseptics, definitely blood this time, cotton, body odor, bleach, other combinations from the periodic table. At the nurse's station, she even smelled mint and found an empty five-pack of chewing gum on the counter. Adiel put it up to her nose and took a deep breath so she could escape, if only for a moment.

"Miss Thomas," the Shah called from somewhere down the hall.

She kept her eyes closed. "Adiel," she said. "Miss Thomas was my father."

"Adiel," he said. "Miss Thomas."

---

[*]Nope. I've lived in midwestern areas with un-air-conditioned schools that would close when the temperature outside caused the temperature inside to rise to 90 degrees F. And if they don't air-condition the schools. . . {Publisher's note: Ridiculous! Whoever heard of such a thing? By inventing such a capacity for cruelty, this writer reveals his own capacity for cruelty. I would prevent this monstrous novel from being published, but it reveals about him things he doesn't want. And I still profit. So he loses.}

She opened her eyes and walked down the hall toward his voice. He stood outside the doorway of the janitor's closet with his right hand on the door jamb. When she got a few steps away, he moved back so she could see. At the back of the closet, what should have been a wall was an open door with a several-inch red-brown smear in an arc toward the open end. There was no light behind the open door.

The Shah cleared his throat. "I don't want to see what's behind that door."

"But you explored the tunnels underneath the Freedome."

"I don't want to know what's down there. Why don't we just assume the worst and leave?"

She looked back at him. "What do you assume would be the worst?"

"Maybe we've already seen it in the pictures," he said. "I don't even want to say."

Far Too Young to Die

Far Too Young to Die

At Fort Wood Military Base, Scheissetete clattered up the ramp to the portable building, a suitcase in his left hand, a folded sheet of paper in his right. Like any good murderer, he hated paperwork, but it was a necessary evil.

When he entered, the two drone pilots and their superior stood in salute as always. Scheissetete recognized one of the drone pilots, a woman, part of their Equality and Equivalence in Conflagration program—I Would Kill for Equality. (It was winning over the liberals.) Scheissetete cared as little for PR as he did for paperwork, though he acknowledged the utility of both.

He handed the sheet of paper to the superior, who read it to himself, then looked at Scheissetete pleadingly, eyebrows straining up. Scheissetete shook his head. The superior waved the drone pilots out, then followed them. Once the steps outside stopped clattering, Scheissetete sat in the chair on the left and took a small CD player from his suitcase. Bob Toose had been a songwriter, even scoring a top-40 hit on the country charts (whiskey, women, a bar fight) before his political career began; he had given Scheissette a CD of his demos, recorded in his basement studio, in the style Bob Toose called "Trepan Alley." As Scheissetete typed in coordinates for the first strike, Bob Toose crooned. He had a warm high tenor; Scheissetete imagined Bob Toose would have made a good countertenor, probably a good candidate for castrato. (After the final papal castrato ban in 1903, Scheissetete's first job was identifying and creating illegal castrati who would claim to be countertenors. Every cut he had made since ached for the pure pleasure of the first time. You can never regain the intimacy of that initial kiss of steel.) Scheissetete danced as he typed in coordinates for the second strike and Bob sang:

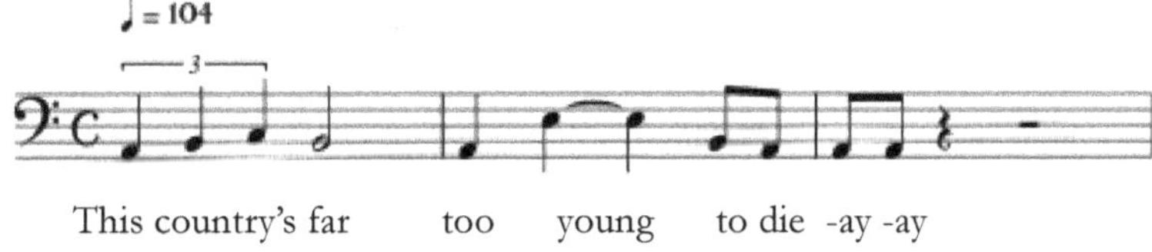

Once Scheissetete had finished typing the coordinates, set the timer, and hit enter to begin the process, he checked his watch. He had plenty of time, so he slow-walked to his car and even shook the hands of the two drone pilots and their superior outside. Necessary sacrifices. Maybe even holy, by one reckoning.

His car was over a half-hour east on its way back to Houston when the bombings began.

Meanwhile, in his private residence at ███████████, Dick Dick Dick Dick Dick sat above an industrial shredder for his monthly defecatory egress. The shredder's grinding reminded him of when, as a teen, he toured slaughterhouses for fun and education. That memory eased the fecal expulsion.

Once he was done exorcising a truncheon from within, Dick Dick Dick Dick Dick called out, "Wife! I am at arms! Prepare yourself for a great dickering!"

Inside the Underbelly

Inside the Underbelly

Adiel stepped into the dark closet. Behind her, the Shah cleared his throat again. She pushed the wall open and felt to the side past it for a light switch but felt the wall's flatness. The power to the facility was out anyway. "I don't suppose you happen to have a flashlight," she said.

"I guess I left it in my other pants."

Adiel went to the nurse's station and tried to open drawers, but they were all locked with little worn brass fittings the size of an American dime.[*] "You don't happen to have a hairpin or a lock-picking set."

"No," he said, "but I do have a Texan Army Knife." The Shah pulled it from his pocket. Texan Army Knives were the length of an index finger and included one (1) short blade, one (1) long blade, one (1) nail file/saw, one (1) bottle opener/screwdriver, one (1) lasso, one (1) replacement belt buckle, and one (1) refillable beef jerky server.

"Why do you have that?"

"I don't have any keys to jangle in my pockets, and I'm not allowed to have coins to jangle anymore because it distracted Bob. Gives me something to have in my pocket. I cut my pinky on it once. Bled like an American."

He handed her the Texas Army Knife. Adiel crammed her thumbnail into the wedge for pulling out the (1) small blade. She tried to jam it into the keyhole, to no avail, then jerked it around in the space between the bottom of the desktop and the top of the drawer. After a few wild moments, she heard a click and slid it open. Inside, she found the tool for shining a light into a patient's ear, nose, and mouth. Adiel held it up and said, "I found a—one of these!"[†]

"Hot damn! You go on ahead and find out what's down there." The Shah pulled up a wheelchair and sat down in it.

From the drawer, she pulled one of the clippy cones for putting on the tool to look in a patient's ear, nose, and mouth,[††] walked to

---

[*] In Texas, dimes were, of course, larger. They did have the good sense to make progressively more valuable coins progressively bigger.
[†] In case the reader is curious, it's called an otoscope. I looked it up.
[††] A speculum.

the Shah, and pulled on the top of his ear so she could look inside. Little hairs, a few flecks of wax.

"What are you doing?" the Shah asked.

"I'm looking for courage." She unclipped the cone and it rattled on the linoleum.

He pulled his head away. "You're thinking of the Cowardly Lion. My brain is in my head. That's the Scarecrow."[*]

"Whatever you need to go downstairs with me," Adiel said. She sounded resolute, but she knew how he felt: she wanted to run or cry or vomit, whatever she could do to avoid moving from the realm of uncertain imagination to certain knowledge. "You're the Shah. You can do anything you want."

The Shah planted his feet and stood. The wheelchair crept away behind him in an arc until one handle tapped the wall. The way he looked at Adiel, she wasn't sure what to do, so she straightened her posture and saluted. He saluted back. "Let's do it."

The closet had a faint bleach and formaldehyde smell, but when she nudged open the door at the back of the closet, a putrid stench overwhelmed. The smells of bodies unshowered for days, if not weeks (which she knew from a one-time depressive boyfriend), the rot of mice dead in the walls (which she knew from her first apartment), moldy and rotten food (which she knew from her first and third college roommates), and something else: in her head, she called it "death." She had encountered death but not this smell.

Reader: We're only ignorant if we look the other way. My Lai, the Indonesian genocide, the treatment of Haitian immigrants at Guantanamo Bay, the Tonton Macoute. If you know the history of the twentieth century, what horrors could surprise you? I don't even need to mention the Holocaust. If you know the history of the twentieth century, you've already encountered what they're about to find: the

---

[*] Were this novel a movie, one of these characters would say upon entering the area below, "I don't think we're in Kansas anymore." (Cf. *The Matrix; Avatar; Honey, I Shrunk the Kids; Little Shop of Horrors; Sex and the City II; Beach Blanket Roulette; Gitmo Bay Bikini Blast 4;* et cetera.) Alas, the independence of Texas has rendered that cliché unusable in this context. And, alas, the challenge of originality.

ends of human imagination.

Adiel held the otoscope in front of her as if it were a cross warding off vampires. Her thumb pressed to light it, and she saw metal-latticed steps going down. Adiel went down one step, then set her feet together on that step. The Shah followed. The staircase shook with Adiel's and the Shah's steps and with their nerves.

She counted the steps down as she went in case she had to climb back up in the dark. Sixteen. "Sixteen steps," she said when they were both at the bottom. Concrete, with concavities and lumps, like any poorly leveled basement floor. Adiel moved the light around to give them a 360-degree view, but the light showed little. Just walls, a grayish brown. She sniffled and got an enormous whiff of whatever she had called death, now a bit more recognizable as varieties of human waste and human wasting. She pulled her collar over her nose and craned her head forward to keep the collar up. "We should follow the smell," she said.

"What direction? It's all around."

The room at the bottom of the stairs opened to a hallway. On both sides of the hallway were cells with doors, solid metal save for a knee-high slot wide enough to put in a food tray, and a glass-and-diagonal-wired little window at throat height. Every glass had fingerprints and weird whitish smears on the insides. The doors were all ajar, their deadbolts sticking out. They were so heavy that Adiel had to shoulder them open. The cells were tiny.

They went in the first four and looked closely. Remnants: dried urine and wiped up but not fully cleaned feces in the corners, bits of curled short hairs and some longer hairs around the floors on and off the shoesole-thin mattresses, no pillows, dried gobs of what she assumed was semen, spots of blood on the floor and walls. And in one of the corners nearest the doors of each of those first four cells, a small bar of off-white soap with dried bubbles, pubic hairs, brown-reddish flecks.

Adiel and the Shah didn't speak, but after they scanned each of these first four cells, they looked at each other, pursed their lips, and shook their heads in a small way. These were the backdrops of the Garza West photographs. The images had become real. For their eyes, the space of terror was no longer alleged. They had already known these things, but now their faces recoiled. They couldn't escape the smell or the way they imagined lying on the mattresses with their shoulders sore against the floor.

With the next six cells on either side of the hall, they each glanced in, confirming what they had seen in the other rooms. At the end of the hall stood a different door: no slot for a tray, but still a square window, again glass with diagonal wires, but spraypainted black on the outside. This door was shut. Its handle was round, the steel stained by many hands. On the door was a sign that read, "No cameras beyond this point."

Adiel and the Shah looked at each other again. This time, the Shah reached forward to open the door. But the knob clicked and wouldn't turn. There was no keyhole. The Shah tried to turn the knob and shoulder it open, but it rattled just millimeters in its lock. "How do we get it open?" Adiel handed him back his Texas Army Knife. He tried jiggering with both blades, the nail file/saw, bottle opener/ screwdriver, even one end of the replacement belt buckle. All to no avail.

In a ceiling corner behind them was a black box with wires that disappeared into the wall. When Adiel went on her tiptoes with her hand against the wall, she could see a little circle that was unlit. The power was out. "I don't think we can get in."

The Shah was pinching his nose. "I don't think we want to."

Adiel took the Texas Army Knife and scraped the spraypaint off the window. By the time she was finished, the pane scratched but translucent, her shoulder ached. She shone the otoscope into the locked room. Streamers hung on the far wall. It took Adiel a few seconds to recognize what they were: one was human ears strung on a wire, another eyeballs, yet another what appeared at first to be jerky and revealed its shape as severed male genitals. American eyes, American ears, American bodies. Maybe Texan, too. In the corner was a dead child's naked body, all ribs and pelvis. Adiel couldn't tell if it was male or female. There was a raw, fringed bullet hole behind the child's ear.

The Shah's face was teary. "We gave them QwikPik cameras so they wouldn't do this."

Adiel remembered she had a QwikPik in her car for this trip. Getting it meant climbing those stairs, breathing the living air outdoors, and forcing herself to return, if she could. She didn't know if she could. She asked, "What happened in here?"

The Shah breathed heavily. "I wish I knew," he said, "because then I wouldn't have to imagine it."

Suddenly, the ground and walls trembled, and a muted boom rattled their ears. They looked around, then at each other. "Run!" Adiel yelled. She ran ahead, holding the otoscope in front of her. Another trembling and boom as they clattered up the stairs, and two more as they sprinted through the hospital wing's halls and exited through a rear door. Dirt and smoke clogged the air. It stank of sulfur and some hellish electrical fire. Through empty air, they saw smoke clouds rising from Beeville in the distance and, outside the fencing surrounding Garza West, red-orange flame and clumps of asphalt and earth.

The Shah pointed to a ditch about 50 yards to their left. "Eyes on the prize!" he screamed. He bolted for the ditch. Adiel sprinted behind him, faintly aware of a cold fire in her lungs and throat, and as a whistling signaled another falling bomb, she leapt after the Shah into the ditch, landing on a haphazard clump of dead bodies.

Softening the Blow

Softening the Blow

Reader, the last chapter was difficult, for me at least if not for you. So I would like to offer an opportunity to come down, as it were, or to rise back up, with an alternative summary of the events and details of the previous chapter. Consider this an act of Critical Incident Stress Management. For fun, education, elucidation, and/or entertainment, pick your favorites and use them in conversation with friends.

In the previous chapter, we witnessed:
- Kinetic strikes
- Targeted strikes
- Palate cleansing
- Limited military coercion
- Or, if "coercion" girds your sinews too sharply: Limited military intervention.
- Discriminate deterrence
- Friendly fire
- The munitionary position
- Texan exfoliating
- Early retirement
- Dirt napping
- Body counting
- Bodies at rest
- Biting the dust
- Crop dusting
- Death by misadventure
- Justifiable homicide
- Awakening to eternal life
- Yielding to the crow a pudding
- Snuffing one's glim
- Making the ultimate sacrifice
- Promotion to Glory
- Collateral damage
- Potential blue on blue
- Armed intervention

- Disarmament
- Carpet bombing
- Revarnishing the floors
- An action
- A state action
- A police action
- Weapons of action
- Assymetric warfare
- A military effort
- A military process
- A military campaign
- A military conversation
- A military dialectic
- Military muscle
- Air support
- An air campaign
- A coalition of the willing
- A coalition willing
- Snafu
- Tarfu
- Kungfu
- Fubar
- Rebar
- A future rapid effects system
- Deterrence
- A surgical strike
- Surgery
- ICU (Important Critical Undertaking)
- A good, healthy spanking
- Conquest
- Drop zoning
- Going to a Texas cakewalk
- Eating at the Cheesecake Factory
- Going west
- Manifesting Destiny
- History

- Honoring one's country
- Honoring one's forefathers
- A black site
- A detention camp
- A contingency operation
- Surging
- VUCA (volatility, uncertainty, complexity, and ambiguity)
- A gray zone
- COIN
- Pacification
- Nation-building
- Liquidating
- Clean bombing
- Coercive interrogation
- Or, if "coercive" shrinks your scrotal aura[*] as fear does: Enhanced interrogation
- Ghost prisoners
- The resulting effect of incestuous amplification
- Neutralization
- Negative health consequences
- Protective custody
- Improper relations
- Reconstruction
- Regime change
- Shock and awe
- Softening

I do apologize for any inconvenience or dismay caused by the previous chapter's unfortunately necessary extraordinary rendition.

---

[*]Males only.

Wreck of Ages

Wreck of Ages

Shrapnel had rendered Adiel's car useless, so she and the Shah trekked into Beeville and found a used-car lot. The salesman and his boss were as devastated and shell-shocked as half their inventory and Beeville itself, but they proved to be good Texan patriots "happy to help" the Shah as long as someone wrote "With Love from Beeville" on a bomb to be used later.

"We saw those bastard American jets," the boss said. "I can't wait to hear how we retaliate."

They got a clunker with no AC, but the Shah didn't complain.

The less said about Beeville, the better. Neither Adiel nor the Shah wanted to acknowledge it as they drove past, and one would not want to distract from the ongoing plot with the desolation and wreckage of Beeville and its residents, alive or newly deceased and desisted, or historical save for one famousish personage who lived in Beeville for a time: Gutzon Borglum (gesundheit). In their car's slow creep through the rubbled historic downtown, Adiel and the Shah passed a monument that they thought had been wrecked by the bombing but that had been wrecked, in fact, when Texas became the Great Independent Nation of Texas. It was a monument to Gutzon Borglum.

There was, perhaps, no greater symbol of Americanness than Gutzon Borglum. The son of Danish immigrants who were also Mormon polygamists—yes, Danish immigrants who chose to be Mormon polygamists—Gutzon Borglum was an essential figure in American art. He was on the founding board of the famous Armory Show of 1913 that first exhibited major works of European modernism for American audiences (including Picasso, Matisse, Kandinsky, and others). But Borglum left the board because of that infusion of modern art: he said it made artists like him "appear provincial." As an insult, he called Marcel Duchamp's "Nude Descending a Staircase" "staircase descending a nude."

After creating an enormous bust of Abraham Lincoln, Borglum became a member of the Ku Klux Klan and was promoted to the Imperial Koncilium of 1923, which something something something, frankly, I don't want to delve too far into the minutiae and minutes of internecine KKK politicking. Anyway, the United Daughters of the Confederacy, with enormous financial backing from the KKK, commissioned Borglum to sculpt an enormous bust of Robert E. Lee as part of the effort to reify the Confederacy in Southern life. At the request of one Helen Plane, he was determined to add an altar to the KKK; she wrote to him, "I feel it is due to the KKK that saved us from Negro domination and carpetbag rule, that it be immortalized on Stone Mountain."

His Stone Mountain bust of Lee was unveiled in 1924, but his domineering attitude proved too problematic for his financial backers, who eventually pushed him out and blasted his bust off the mountain; Lee, a loser who has been overrated by the historical inventions of Southern dead-enders, lost yet again. Below, an image in reconstruction:

Stone Mountain would go on to become "the sacred site to members of the second and third national klans," according to one American writer, and the official mural was officially opened on the 100th anniversary of the assassination of Abraham Lincoln.

But Borglum was not deterred. He was, in fact, inspired. "Art in America," the Danish immigrant and child of Mormon polygamists once said, "should be American, drawn from American sources, memorializing American achievement[*]." He then went on to design, sculpt, and create Mount Rushmore, which includes, as we all know, George Washington, Thomas Jefferson, Theodore Roosevelt, Abraham Lincoln, and, if you look closely, the corpse of actor Martin Landau.

While Borglum worked on Mount Rushmore,[†] he lived in Beeville, Texas, then of the United States. Long before Independence, Beeville boosters erected a small monument to Borglum. After Texan Independence, however, a mob of Beeville residents vandalized and defiled the memorial to Borglum for his Americanness, while, later, in other Texan cities, memorials went up to Borglum for his artistic work in support of the Confederacy, the shining ideal that inspired Texan Nationhood.

Adiel and the Shah drove past the destroyed Borglum monument in Beeville, thinking it had been damaged by the bombs, and, on the highway back to Houston, made no substantive note of a sign encouraging them to visit another small town to see its monument to Gutzon Borglum.

The drive was quiet but not peaceful. The bombing had damaged Beeville's water lines, so Adiel and the Shah remained skinned in dust from their wrists to their necks, down to their feet. Only their faces and hands had met any rinsing, and even though they had blown their noses repeatedly, neither could get rid of the feel of dust or the smells of electrical fire and death. From time to time, the Shah wiped his thigh, and dust rose to eddy in the wind. The sweat on Adiel's back, under her breasts, and in her armpits felt almost like relief: she hadn't been turned to dust herself. The open windows meant wind was loud in her ears, and along with the car's unhealthy shocks, her thoughts were zeroed by distraction. She drove under the speed limit; at 200 gallops per hour, the engine rattled the car and clamored for rest. At times, Adiel forgot herself in the present so fully that, when the Shah

---

[*]Mormonism is, of course, a kind of American achievement.

[†]By coincidence, Teddy Roosevelt once called the art of Borglum "first rate."

sniffled, she noted to herself, *oh yeah, he's in the car.*[*]

Several times, military vehicles, police, and ambulances passed them in the other direction, toward Beeville, speeding and screaming with horns and sirens. When Adiel and the Shah passed Victoria, Texas, on The Great Independent Nation of Texas Highway 59, he said something she couldn't hear. She asked him to repeat it.

"It was just a child," the Shah said. "It was so young."

Adiel didn't say anything. She just nodded. She'd seen the bodies in the ditch, had lain among them as the bombs continued dropping, had lain among them after the last bomb, her body still a quaking cramp waiting for the next blast until whatever instinct or reason allowed her and the Shah to finally move and climb out. She'd seen how they were young—teenagers, some maybe in their early twenties—how they held each other as if their arms and hope would protect them from the bullets that would put them in the ditch. She noticed the eyelashes of the dead. She'd smelled and felt these people more intimately than anyone or anything else in her life.

"What do you want to do?" she said. She hated the pain of talking, the headache that felt like forceps against her temples, the bellowed air of nausea that came and went.

"Nothing."

"Texas tried to kill us. We survived. You're still the Shah."

"It could've been America."

"But it wasn't. You know it wasn't." He didn't say anything, so she repeated, "You're still the Shah."

"My father was the Shah," he said. "I'm not him."

Adiel moved her hands down the steering wheel because it was too hot from the sun. "I know."

"No," he said, "you don't." The Shah coughed several times until he hocked up phlegm and spat it out his window. The windstream sent it back inside the rolled-down backseat window. "When I was

---

[*]After independence, Texas altered its measure of automotive speed to "gallops per hour." The nation refused to produce a conversion system, but rough estimates put 200 gallops per hour at 60 miles per hour. "Gallops per hour" seem to have no relation to "horsepower" beyond the rhyme.

eight, long before he was the Shah or Texas was independent, he had a big party. Lots of men smoking cigars, lots of women in fancy dresses. People would just leave their glasses of champagne and whisky sitting around with a little left and take a new one from a waiter, so I finished off what was left of a lot of them. A lot. He made me wear a little suit because it was fancy. I started to get sick from all the liquor, and when I was just about to sneak away to the bathroom, he grabs me so he can show me off for some reason. He drags me to a circle of old men and fat men in tuxedos. I remember one kept offering me a cigar as a joke, but I don't even remember why Poppy brought me over. I tried to tell him I needed to go, to go go, but he keeps hushing me, and I convinced myself that if I peed just a little, I'd get a little relief and nobody would notice. Instead," and here the Shah laughed a mirthless, dust-clotted laugh, "I proceeded to throw up and—and shit myself at the same time."

"That's awful," Adiel said, and it was awful to her, but saying "That's awful" in light of what they'd been through and seen that day made her eyes rim with tears.

The Shah shook his head. "That's not the awful thing. I've never told this story, but Poppy used to tell it all the time. Now, I'm covered in throw up, and I smell like shit, and he can't hide in front of his friends that he's just furious. Of course, he can't spank me because my pants are full of shit, so he drags me toward the bedrooms, and he tells me not to change out of my clothes. He even tells Lila, one of the ladies who works for us, to watch me and not to change me or let me change or even wash myself off. And, so help him God, if he came back and found me cleaned up, he'd fire Lila and make sure she'd never work again, and he'd get our cook deported. I don't even know where Manny was from. Poppy called me his Shitty Little Boy, and when he went back into where the party was, I heard him call me Shitty Little Boy real loud and laugh big like it was all a big joke."

"Jesus Christ. What a monster."

"Not all the time. But Lila said he could fire her if he wanted, and she cleaned me up and put me to bed.

"But I was still sick, and I woke up in the dark ready to barf. I hear this weird noise, so instead of going to the bathroom, I follow it to the library. The closer I get, it sounds like hooting and hollering, but also like some pain sounds. Not screaming exactly. I open the door, and I see Poppy from the back. He's naked, and he's at his desk, and there's a bunch of dudes around him in open bathrobes. I just, I was staring at his—his balls. I'd never seen a grown man's balls before, and they were just so big and droopy and hairy. I was just so shocked by them. Somebody noticed me and called out, and Poppy turned around, and I saw the face of the girl he was having sex with. I mean, she was a girl. Like, maybe not even a teenager. Her face was red, and I don't know if she was crying or not. Poppy had this penholder that had two pens sticking out, and her head was in the penholder with the pens on both sides of her neck. Next thing I remember, Poppy escorted me out, and the door got slammed."

Adiel's cheeks hurt as if she were crying, but she wasn't crying. "What did he say about it?"

The Shah shook his head. "I don't remember if he said anything or not. I mean, it feels so real, but it feels like a dream, too."

"You must have wanted to kill him."

"No," he said nonchalantly. "I just wanted him to like me. I wanted him to tell other people he thought I was awesome. After he died, I hoped somebody would find a private diary where he wrote about how much he liked me."

Adiel closed her eyes for a moment even though she was driving. She opened them, and the landscape looked the same. Soon, the Houston skyline would appear, and they would have to do something.

"I mean," he said, "every once in a blue moon, when I'm real tired and I've been doing Shah work all day, I imagine just nuking the hell out of Texas and America and the whole world. But that always passes."

She tapped his bicep. "We'll be there soon. We could do something like that. Better than that, I mean."

He shook his head. "I just want to forget everything."

"You could change it from the inside," Adiel said. "The way people get better by changing themselves from the inside out."

The Shah stared out the window. "Maybe," he said. "Everything dies eventually."

Neil's Own Self

Neil's Own Self

Neil awoke, who knows when, with an awful headache echoing out from the back of his skull. Except echoes were supposed to get quieter with each return. Every time he blinked, pain pulsed back, as did an afterimage of the room's lights.

Reader, you've seen some movies. So let's forgo the necessaries of this scene: nurse comes in and informs him what happened and how he got here, doctor tells him his injuries (concussion, shoulder contusion, some bruised and cracked ribs), he asks for details and is told it's time to rest, there will be time for all that later, a close-up shot of his worried face. Let's get to the good stuff, shall we?

Neil thought at first he was hallucinating the sound. He'd had ringings and bass thuds at intervals throughout the morning. But he was pretty sure the heavier steps in the hallway and the blips and static of walkie-talkies and the jangling were real. And it turns out they were. The nurse (she smiled a lot, evidently happy to treat a celebrity and now to be visited by another) opened the door, leaned her head in, and said, "You've got a visitor." She said "a visitor" with the giddiness of a young boy telling his younger brother he has a present, knowing that said present is just freaking awesome.

In came the suit and cranium of Dick Dick Dick Dick Dick. His face seemed pained, as if Dick Dick Dick Dick Dick were constipated. Around his eyes fired little tics. It took Neil a moment, but he realized that Dick Dick Dick Dick Dick was trying to extend an image of empathy.

"Oh, Neil, it's just terrible what happened to you."

"I'm not totally sure what happened to me."

"They haven't told you?" Dick Dick Dick Dick Dick put his hand on Neil's shoulder. The hand felt like an ice pack.

"They told me. I just don't get it. Why would an American try to kill me?" After every blink, Neil's vision had little floating phosphenes. Still, he could see the pinpricks of burst blood vessels in Dick Dick Dick Dick Dick's face, the throbbing vein in the center of his forehead that presumably carried all the bile from his brain to his mouth.

Neil wasn't sure where that feeling of rage came from.

"We're investigating," Dick Dick Dick Dick Dick said. "We think they did it to make it look like we did it. We'll make sure they hear from us for trying to kill you."

Neil's arms instinctively closed against his sore ribs. "Are you here to finish the job?"

Dick Dick Dick Dick Dick looked like he was trying to look taken aback. Neil assumed he hadn't been taken aback in years, if ever. "Neil, we've had our disagreements, but when they said on the news you were dead, everything in the Grand Office of the Shah just stopped."

"I was dead?"

"Of course not, thank heavens, but the early news reports said you were the target and were unaccounted for. And when you were accounted for alive, I rushed down here first thing." Dick Dick Dick Dick Dick squeezed Neil's shoulder. Perhaps it was meant to massage, but it pinched, and Neil's head jerked toward Dick Dick Dick Dick Dick's hand. Dick removed it. "I just wanted to tell you we'll get the bastards who did this."

Neil shook his head. "Bad things happen in war, right? I should have known that was a threat."

Dick Dick Dick Dick Dick walked to the door, peered through the vertical window, then walked back to the bed. "You know," he said in a quiet growl, "someone in our offices proposed something bad happen to you, but I shut it down. Think of me whatever you think of me, but I'm not that kind of monster."

"So you admit you're some kind of monster."

Dick Dick Dick Dick Dick smiled, his mottled face nearly a Hieronymus Bosch painting come to life. Maybe just the right panel of "The Garden of Earthly Delights." "To thine own self," he said, "be true. To what, exactly, are you true, Neil?"

Neil had never noticed how thinly haired Dick Dick Dick Dick Dick's eyebrows were. Little white hairs separated by bald schisms. "To myself," Neil said. "To Texas. To the truth." The words didn't sound as noble as he'd hoped.

"Then we're on the same page. It shouldn't be hard for us to reëstablish a working relationship at all."

"I don't think I want a working relationship with you."

"Why not? You work for W-ANK, but, really, we both work for Texas." Here Dick Dick Dick Dick Dick leaned down, breath full of onions. "And I am Texas, so we both work for me." Dick Dick Dick Dick Dick walked to the window and peered through the blinds. "So many media trucks down there. They all want your story, Neil. And you've got two options: brain-damaged kook, or hero. What's it going to be?"

The End of a Sensing

The End of a Sensing

Reader, as you know, one of the great things about a novel is that you can finish it anytime. Quit when the quitting's good, whether you get tired of it halfway through, or if you save the last twenty pages for later because you just don't want it to end. Of course, tossing a novel aside can be hard to do. You've already invested all this time, all this energy, even if you dislike it. You want that sense of accomplishment; you want your hope to be redeemed.

Reader, because the real author of any novel is the reader imagining it, have I got a deal for you! You can have the ending you'd like. I offer the following options:

1) For however you want the novel to end, I offer the blank page after this chapter. Pretend it's the flyleaf if you have to, close the book, close your eyes. Imagine how you want the novel to end. It's done. After all, no matter the writer, every book belongs to the reader. So write your own ending.

2) For those who want the happy ending, read the next chapter, close the book, then return it to your local library, or shimmy it under that uneven table leg, or pass it on to that friend you dislike. "Oh, it's amazing!" you can say, then go get brunch as everything is back to normal.

3) For those who want to know how it ends, it would only be polite to read through what I wrote, right? You want to be polite, don't you? You don't want to be rude, do you?[*]

There you go! Three options. Now I set you forward on whatever adventure you choose. Or, to avoid potential copyright lawsuits: opt for your own undertaking.

---

[*]This kind of coercion doesn't work on the kinds of readers who would choose the first two options, so I don't feel bad trying it.

AN ENDING

AN ENDING

FINE

The Happy Ending

Adiel drove past the exit for the Freedome and the Grand Office of the Shah. When the Shah asked where she was going, she said she thought she'd be dropping him off where she'd picked him up, where the tunnel underneath the Freedome let out.

"No," he said. "You and me, we're walking in the front door."

So Adiel turned around at the next exit and came back the other way to take the Freedome exit. She drove right up to the front gate. Soldiers swarmed the car, rifles out, but when they saw the Shah, they stood up straight and saluted.

"At ease, boys," the Shah said. "Miss Thomas and I are heading in. If you could kindly open the gate, I'd be real grateful."

The soldiers hustled and opened the gate. Adiel eased the car up the roundabout driveway that led to the front door. Something in the front left wheel was squealing. "We'll get that fixed," the Shah said. "And we'll get AC installed. And we'll send money to that car salesman who let us take it. In fact, we'll send all kinds of money to help Beeville."

Adiel smiled all big. "It sure is a wonderful life."

The Shah led her inside the front door, down hallways and through metal detectors (she still had to go through two of them, though he didn't), all the way into the Grand Office of the Shah. Inside, Dick Dick Dick Dick Dick sat at the Shah's desk, and Scheissetete and Bob Toose flanked him.

When Adiel saw ███████████, she said, "You're ███████ ███████!"

Her comment required some explanation and back and forth, culminating in ███████████ avowing that he would have gotten away with it if it wasn't for this kid reporter.

The Shah called into the hallway, "Guards!"

Armed guards, the Good kind, entered. "Yes, sir?"

"Arrest these men!"

Dick Dick Dick Dick Dick, Scheissetete, and Bob Toose clamored and claimed their innocence, but the guards arrested them all the same. The Shah had ordered it.

Over the ensuing months, the great public trial of Dick Dick Dick Dick Dick, Scheissetete, and Bob Toose played out in detail on all television stations. The nation of Texas was glued to it, as was the nation of America: the Shah had declared peace between the nations, a real peace, and insisted that the Americans see the warmongers and criminals brought to justice. Texas remained independent but became great friends with America and even started calling it The United States again. The Shah apologized and even cried publicly for the violence and lives lost, agreeing that he would step down due to his role. The nation loved him and, in the first Shahidential election, overwhelmingly elected him via write-in vote. Humbly, he returned to power.

Rehired by an apologetic Margot Nought, Adiel S. Thomas covered the trial. Media coverage swayed Texans from their support of the regime and toward justice. For her efforts, she won an Alice Walton Award, the Texan equivalent to a Pulitzer, and her book about her experience and the trial was a finalist for the Jerry Jones Book Award, the Texan equivalent to a National Book Award. (She was happy that the JJBA winner was the memoir of a noble military man.) Neil O'Chisholm healed from his wounds in time to cover the trial to great acclaim, and *The Age* magazine named him their Man of the Year.

In short, Texas was made great and restored to normalcy.

A Brief Reminder, Blah, Blah, Blah

Brief Reminder for the Happy Enders

That's it! Close the book, do with it what you will, and go about your day, back into your life. Dishes, swing sets, the HOA. Book's done! The rest is tedious acknowledgements!

Are they gone?

A Great Throat Clearing

A Great Throat Clearing

Nrsrshshnxnrsnunxxsnxsnuxsnunrnuxsrxxxxnrsurxnnrhnrrsnsnrnhuxhxxxrxunrnhuhuhunuhrhhunrnrrsurhhrnxsnrnuurnusruunuhxruhsxhhnnhruxhrxrrxhursxuhrxrsxnhnnrusssusnruhxxhrhhrnsxsxusnhnhunnhshrsshshxnhshhnunhnxuuhhurnhhsssnrrsrunsshrnnhusuxuurrrnssnnurusxnhrrrnrhsunsnrrsrhhxnhunuunnhuxxhnsuhxhhrxrrurrhhhsuhsurnnhnrnsnuruhnnsrhrxnrxruxsxxxrurusuunsshhnxnuuu.

Lorem ipsum dolor sit amet, Kissinger adipiscing elit, sed do eiusmod tempor incididunt ut Hague et dolore magna aliqua. Murderer non arcu risus quis varius quam quisque id. Enim nulla Cambodia porttitor lacus luctus. Fringilla ut Murderer tincidunt augue interdum velit euismod in Syria. Auctor neque vitae tempus quam pellentesque nec. Guillotine ipsum nunc aliquet bibendum enim facilisis. Purus gravida quis blandit turpis. Sed arcu non odio euismod Allende at quis. Turpis egestas sed tempus urna et pharetra pharetra massa. Argentinian disappearances quis varius quam quisque id diam. Orci nulla pellentesque dignissim enim sit amet venenatis urna Guilty.

Okay. We're ready to move on.

Onto the End

Onto the End

Dick Dick Dick Dick Dick sat at the Shah's desk, and Scheissetete and Bob Toose flanked him. Bob Toose slid another glossy 8x10 in front of Dick Dick Dick Dick Dick. "What about this one? Bona fides: loves the war, very big on wearing the flag pin, pretty normal looking."

"Negatives," Dick Dick Dick Dick Dick said: "really anti-sodomy. It's always a Thing with him. Everybody gets tired of hearing about it."

Scheissetete cleared his throat.

"Plus," Dick Dick Dick Dick Dick said, "there's a rumor that, in some sodomaniacal communities, his name is used as a slang term for some kind of sex goop."

Scheissetete fed the 8x10 into the shredder.

"God," Dick Dick Dick Dick Dick said, "I love that noise."

Bob Toose slid another 8x10 in front of Dick Dick Dick Dick Dick. "Bona fides: pro-war, stern, very good at timing his hand gestures."

Dick Dick Dick Dick Dick shook his head. "Too asexual. Makes a weird noise when he swallows. You can see people recoil when he does it. Remember that time a white fleck just hung on his lip for ten minutes?"

Scheissetete fed the 8x10 into the shredder.

Bob Toose saw Dick Dick Dick Dick Dick's shoulders ease at the sound. He slid another 8x10 in front of Dick Dick Dick Dick Dick, but before Bob Toose could say anything, Dick Dick Dick Dick Dick said: "Too ethnic. Not Texan enough. We don't want to lose support." Into the shredder.

Dick Dick Dick Dick Dick moved against the chair as if rubbing an itch along his spine.

"You know," Bob Toose said, "at this rate, we're going to end up replacing the Shah with a cardboard cutout of the Shah."

Dick Dick Dick Dick Dick sat back, the Great Throne of the Shah sighing under him. "There are worse ideas."

From the bottom of his dwindling stack, Bob Toose slid in

front of Dick Dick Dick Dick Dick another 8x10.

Dick Dick Dick Dick Dick's veins thickened. "Jefferson Williams? He's the nominal opposition! He's lukewarm on the war at best! He even said something negative about Garza West for the press! Why on earth would you propose him? How can we trust him to do what's right, vis-a-vis war?"

"Remember when he was campaigning for his governorship and everyone said he was tough on crime?"

Scheissetete grinned and nodded.

"You're right," Dick Dick Dick Dick Dick said. "He went home to oversee the execution of a retarded man.* Besides, he's one of those who believes war is fine as long as you fight it the right way. They always come around. Scheissetete, put Jefferson Williams in the good-maybe pile."

"Great," Bob Toose said. "That's two."

The other in the good-maybe pile was Dick Dick Dick Dick Dick.

From the hallway outside they heard the little statics of walkie-talkies and heavy steps on the carpet that made *fwumph* sounds. They looked to the door and were staring at it when it opened and in came. . .

---

*I just want to note: I feel gross for writing the r-word. It's in character for these people, though, and I'm close to done spending another moment considering them, because it means considering whatever ways I might be like them. I just want to be done with this—the novel, its referents, imagining the sort of reader who might enjoy it all.

. . .in came. . .

. . .in came. . .

(It's exciting, isn't it!)

. . .in came one of the Shah's guards. "Sirs!" he said, saluted, clicked his heels together, and clapped his arms at his sides. "The Shah is here!"

Dick Dick Dick Dick Dick stood, joining Scheissetete and Bob Toose in standing. As it happens, they waited standing for quite a while. Fifteenish minutes. By "here," the guard meant "on the premises," which meant at the front gate of the Freedome. The guard maintained his erect posture, staring at some point above the head of Dick Dick Dick Dick Dick. Bob Toose worked away at a hangnail on his middle finger with his thumb and, for a few moments, tried to unwedge some shred of food from between his teeth. After the first few minutes, Dick Dick Dick Dick Dick grunted every so often, a little louder each time. And Scheissetete either reminisced to himself over tortures once done or imagined tortures that would be done. It's hard to tell what exactly he thought, and I don't want to risk omniscience again where he is concerned.

Finally, they heard in the hallway the janglings and clickings of the guards: the Shah was here. Here here.

The Shah appeared in the doorway, then closed the door behind him. "I'm surprised you even let me in the building."

He looked terrible. Bob Toose couldn't believe it. The Shah's hands and most of his face were clean, except for smeared blotches near his ears. Dust and dirt caked his dress shirt and jeans; his neck looked as if it had been smeared with foundation darker than his skin. Little cuts and a scrape colored his forehead. Visible amoebas of some dark rust splotched his shirt. He patted his leg, and a cirrus of iotas rose from his clothes and fell.

Bob Toose, Scheissetete, and Dick Dick Dick Dick Dick stood quiet a moment too long. The jig was up. That didn't stop Dick Dick Dick Dick Dick from trying. "Thank God you're alive! Bob, go hug him!"

Bob Toose walked over to hug him, but the Shah held out his hand: Stop, in the name of the Shah.

"You don't need to pretend. You tried to kill me."

"Shah," Dick Dick Dick Dick Dick said. "Of course not!

Those were American jets that dropped bombs on Garza West and Beeville. We're still waiting for satellite confirmation, but early reports indicate it was American pilots."

The Shah looked at Bob Toose. "Under Dick Dick Dick Dick Dick's command?"

Bob Toose glanced at Dick Dick Dick Dick Dick, then back to the Shah. "Of course not."

"Either y'all are worse liars, or I see it better."

Dick Dick Dick Dick Dick sat back down in the Grand Throne of the Shah and leaned back. "I guess you're just too smart for us now."

"So you admit it," the Shah said. "You killed Neil O'Chisholm and tried to kill me, too." He stepped forward to the desk and pointed at the good-maybe pile. "And these are your next targets?"

Bob Toose walked to the desk, right next to the Shah. "Neil O'Chisholm isn't dead. He survived. And besides, that wasn't us." He looked to Dick Dick Dick Dick Dick and tilted his head forward encouragingly, like a dog wanting his person to throw the ball he's just dropped.

"Technically," Dick Dick Dick Dick Dick said, "we contracted Neil out."

Bob Toose's arms and legs went weak. He leaned forward on the desk. "You said you couldn't confirm or deny."

Dick Dick Dick Dick Dick shrugged. "I lied."

"You lied to me!"

"Get over it, Bob. I lied. It's not like I killed anybody."

"But you did! People died in that bombing!"

"Potato, potato.* And no, those aren't the next targets. Those are your potential replacements."

"You can't replace me! I'm the Shah. Right?" He looked around for some kind of confirmation. "Where the hell is Holly Unlikely? What did she have to say about any of this?"

"She moved north to become a university president†."

---

*For clarity's sake: Dick Dick Dick Dick Dick did not say "Po-tay-to, po-tah-to." He said, "Po-tay-to, po-tay-to."

†Harvard, not Haverland.

The Shah's eyes narrowed. He leaned forward and put his hands on the desk. "Get out of my throne."

"Make me." Dick Dick Dick Dick Dick put his one good arm behind his head.

The Shah stood up straight and crossed his arms. "I'm the Shah. Get out of my throne."

"You're not the Shah anymore. You're just a daddy's boy who had a lucky run, John Walker Sidney George, Junior."

Bob Toose left out a little puff of breath. He hadn't heard the Shah's actual name in a long time.

"So you're just going to kill me and replace me, is that it?"

"No," Bob Toose said in a very rare show of sarcasm. "He'll contract it out."

"He's right," Dick Dick Dick Dick Dick said. "I'll just contract it out."

Scheissetete grinned and moved a step closer to the Shah.

"I may not even have to contract it out that far."

The Shah stepped back, and Bob Toose moved between the Shah and Scheissetete.

"Wow," Dick Dick Dick Dick Dick said. "You inspired Bob Toose's first moment of bravery. Unless you count screwing Maude Lynne as brave."

Bob Toose slapped the table. "I've never done that. How did you know about that? Besides, what's the bravest thing you've ever done? Order somebody to order somebody to assassinate someone?"

Dick Dick Dick Dick Dick rose to his feet. "You have no idea what I've done! And you have no idea what I know. I could tell you things about yourself that would turn your pubic hair white."

"My pubic hair is already white!"

The Shah leaned toward Bob Toose. "You and Maude Lynne?"

"Yes." He grinned at the Shah. "We declassified the strategic map of ▮▮▮▮, if you know what I mean."

"Wow," the Shah said. "Across the continent."

"You and the reporter?" Bob Toose's hands mimed *flagrante delicto.*

The Shah put on a serious face and shook his head.

"No," Dick Dick Dick Dick Dick said. "He just tried to fuck us. Thought he'd get his itty-bitty little jibber wet striking out on his own." He leaned forward. "Your Poppy was a real man, and the Shitty Little Boy wanted to try and be just like him. But he was better than you."

The Shah's face went red. He tried to run around the desk to get his hands on Dick Dick Dick Dick Dick's throat, but Bob Toose and Scheissetete tackled him.

"You killed all those people! You had them all thrown into a ditch! You knew what they were doing at Garza West all along!"

"Of course I did! Not every little thing, but enough." Dick Dick Dick Dick Dick gestured to Scheissetete to let the Shah up. "Because nobody can know everything. Some people have to do the worst and know the worst so everybody else can live their dismal lives. Dishes, swing sets, HOAs! If punishment isn't cruel and unusual, it doesn't work! Texas is free because of me. According to the Christians, Christ died so everybody could live. Me? I kill so everyone else can live."

Scheissetete and Bob Toose picked up the Shah. They each took one of the Shah's arms and led him back to the side of the desk facing Dick Dick Dick Dick Dick.

"So you're going to kill me, too?" the Shah said. "And maybe Bob if you have to, and Scheissetete?"

Scheissetete laughed in a high pitch.

Dick Dick Dick Dick Dick: "I don't think I'll ever need to kill Scheissetete."

Bob Toose felt goosebumps on his arms and sweat in his armpits.

Dick Dick Dick Dick Dick pulled a revolver from his jacket and held it down by his side. "As for you, I'd like to give you a choice. You die a martyr for us, or you continue living as a hero for us. What'll it be, Junior? Or do I call you the Shah?"

Bob Toose imagined himself letting go of the Shah's arm, leaping over the table, disarming Dick Dick Dick Dick Dick, firing a single bullet into Scheissetete's heart (or where one might be) and re-throning the Shah. But he kept holding the arm and waiting for the Shah's decision. Bob Toose had never acted alone.

The Shah craned his neck and looked to the reproduction of the portrait of his father.

À Point

À Point

Since she had hired her first cook and first housecleaner, Maude Lynne had vowed: she would never cook or clean another day in her life. Both were below her station. But in firing her housecleaner, she didn't feel the great pleasure she'd felt at prior firings, so she fired her cook as well. Again, no great pleasure, and now she was hungry.

But she wasn't just hungry: she was ravenous. She wanted to gnaw on meat and taste its juices. She even imagined herself in the pose of one of those prisoners from one of those photos, on her knees, juices running down the sides of her mouth. As improper as anything she'd ever thought, and what she wanted more than anything.

Maude Lynne had memories of cooking—after her father left, Maude had to cook many nights her mother couldn't be bothered to get out of bed—but never steak. She didn't even like to be in the kitchen when her cooks prepared food, so she had no memory even of steak being prepared. Thankfully, she had cookbooks, all in French. In college, she had done a year's study abroad in Paris and brought home cookbooks—not because she imagined preparing food from them, but to decorate her future homes in culture. She remembered the phrase—à point—meaning steak cooked medium rare. She had always loved both descriptors: Maude herself was both rare and to the point.

Be careful not to overcook, and let the meat sit. Be careful not to overcook, and let the meat sit. She let the pan heat until smoking, something beautiful about the acrid smell, and cooked each side for about a minute. While the meat sat, she paced. Her hunger gnawed at her. Finally, standing at her kitchen island, she knifed off a square and discovered the steak was not *à point*. It was, as the French said, *saignant*. Bloody. Her teeth tore into it, and she breathed deeply, eyes closed, as the juices lived in her mouth. Maude Lynne had discovered a new life.

The Return of El Polla Grande

The Return of El Polla Grande

Adiel S. Thomas was so tired when she walked into her apartment that she almost went straight to bed without a shower. She dropped all her things just inside the door and stood, waiting for some event or synapse to force her to move. But nothing came. She'd had the dumb idea to actually go pick up the Shah, actually drive him to Garza West, actually go into the facility, actually go down into the area of torture and death, actually get bombed nearly into oblivion as she lay on corpses. A series of wrong choices. Somehow, all the choices in her life led her here. She had never chosen right, and now she couldn't decide if she should go sleep as long as she could or shower until the water went cold. Maybe she would do nothing, stand until her legs failed, take choice out of the equation.

Outside, against the window facing the alley—more accurately, facing a brick wall and a skeletal fire escape—two sparrows were either mating or fighting. It seemed like both. Adiel watched. Watching was exhausting.

If she went to bed, she'd have to wash the sheets afterward, then shower, then put the sheets back on the bed, then look at her résumé and look for jobs. Life would go on, one thing after another. So she would shower first.

In the bathroom, she peeled her sweaty, dirt-threaded shirt off and nearly tossed it in the hamper, but she never wanted to wear these clothes again, and she didn't want the evidence of this day to spread to her other clothes. A shame, really. She liked these pants. So she went to the kitchen, unballed a creased plastic bag from the grocery store, stripped down, and crammed all of her clothes inside. A pant leg and sock surged out of the top, so she got a garbage bag from under the sink and dropped the whole mess in. But then the bag lumped there on the kitchen floor, so she opened her front door and tossed it in the hall. She'd deal with it later. Or someone else would. Garbage ended up somewhere.

Adiel gave her shower a minute to warm up, then sat down in it. When the water hit her hair, the smell of dirt and sweat and death rose. She let the water run over her, not quite ready to wash everything off, but once the water cooled a bit (in this building, it was never warm for long), she worked herself to standing, tilted the handle a bit more to the left to warm it up, and scrubbed. She was very aware of each part of her body, how each could be detached and made into something else. Water went up her nose, and she blew snot and blood on her fingers.

She'd really liked those pants. She was crying. Why was she crying over those pants?

The water got cold and wouldn't warm with any more tilting of the handle, so she shut it off. Adiel and the faucet dripped.

She gave her wet hair a cursory rub with the towel, brushed her teeth until her gums bled. When she spat, she realized how thirsty she was, so she went to the kitchen and gulped a full glass of water, filled another and drank it a little slower, and then a third until she felt bloated. Then she went to bed, too tired to wrap her hair or put a towel down on her pillow.

But Adiel couldn't sleep. She couldn't even get herself in the mindset to go to sleep, exhausted as she was. After a good long while of rolling over several times, sliding one arm under the pillow to only moments later lay it parallel to her body, she got up and turned on the TV in the other room. When she was a child, after her mother died, her father would stay up late with the TV on. Sometimes he'd fall asleep, and, in the morning, she'd find him in his chair. The noise of the TV coming through the walls, just low enough that she couldn't understand the dialogue, put her to sleep most nights. Maybe that would work now: she turned the volume down and went back to her bedroom, a little chilly but with little hands of sweat at the back of her neck and under her arms.

But she'd left the volume too loud. She could tell when it was a commercial for shampoo or women's razors, when the scene was dramatic or lightly comic, when characters were giving expository information. She could make out words and sometimes entire sentences, and once she hummed dully along with a commercial jingle for a truck, surprised to realize how well she knew the song.

And then the interruption: Breaking News. Adiel was so used to Breaking News—it broke so often on the news channel and at work that it could be difficult to tell which news was actually news—but not on this station. This was an evening soap; they didn't interrupt evening soaps with news. She focused on actually listening, and the anchor said they had a major update on the bombing at Beeville and Garza West, that the Shah had been there, that in a moment they would go live to the Chamber of Dissemination at the Freedome, where Bob Toose would be making a statement.

Adiel knew: it would be nothing about the torture, nothing about the dead bodies and streamers of body parts, nothing about the trench of bodies alongside the facility, nothing about Adiel and the things she couldn't forget. The Shah would be dead (probably by Dick Dick Dick Dick Dick's orders, though that would go unmentioned), and soon she would probably be dead, too. Outside, it was night with its dark sky and the yellow glow of streetlamps. She sat up to listen.

Then, the voice of Bob Toose: "We have terrible news and good news, for sometimes the terrible news gives us our good. We are sad to report that the Shah himself was visiting Garza West during today's bombing by the dastardly Americans. He was there to give his personal oversight of the accusations about torture there, but we are very happy to report that the Shah survived with only minor injuries."

The Shah survived? They didn't kill him when he returned to the Freedome? Did that mean he could actually tell the world what he saw and what they did? Adiel forced herself to standing and went to the living room to watch.

"We are sad that the Shah was nearly killed, but we are happy that he will be able to tell the world tomorrow what happened."

A wake of relief spread in Adiel. He was still alive. Maybe the Shah would actually tell the world.

When Bob Toose left the podium without taking questions, the network went to a panel of analysts. Adiel turned off the TV— nothing to be learned there. The moment the TV's little center dot disappeared, the phone's ring startled her.

Adiel answered. A voice on the other end said, "There's a car waiting for you downstairs. The Shah would like to see you."

She hadn't known she had any adrenaline left. She said she'd be down in a minute.

The Shah would like to see her. Another wave of relief, followed by fear: maybe she was about to be killed? And maybe the Shah wouldn't survive his wounds, as it happened? Maybe he had somehow decided to forget it all, just as he wanted. All futures seemed possible; all presents seemed possible. That terrified her.

Adiel went to get dressed. That pair of pants was in the garbage in the hall, and again she cried, for the dirt and blood on them and her. The grit of dirt felt like it was still in her nose, no matter how much she cried and snotted into tissue. But she got her eyes dry enough, got into jeans and a bra and a t-shirt—she didn't even think of dressing up for this trip to the Freedome—and went into the hall, where her neighbor Otis, in a black suit, held up the bag of garbage.

"Otis," she said. "You."

She'd only ever seen him slumped, shoulders pulled inward making his chest concave, but now he stood up straight. The arms of his suit jacket were tight. "Your car is waiting downstairs," he said. "There's nothing in here you want?"

"You," she said.

"Yeah," he said. "I needed work. It pays good."

"You can throw it away."

He followed her to the elevator and waited alongside him. When the doors opened, Otis nodded. She went in, and he stayed outside. "See you tomorrow," he said. He had no idea.

Outside her building, in front of a new dark blue sedan, stood Cody, also in a black suit. He held out car keys.

"You, too?" Adiel said.

Cody was more direct than Otis. "Work is work. This is your new car, compliments of the government of the Great Independent Nation of Texas." He handed her the keys. "All the paperwork is inside. You know how to get there?"

She nodded. "Front entrance?"

"Any entrance will do. They're expecting you."

She put one leg inside the car and stood. "How long?"

"You can get there whenever you'd like, though this evening is preferable. And don't try to run. They're watching you."

"No, how long have you—you and Otis been—" she nodded

at his suit.

"Texan at heart. Government men by the grace of God. Since last Tuesday."

The car smelled new. Would they give her a new car, only to kill her? Maybe this meant they wouldn't kill her here. Maybe this meant they would let her live. Adiel was incredibly tired and incredibly tense. She adjusted the seat and mirrors, checked the glove compartment and found the title with her name and address on it (the o and m of Thomas transposed into *Thmoas*), turned on the headlights. She'd never owned a car so comfortable or quiet. She wasn't sure she owned this one.

The entire drive, every pair of headlights harbored an assassin: those that followed her for three blocks, then passed her; the ones that matched her speed in the left lane before turning off or speeding ahead; the ones that passed her with their lights too bright, seeming directed right at her eyes. But she arrived at the front gate unharmed.

She pulled her car next to the little guard house. It looked like a shed, but spotless. A guard with a bayonet—for show? Weren't bayonets obsolete?—stepped out and leaned down to her window. The guard, handsome, his hat pulled down so it seemed he didn't have eyes, said, "Miss Thomas, we can park the car for you from here."

Once, Margot Nought had driven Adiel to a steakhouse downtown for a "working lunch." Adiel ate a salad and drank, at Margot's suggestion, two old fashioneds. The "work" of the "working lunch" meant that Margot gossiped about Adiel's co-workers, which made Adiel feel special at the time, until she realized after work that Margot would gossip about Adiel to other co-workers. I include this story because Margot had used the valet parking; Adiel had found the servitude of it a little disgusting but had also imagined herself one day using the valet, the pleasure of being able to afford the help.

So she went, only to feel a little grosser as another guard, crisp as pages of an untouched new book, drove her in a golf cart up to the front door. Adiel's hair was still damp, and she could feel it frizzing. Then, realizing she was thinking about her looks after all she'd seen that day, her whole body echoed again its exhaustion. She hated these people, and she hated herself more. Or, at the very least, she felt more power in hating herself.

Inside the front door, the guard on the door side of the metal detector asked for identification. Adiel panicked: she hadn't brought any. And she'd driven her free new car over without her driver's license, which felt suddenly like a grave crime: driving without a license. They'd be looking for any mistake she made. They'd use anything against her. Unless the Shah really was going to change things, which she couldn't believe at that moment[*].

But they let her through. They knew who she was, they were expecting her, and, once they determined she had no weapons, they let her through. A guard led her down the hallways she'd walked in once before, in awe, and now she saw the tedium of work (the guard's shoulders had been trained to stay at attention, but he tilted his head to pop his neck), the little scuffs in carpeting and marble, the ill-gotten gains of gold light fixtures and heavy, spotless vases given as gifts in honor of whatever new international relationship. Adiel imagined herself smashing one tall, thin, elongated vase but walked on quietly behind the guard.

He led her to the Grand Office of the Shah. The door was closed. The guard knocked twice, and a muffled "Come in" responded. The guard opened the door before her, then closed it behind her.

The Great Throne was empty. The Shah sat instead, torso caving inward, on the sofa facing the door. He, too, had showered. His white dress shirt rounded in ways that made it seem a size too large for him. The sleeves were rolled up. "Thanks for coming," he said. He gestured to the facing sofa. "Please, have a seat."

Adiel stood by the door. "You're still the Shah?"

He nodded. "Please. Have a seat."

She did.

"I see you dressed for the occasion," he said.

"Am I here for good news or bad news?"

"It was a joke," he said. "I don't care how you dress."

"Just tell me why I'm here," she said. Her throat crackled. "I

---

[*]When Texas became independent, they made driver's licenses optional (for certain kinds of people), so Adiel had nothing to worry about in that regard.

really need to sleep."

"You and me both." The Shah leaned forward and put his arms on his thighs. Adiel could tell he was struggling just as much as she was. He whispered. "The short version is that they're going to let me stay the Shah. I'm going to try to change things from within, like you said."

Adiel rubbed her cheek with the heel of her hand. "They're going to let you?"

"I don't have a lot of options. Really only two." He let his head hang down. She saw for the first time how, underneath the criss-cross of brown and gray hair just behind the top of his head, a bald patch showed through, pale skin with a group of mica freckles. "You like the car?"

"I don't know," she said. "I guess. It's nicer than any other car I've ever owned."

"Good." The Shah leaned back and tried to smile at her. Adiel could tell his face wasn't having it. "That's something. So everybody gets what they want. I get to stay Shah and stay alive, I get to try and change things from the inside, and you get a car." He half-heartedly waved his hands. "A brand-new car!"

"And to stay alive," she added. "As long as I do what I'm supposed to."

"That's life for everybody. As long as we all do what we're supposed to, we stay alive. Until we die."

Adiel picked at a thread on the armrest. "That's what they told you?"

He nodded. "Please don't pull on the thread."

She kept picking at it. "And I'm supposed to stay quiet."

The Shah shook his head. "Live a good life. See things, do things, whatever makes you happy. If you want to travel, there can be a fund."

The thread came out of the armrest and left another short thread sticking out. "Sounds great. I imagine I'll have nightmares and look over my shoulder every time I heard a loud noise or footsteps, but it sounds like a great life. Can I have this couch now that it's ruined?"

"We all do the best we can," the Shah said, trying a surly, raspy voice. "That's what Dick Dick Dick Dick Dick said."

"You need to work on your imitation." She looked up at the reproduction of the painting of the first Shah on horseback, the horse rearing, the Shah holding forward a sword, leading captured prisoners free. She pointed so the Shah looked at the reproduction. "It's not what it used to be. Texas. Were we good once?"

"My dad liked to talk about JFK. JFK wasn't supposed to be president. He was supposed to be a journalist. His older brother was supposed to be the President, but then he died. So John got to be president and screw Marilyn Monroe and get killed by the ███." They looked at each other. "I don't think I was supposed to say that."

"I won't tell. Who would believe me?" She looked back up at the painting.

The Shah nodded but didn't laugh. "The Era of Texceptionalism. The end of the Shah."

The far door to the room opened, and Dick Dick Dick Dick Dick entered, followed by Bob Toose and a man Adiel recognized. But before she could say anything, Dick Dick Dick Dick Dick said, "Are you going to stay quiet or not? We have a lot to take care of tonight, more important things than this!"

Adiel stared agape at the man, non-Dick Dick Dick Dick Dick and non-Toose edition. She felt utter deflation. They wouldn't have to kill her at all. They'd done everything from the beginning, from before the beginning. They were like God, but more immediately consequential. "You're El Polla Grande."

The Shah turned in the sofa to look at the man. Dick Dick Dick Dick Dick and Bob Toose stared at him, too. The man's lips curled upward as he held in a laugh. His face went bright red before he bent over and burst out laughing.

Once the man's laughter dimmed to a giggle, Dick Dick Dick Dick Dick said, "What the hell is El Polla Grande?"

The Shah said, "It's a chicken place southwest of the city." He looked to Adiel as if she could confirm this. "I saw a sign for it on the way back today."

Now everyone looked at the Shah.

"What?"

El Polla Grande, his giggles reduced to titters, said, "Well, howdy y'all, como estas? Me llamo El Polla Grrrrrrande!"

The eyebrows of the three other men arched, and their heads moved back in shock.

El Polla Grande, in a slim black suit with a slim black tie, the loose folds of his throat narrowed at the top button of his shirt, came over to the sofa, sat down next to Adiel, and put his arm around her shoulders. In a different accent, one she couldn't quite place—French? German? Swiss? Alsatian? Was Alsatian a word?—said, "We've met already." He extended his free hand. "Scheissetete. Pleased."

"Scheissetete?" Adiel said.

Bob Toose and the Shah each had eyebrows that looked like they were trying to reconnect with each other, but Dick Dick Dick Dick Dick's face went through anger to recognition. "Scheissetete! You're the source! You worthless cunty sack of horseshit! You gave her the photos of Garza West and the bombings in Pittsburgh! You no-good, traitorous son of two whores!"

"Wait," Bob Toose said. "You're the leaker?"

The Shah laughed, then fell onto his side on the sofa and kept laughing, much in the boyish manner that El Polla Grande—Scheissesomething?—had laughed. Now, ScheissePolla smiled, and it looked to Adiel like a genuine human smile. That terrified her more.

"Why the hell are you laughing?" Dick Dick Dick Dick Dick asked the Shah. "Are you a traitor, too?"

Once the Shah could breathe, he said, "I understood before Bob did, and I'm so exhausted."

"What's your name again?" Adiel asked. "Not El Polla Grande."

"Scheissetete. Technically," he said, "I'm not a citizen of the Great Independent Nation of Texas, so I cannot be a traitor. Legally speaking."

"Since when do you care about the law?" Dick Dick Dick Dick Dick asked.

"I was going to ask the same thing," Bob Toose said.

"I don't care, *per se*," Scheissetete said. "I just find it interesting. Like anatomy. If you peel the skin from the body and look inside, you find all these mechanisms. These tendons and muscles, and an actual heart. But you never find the core of pleasure and pain. For me, that's the law: all those mechanisms. Pleasure and pain, the real core of life, exist beyond them, unseeable."

"Jesus Howard Christ the Fourth," Dick Dick Dick Dick Dick said. "Now you're into philosophy, too? Tell me why I shouldn't have you killed."

Scheissetete looked up to the ceiling and bobbed his head back and forth as if he were doing calculations. "Logically: I've done nothing wrong and nothing to harm you. Practically: I'm the only one in here with a gun. Additionally: I know what makes you tick. I'm not essential to you, but I serve a necessary purpose."

Dick Dick Dick Dick Dick went to the Shah's desk and pulled open a drawer. "Rats," he said. "No gun. You've planned for this." He plopped down in the Great Throne of the Shah.

Adiel spoke, to her surprise. "Why would you leak photos that would hurt Texas?"

"I was doing everyone a favor. A surprise. We always need to know the limit. You always do the worst thing you can, and you see how people react to it. If they revolt, you backtrack and prosecute the lowest on the pole. You have met the limit. Most of the time, though, they don't revolt. They don't know how. They adjust. If they resist, you apologize, and when you do it again later, they feel helpless. Most of the time, though, they'll just go along so long as they can get a decent sandwich somewhere. If they don't react to the new limit, you continue to move it."

Bob Toose: "But people care! They're marching in Austin!"

Dick Dick Dick Dick Dick: "They're always marching in Austin."

Adiel: "He has a point."

The Shah stood and stared at Scheissetete. "But the purpose of war is to keep doing it until we get it right!"

Scheissetete shrugged. "We have different understandings of what's right."

Adiel shook her head and looked at the Shah. "You're going to change this from within? It's a deal with the devil."

Scheissetete hugged her tighter. "Darling, the devil is usually the only one who's dealing." He looked at Dick Dick Dick Dick Dick. "I think she's made her decision. She won't be quiet."

The Shah's eyes flared. He went to his desk, where Dick Dick Dick Dick Dick sat. "No! She's a good person. She won't talk!"

Scheissetete said, "A good person would talk."

Dick Dick Dick Dick Dick didn't look at the Shah. He stared at Scheissetete and Adiel. "Where should we put her? Huntsville, NTSH, or the Great Beyond?"

Adiel's stomach roiled. She couldn't move. Not because of Scheissetete's hug of her shoulders; she just couldn't will herself to move. Run, she told herself. But she couldn't. They had no idea that she'd never do a thing. She'd be this tired forever, until she reached her last sleep, whenever that might be. Scheissetete was right: she'd go along to stay alive.

"They all have their charms," Scheissetete said. "I've heard delightful things about NTSH, and the prisoners are evidently even harder to live with than the guards."

"No!" the Shah yelled. "She'll be quiet! We gave her the car!" He stepped over to Adiel and squeezed her free shoulder. "It has cruise control. Great AC! Tell them. You'll be good." When she looked up at him but didn't say anything, he went to Bob Toose. "Bob, help me out here!"

Bob Toose's mouth opened, but the Secretary for Conflagrational Elucidation said nothing.

Dick Dick Dick Dick Dick pulled a pen from the decorative penholder on the desk, there for decorative signings of orders and bills, and tapped it on the desk. "I lean toward the Beyond."

The Shah squealed, "No!"

The sound of his squeal echoed for Adiel with the sounds of planes overhead, of weaponry falling downward. "I'll be quiet," she said. "You can trust me to be quiet. But I don't want the car."

"That sounds like Huntsville," Scheissetete said. "Or Beto."

Dick Dick Dick Dick Dick nodded. "Beto's rough. I have a live feed I can watch from my bedroom. For educational purposes."

The Shah slumped to the sofa facing Adiel and Scheissetete, shaking his head. His eyes were red and teary. "Adiel, please, please just say you'll take the car. It's a nice car. You said it yourself—it's the nicest car you've ever owned."

Adiel shook her head. "I'll stay quiet. Nobody would believe me anyway. But I don't want the car. Please don't make me keep the car."

Bob Toose stood and held one palm out toward Dick Dick Dick Dick Dick and the other toward Scheissetete as if they were aiming guns at him and he wanted to calm them down. "How about this? She stays quiet, but she doesn't keep the car, and we just blackball her."

Dick Dick Dick Dick Dick and Scheissetete stared at each other with pinched faces. After a few seconds, Dick Dick Dick Dick Dick sat back in the Great Throne of the Shah and put his one good arm behind his head. "I guess blackballing's fun."

Adiel's body went limp. She'd have a life, of a sort.

"Thank you," the Shah said, and bawled.

"Have some dignity," Dick Dick Dick Dick Dick said. "This is your Grand Office."

While the Shah whimpered, Dick Dick Dick Dick Dick and Scheissetete went to one another and hugged. "I could never stay mad at you," Dick Dick Dick Dick Dick said.

"I know," Scheissetete said. "I know all too well."

Bob Toose called for a guardian to escort Adiel out of the building. She was leaving the room when she turned and said to Scheissetete, "What did you learn about the limit?"

Scheissetete smiled. "We have not reached it."

They let Adiel walk home. For much of the walk, she regretted not keeping the car. Even though she had no money on her and wasn't sure if she had cash at home, she hailed a taxi after a couple of miles of walking through streets with too few streetlamps. At the curb in front of her apartment, she told the driver to wait and went up. In her apartment, she saw someone had wiped her purse clean of dust and placed it on the counter. An envelope with a rubber-banded wad of cash stuck out. They wouldn't let her live without a payout. The payout implicated her. She should have asked for—for what? There was nothing she wanted, nothing right they could give her.

She pulled a bill from the wad, took it down to the driver, and said, "Keep the change."

As she walked back to her building, Adiel heard the driver say, "Holy shit!" She went upstairs, lay down on top of the covers, and slept the sleep of the condemned.

Two Years Later

Two Years Later

No, Really, Two Years Later

Adiel carried a short stack of video cassettes into her boss's office, set it down on his desk, and put five to the left of the floppy pink dildo and two to the right of the flopped pink dildo. "These two are no good," she said. "One has bestiality, the other has an underage character. I think I've seen the actress in other stuff. She's not actually underage, but it's a big plot point in this one."

Felix, her boss, grabbed the two and put them in a box behind his desk. "Private sale it is." When he sat back up, he coughed his asthmatic cough. He had moved to Texas long before the war for its dry heat. The white hairs on his head and in his scraggly beard caught the light. He was probably going to have this job for the rest of his life, however long or short that might be. Adiel, the same.

Adiel showed him the cover of the video on the top of the stack of five. "This one I'm unsure about. You'll want to watch the scene seventeen minutes in."

He took the video and examined the cover over his glasses. "Great. I get to take work home with me. 'The Dongest Lay.'"

"The Whoremandy Beach scene involves a vagina cannon that mows down the men who come near it. It probably violates Statute 421, but it's your call."

"I went to Columbia for this. *Cum Laude*."

Felix remained one-dimensional, a plot device in Adiel's life. Every time she brought him a video that needed his finer understanding of Texan obscenity laws, he read the title, she summarized it, and he said, "I went to Columbia for this. *Cum Laude*." She had a job, so she had a boss. Work was work, and then she went home, thank God. Much of the time outside work, she didn't think about her job. The Shah's people—and/or Dick Dick Dick Dick Dick's and/or Scheissetete's and/or Bob Toose's—had done a bang-up job of barring her from any meaningful work other than what the raggiest alternative newspapers offered, and she wanted as far from journalism as possible. So she worked for a sex shop, Longhorns and Red Raiders, the largest in Lubbock, watching new videos to make sure they could be sold legally in Texas. She got to judge what was moral, or at least legal. Prudish carveouts in Texas and Lubbock County meant the shop had to be careful. The occasional raid, more for show than enforcement, and for restocking the prurient needs of the police, meant her job was necessary.

Luckily, she could read on the job and do crosswords and try not to think or remember. When she had to pay attention to the videos, they offered diversion that sometimes lodged in her thoughts—could one describe those legs as *akimbo?*—so she wouldn't have to think of other things that this recounting has already recounted.

Two days prior to this particular scene, though, she thought of what she assumed would be her own imminent death. Two days prior, everything stopped when the news was announced: the Shah had suffered a massive heart attack and passed away.

The Shah was dead. Allegedly.

Adiel didn't know whether he had actually died or not—whether Dick Dick Dick Dick Dick and Scheissetete had killed the Shah, or he'd died, or they'd simply stowed him away in Beto prison or some other so the Shah would suffer and Dick Dick Dick Dick Dick could watch—but she'd had to listen to co-workers, strangers in the grocery store, people at the corner gas station out the window of her second-floor apartment (furnished and aromatically compromised on the best of days): she'd had to listen to assorted Texans mourn, interestedly or disinterestedly, and she couldn't tell anyone how terrified and skittish her own mourning was.

After the day at Garza West, he'd been a different Shah. Still charming in his way, but when he was shown on television, more detached and serious. He seemed like a man who'd seen things. People seemed to read this as honor. Mostly, she tried to ignore the news.

And now he was dead, or "dead," and the country seemed panicky. He had no heir to replace him as Shah; some wanted an election, and others wanted the powers-that-were to choose. A lot of people didn't seem to particularly care, as long as things stayed the same or got a little better or didn't get too much worse. The war had ended and a treaty had been signed. All of Texas' and America's wars were far away;

some of them were wars between Texas and America, fought by other nations. The GDP was good, and oil was flowing and selling. Even some American movies were starting to show at theaters in Houston and Dallas, Adiel heard. Not in Lubbock yet, but people in Lubbock seemed excited at the prospect of Hollywood.

"Why don't you take off early?" Felix said. "You look like you've been run roughshod."

That was Felix's one personality trait that accompanied managing a sex store: daily innuendo. If Felix had a different sort of charm, one might interpret it as flirtation or harassment rather than a way to pass the time.

Adiel grabbed her purse, double-checked that the small can of mace was on her keyring, and started to head out. The phone rang behind her in Felix's office. She heard the niceties, then Felix said, "Holy shit!" He hung up and jogged past her into the store's video area, said, "Hold up" to Adiel, and grabbed the remote from the counter. Jason, the only full-time clerk, was ringing up a group of frat boys in polo shirts (or frat-boy types, not that it mattered to Adiel whether they were officially affiliated or not), faces striped with tan lines from their sunglasses; they were buying several videos and a variety of sex toys. Props? Actual generosity toward their partners or themselves? They wore big, showy grins on their faces.

The TV in the corner always showed new releases, either muted or on low volume, depending on Jason's level of tolerance. He also liked to read at work, mainly stagey historical fictions of palace intrigue, and he was easily distracted. Felix futzed with the remote, stopping the video and switching the screen from video to live TV: the news. Neil O'Chisholm looked dapper, slender and tan against his white collar, hair newly streamlined and gelled upward, head an elegant cube. When he had returned to television after the bombing that attempted to take his life, he had been a particularly forceful critic of Adiel's work and the miniscule antiwar movement, and an ardent proponent of the Shah.

"—announcement is coming shortly, from the Director of Disseminations Bob Fugate, only on your number-one Texas news source, W-ANK. In fact, let's go over to the rest of our panel, where

Bob is ready to give us the scoop. Bob?"

The other Bob, Bob Toose, was gone from his job, "promoted," as it were, to be the first Ambassadorial Emissary to Fiji.

The shot moved to Bob Fugate's bald bullet head and glasses with frames that always caught a glint of the light. "Neil, I'm so honored to be here with you at W-ANK, and to give this news to the Great Independent Nation of Texas about our new Shah."

"So the government has already decided?"

"Yes, Neil, it has. It has long prepared for any contingency, because planning for any and all and every contingency is necessary preparation for the future. The government can't predict *the* future, but it can predict *every* future. Nothing that happens is unknown. Nothing that happens is unpredicted. So the government has long had a process and prospects in case of the untimely, terrible demise of the Shah."

"Before you tell us who the new Shah is, I understand you have news about the late Shah's funereal celebrations and revelations."

"Yes, I do. Given the Shah's well-known humility, the government has decided that he will not lie in state."

"Dude," one of the frat boys said. "I wanted to go see him."

Adiel shook her head. She said, quietly, "He's not dead."

Felix asked her what she said; she told him it was nothing.

"As I understand it, the Shah died interstate," Neil said. "Is that correct?"

"Yes. But even though he died intestate—"

"Interstate," Neil interjected.

"—we knew he didn't want to lie in state. But to honor him, the government will have a week-long funeral procession which will tour the Nation, starting today."

"So people will be able to see the processional."

"Oh, yes. And in concert with gas stations around the country, the government is providing a one-cent tax on every gallop of gasoline purchased during this week to honor his memory. We're calling it 'Texceptional Savings Week.'"

"A beautiful way to honor one of our greatest Shahs," Neil intoned. "So tell us who we will honor as our new Shah."

"We are delighted to bring in a man who is a real leader, charismatic, and, most importantly, a reformer. The government admits that mistakes have been made in some areas of foreign policy and strategizing for conflagration, and we want to continue to honor a real reformer who's tough on crime and who believes in fighting war the right way: Mr. Jefferson Williams, who we will now know as the Shah."

The news went straight to Jefferson Williams, newly and forever known as the third Shah of Texas. He spoke at a podium emblazoned with the Seal of the Great Independent Nation of Texas (its Latin slogan circling: *Inpulsa et Tremendum*). Adiel didn't really listen; she imagined instead the Shah—the second Shah—imprisoned, and as the space of the prison she saw Garza West: fundamentally now a prison for one, maybe still haloed in a haze of dust or flies. Only a few phrases from the new Shah's speech registered: "no more raping of nuns," "smarter bombs," "honoring the Texceptionalism of the founding," the word "reform" repeated many times. Adiel entertained ideas of driving to Beeville, of trying to get back into journalism, of leaving Texas to live in America or Mexico or Canada. But she knew she would continue to live as she was living: she would twitch for a while at every creak of floorboards, at every car that moved to close to the bus she was on, at men with backpacks who got on the bus with shifty eyes. But what she didn't know, and what I can tell you, is that she would keep on living, well past the end of this accounting, into one of the futures already predicted by the government.

That was her punishment: a life of imagination.

Before she left work, though, the new Shah's speech came to a close with applause as the camera panned out to a crowd of journalists for questions. The new Shah, his every move and act empowered, pointed to one, sleeves rolled up, glasses and lanyard glinting.

"Sir," the journalist said, "Your Greatest Honor, there are rumors that your Shahdom might commence investigations into the acts and behaviors of the previous Shahdom, including those related to Garza West. What do you say to those rumors?"

The new Shah cocked his head and made a face of thinking. He seemed so human. "The past is past. We cannot judge men for what, in the present, we may think are crimes now, but were acts of the past. It was a different time. We need to look forward as opposed to looking backwards, for if we look backwards while moving forward, we will fall either forward or aslant to time, taking Texas off its path of Texceptionalism."

Maybe, Adiel thought, some people would rise up. Someone would speak out, and people would follow. Not her—she had no energy to give, to lead, to investigate. If someone led, and others followed, she would join. But someone would have to start.

The camera turned to Maude Lynne. She wore no jewelry, but her lips glistened red. She held up her pen, which the news once said had cost millions: a Vulgar Sanguis, crusted with diamonds that were coated in a thin layer of blood.

"Tell us, Shah," she said. "Who do we fight to maintain the great Texceptional glory of Texas in patriotic grace?"

Adiel zoned out.

At the end of the question-and-answer session with the new Shah, the frat boys applauded; Felix and Jason applauded. A lot of people were happy. "Now," the new Shah said, "let us watch as the deceased Shah's processional begins." He turned to a screen next to him on the stage, which showed a view from the sky as a line of cars rolled out of the Freedome and eased through the streets of downtown Houston. The image of the new Shah watching the old Shah became an inset picture on the screen, and everyone in the shop watched Neil O'Chisholm watching the new Shah watching the old Shah, son of the First, whose image on textbooks everywhere led the nation forward to its predicted-but-uncertain future and whatever limit it might meet.

Acknowledgments

This novel wouldn't exist without help from the following people, so if you dislike it, please blame them.

I've been lucky to have so many great writing teachers—special thanks to Michael Griffith and Brock Clarke, who are exceptional. I couldn't have kept going over the years without David Jauss, Speer Morgan, Trudy Lewis, Marly Swick, and Leah Stewart, who were always supportive. Thanks to Earl Ramsey for saying yes despite common sense, for tolerating my bad opinions on Virginia Woolf, and for introducing me to *Tristram Shandy*. Many thanks to Nicola Mason, who taught me to edit.

I'm grateful to my colleague Roger Gilbert for his friendship and assistance. Thanks to Stuart Davis for his mentorship and feedback on the novel. Special thanks to J. Robert Lennon for essential revision advice. Thanks to Julianne Lynch for her kind, insightful feedback. Karen Kudej and Victoria Brevetti I thank for tolerating my jokes. Thank you to my colleagues in the Department of Literatures in English at Cornell.

Many thanks to my students, far too many to name: teaching makes me more creative and more intelligent.

Thanks to Mark Falkin for believing in the novel. Thanks to Kevin Brockmeier, Jacob Appel, Brock Clarke (again), Jen Fawkes, Daniel Peña, and Emma Berquist for their very kind words.

Thanks to John Manuel for excellent editing feedback and a lovely demeanor. Many, many thanks to Paul Brooke and Kyle McCord at Gold Wake for everything.

Thank you, Mom and Dad, for never insisting that I veer away from writing. Thanks, Mom, for getting me into books; thanks, Dad, for shaping my sense of humor, for better and for worse. Thanks to my brother Jim for an entire life and for his feedback on the novel. I'm sorry I sat on your globe. Infinite gratitude to my brother John for his advice, his support, and the fabulous illustrations and cover design. I'm not sorry I pooped on your Chewbacca.

Enormous thanks to Nick Friedman: this novel doesn't happen without your constant encouragement of even my dumbest ideas. Thank you for the rocking horse. And you're a great encourager.

And, finally: so many thanks to Charlotte Pass. Your belief in me makes no sense, but I guess that's the nature of belief. You're the very best.

Biography:

Originally from Arkansas, Charlie Green is the author of the poetry collection *Feral Ornamentals*. He teaches in the Department of Literatures in English at Cornell University and earned his Ph.D. at the University of Cincinnati. His writing has appeared in *Image, The Southeast Review,* and *New England Review,* among other venues.

One Last Review:

Set during the never-ending war between Texas and America, Charlie Green's madcap debut novel, The Shah of Texas, serves up a trenchant satire of the United States's military involvement in Iraq that is simultaneously hilarious and deeply unsettling. Featuring a cast of compellingly deranged politicos and propagandists, including the Nixonian demi-Shah, Dick Dick Dick Dick Dick, and his hyenic assistant, Scheissetete, *The Shah of Texas* introduces readers to an alternate history that feels all but alternate as it lampoons our nation's military-media complex. Through the lens of Texceptionalism, Green creates an unpredictable (and skillfully illustrated!) literary universe truly unlike any other: a cross between *Tristram Shandy* and *1984* that is guaranteed to shock, awe and entertain all but the most zealous of jingoists and war-mongers."

—Jacob M. Appel, author of *The Man Who Wouldn't Stand Up*